# WAR
## OF THE
# REALMS

*Neekita Chand*

ISBN 979-8-89130-293-8 (paperback)
ISBN 979-8-89130-294-5 (digital)

Christian Faith Publishing
832 Park Avenue
Meadville, PA 16335
www.christianfaithpublishing.com

Printed in the United States of America

For Abilash Chand

The gentle whisper of the rain as we ran on
the muddy road on our island,
*peace* in the wilderness.

The light of heaven, a guide on our path,
*courage* in the darkness.

The radiance of our Creator, our source of strength,
*serenity* in the eternity.

# CHAPTER 1

"Holy holy holy is the Lord God Almighty, who was, and is, and is to come," the angels sang before God and glorified him. I stood next to the elites as the angels sang before God's throne and praised him. This is the first time I have seen the throne room filled with so many elites, seraphims, cherubims, and elders sitting on the upper floors of God's palace. Michael and Gabriel stood guard on each side of God, enjoying the celebration.

"What are you thinking about?"

I turned and saw Gelin standing next to me in his armour. "I have never seen the palace filled with so many angels at once. I'm not one to sing and dance."

He chuckled and followed my gaze to the elders sitting upstairs. "Neither am I," he said. We stood there as the angels worshipped God in song and dance.

"Your mind is somewhere else," he said as if reading my mind.

"It is," I said. "A lot has happened since Alvinor. The last war we fought was just the beginning. I can't help but think that something bad is looming ahead. We should be on the field right now and fighting the demons."

Gelin didn't say anything. He nodded and turned his attention to God.

The procession ended, and I made my way to the grand citadel. The citadel was quiet, and I walked to the battle arena. I summoned my bow and began to practice the defensive technique that Izralina taught me back on Alvinor. I have grown stronger in my skills since being in heaven. I do miss Alvinor and being in the observatory. There are many more elites here in heaven, and they have helped me in my combat and weaponry skills. Satan's defeat in the last war has given me the momentum to grow stronger and know that his legion can be defeated by the elites. I spun my bow around, and it met Gelin's lance.

"Say it," I said, knowing that he was holding back in the palace. I spun my bow around the other way, and he blocked the attack again. "Very good, Arden."

"You are striking your bow with much more intensity."

I stood still and sighed. "Gelin, you are not here to compliment my weaponry skills!"

He studied me for a moment and summoned away his lance. "Very well," he said.

"I understand that since our last victory, you have been wanting to descend on earth and battle. I also know that you are upset with what happened with Zaphael, but that was out of your control. He is not coming back. You have to stop blaming yourself. There will always be demons to cast out and humans to save and protect. But sometimes, you have to stop and step back. I have seen you in the throne room. Your mind is elsewhere, you're thinking about your next battle rather than focusing on being in God's presence and spending time with the other elites. You are in heaven, enjoy being here. There are other elites fighting the demons, you don't have to assume all the responsibilities."

"I do not want to stop, Gelin."

"I know we won the last battle, but we only made Satan more angry. His retaliation has been swift. He has instigated more wars through his human agents, and the commanders are more involved in these wars more than ever. I am only warning you, Arden. Do not run ahead of God. I know what it is like to defy orders and go your own way, and I suffered the consequences of the decisions I made. We are all in this together, as a team. You are not alone in this." He gave me a reassuring smile and joined the elites in the citadel.

I summoned my bow away and decided to go for a walk beyond the tree line. Since my time in hell with Satan and seeing Zaphael as a commander, I have become more aggressive and angry when I fight with demons. Was Gelin right? Am I running ahead of God? All I know is that since the last victory with the demons on earth, I have gained momentum, and all I can think about is casting out demons. I have been training harder with the other elites, and I have grown stronger. I have not seen Zaphael since our last encounter on the battlefield on earth. I wonder if he regrets his decision.

The light in heaven was different from the light on earth. I miss the sun's warmth on earth, and I miss walking by the ocean. There are no oceans in heaven. I spend more time on earth than in heaven. I love sitting by the beach after defeating demons. Being on earth gives me peace. I love watching the humans interacting with each other, praying and worshipping in churches, and being set free from Satan's grasp. I walked deeper into the forest, surrounded by tall green trees, and found myself on the edge of a meadow. I sat in the middle of the meadow, admiring the flowers and barely saw the tower of the grand citadel. All was quiet around me, and I felt peace that surpassed all understanding. I lay down on the field and closed my eyes.

It was hard to tell how long I have been in the meadow. It is easy to tell time on earth. Heaven exists beyond time; everything is eternal here. There is no need to rush or hurry here. The humans I see on earth always seem to be in a rush, but then again, they live inside of time. The light in heaven is eternal and constant, very much different from the starry blue and orange sky above Alvinor. I wonder what is happening on earth? I did not have to lay out my hands to observe earth like I did when I was on Alvinor. The elites showed me another way of observing earth from heaven. I opened my eyes, and I focused on earth. I could feel myself still lying down on the field in heaven, but I found myself looking at humans rather than the field. I could see the humans walking around the Sydney Harbour Bridge in Australia. I remember coming here, standing on the top of the bridge with Emrail. It was daylight on earth, and the sun was at its peak. Suddenly, the vision pulled me in, and I saw Kitana come into view. This is strange, I have never experienced having a vision like this before. She was standing next to her partner, Aaric. I focused on them deeper so I could listen to what they were saying.

"Have you thought about setting a wedding date yet, Kita?"

They sat down on the steps near the Opera House, and he held her close. "I need more time, Aaric. These past few weeks haven't been easy for me. I have been experiencing more visions, and I just need time to understand what is happening to me. I need to know that you are not marrying someone who is crazy."

Aaric chuckled and kissed her forehead. "You are not crazy, Kita. Take all the time you need."

She smiled back and hugged him. I saw her eyes, and I could see uncertainty in it.

I found myself drifting out of my vision, and I gasped. He stood with his gold staff, and his eyes looked amused. "Lord!"

"At ease," he said. "May I join you?" he asked.

I gaped at him and nodded.

"Are you surprised?" he asked.

"Yes," I said, bewildered that God is sitting with me in a meadow in heaven.

"I am not always on my throne. I like to walk about in heaven and talk with my people, that includes the angels too."

"I just did not expect you, it is a good surprise, Lord," I said.

He looked around the meadow, exploring its beauty. "It is nice here. What brings you here, Arden?"

"It is peaceful here." I gestured around the meadow.

"But there is more to this?" he asked, fixing his gaze intently on me. "Arden, I may be the God of the universe, but you can tell me anything. I am your father and your friend. I am here for you."

I hesitated before him, but his eyes were filled with so much love, and he waited patiently for me to speak.

"Alright," I said. "I have been feeling very restless lately. Ever since the last battle on earth, all I can think about is casting out demons. It's just this feeling of rush that I feel, and I feel like the longer I am here, the more humans are in danger on earth. Being on earth gives me more peace knowing that I am doing something, rather than not doing anything in heaven. But you already know all this, don't you."

God chuckled and nodded. "I created you. I know everything, Arden. It does help for you to talk about it though. It is okay for you to feel this way. The other elites have been here for much longer than you have been. You have just experienced a taste of what it is like being an elite. I believe your experiences on Alvinor, in hell, with Satan and Zaphael, and the recent victory has both overwhelmed you and excited you."

"But?" I asked, knowing there was a but ahead.

"But you do need to understand that you have nothing to be fearful about. There are legions upon legions of elites that are protecting humanity. That does not make you any less important. I have created you for a purpose, remember. I have made no mistake. Your recent encounters with the demons have rattled them. You have grown much stronger since your time on Alvinor. You need to trust that I am in command and that everything is under my control," he said reassuringly. "And…you must not run ahead of me," he added.

"That is exactly what Gelin told me," I said.

"Wise words to abide by," he said.

"Lord, I do not intend to run ahead. I just feel like I should be on earth more than in heaven. I have only been on earth a few times since that battle, and I feel like I can do so much more."

"Okay," he said.

"Okay?" I asked, feeling surprised.

"Yes. I have assigned you to a human. You are to protect her, watch over her, intervene only when necessary, but you are to never interfere with her free will. Her name is Kitana Denali. You may know of her during your time on Alvinor."

"I have. I have been having visions of her lately. If I observe earth from heaven, the visions draw me to her."

"Yes," said God. "I assign each of my elite angels to humans on earth. Sometimes it is one elite to one human. Sometimes it is one elite to many humans, and sometimes it is many elites to only one human. When it is time for the elites to protect the humans that I have partnered them with, the elites begin to have visions, and once I command them, they descend on earth. I have chosen you to be Kitana's elite angel since I first created you. You needed to train first and learn about earth and about humanity first before you were to learn of this part. Kitana is important to me, and as you have witnessed, she is also a target for demons. She is one of mine. I want you to get to know her, observe her from the spirit realm, protect her from demonic interference, and most importantly, never interfere with her free will as I have said."

"When can I descend?" I asked, feeling eager to descend to earth.

"Soon," he said.

I bowed my head in reverence, and he smiled again. He stood up, picked up his gold staff, and walked away. His powerful and loving presence stayed with me, and the restlessness I once felt was no more. This explains a lot about Kitana and why I have been having visions of her lately. I must wait until God has commanded me to go down to earth. Since the last battle, I have only descended to help the other elites fight the demons, but being assigned to protect a human is a brand-new thing. I could not help but smile, knowing that there are new adventures ahead. I got up and went back to the grand citadel, hoping that Nikolai and Valiana might be there.

Elites walked about the grand citadel; their voices and laughter echoed across the hall. I have only met some of the elites since I ascended from Alvinor. There are legions upon legions of elites to get to know in heaven as well as on earth. I spotted a familiar face, and he beckoned me to him.

"Quiff! Good to see you!" I said.

"Great to see you too, Arden," he said, beckoning me to follow him upstairs to the upper levels of the grand citadel.

"I have been quite busy helping the other elites in Reynak. I have been assigned to intelligence. What have you been doing?" he asked.

"I have only been down to earth a few times to help the elites, but nothing big has happened since the last battle on earth with the commanders. But something new has happened," I said cheerfully.

"Oh?" he said, arching his eyebrow and giving me a curious gaze.

"Well, yes…" Before I could finish my sentence, I saw that we were walking into a room, and I saw Nikolai and Valiana sitting with Izralina and Elandriel. They cheered as I walked in, and I joined them. It has been a long time since I have seen Izralina and Elandriel in heaven.

"Great to see you, Arden!" said Elandriel. "We have been occupied in Reynak with Quiff here," said Izralina.

"Anything new?" I asked.

"That is classified," said Quiff. He laughed and sat next to Elandriel.

"Since when did missions become classified?" I asked.

"Some missions are classified as commanded by God," said Izralina.

"Understood," I replied, feeling curious about their mission.

"I take it that you have been busy with helping the elites on earth?" she asked.

"Yes, I have," I said.

"Well, I am sure that since our last victory, the demons must feel quite intimidated by you," said Elandriel.

I smiled back and noticed that Nikolai and Valiana were quiet. "Well, what about you two? I rarely see you two in heaven. I only come across both of you now and then here in the citadel."

Nikolai looked at me wistfully, and Valiana remained quiet. "I'm sorry, Arden, but we are also on a classified mission, as commanded by God."

I remained quiet for a while, wondering why I was not sent on a mission by God just like the rest of the others, but then I remembered that I have been assigned to Arden. God did not tell me that mission was classified. I was about to tell them about my encounter with God and about Kitana, but then another familiar face walked inside the room, and we all stood up.

"Vintore," said Elandriel, acknowledging him and the others did the same.

"At ease, elites," he commanded. Vintore was the first angel I met when God created me. I saw him as my leader among the elites, knowing that others felt the same respect and admiration for him. He got injured very badly on earth during the last battle, but the angels in heaven were able to heal him. He has been one of the angels to continue to train me in heaven.

"I require all of you in the battle arena outside," he said. We followed his lead down to the battle arena and stood in a circle. We waited for him to speak in anticipation.

"Elites, I am well aware that all of you are assigned on missions. We all know how important time is, especially for humanity. Some of the elites, including myself, have known for some time of God's plan for the realm between heaven and earth. I have been commanded by God to share this with you. I am to put together a team of elites for a new mission as commanded by God." Vintore gazed at each of us intently, trying to discern our thoughts. We all waited patiently for him to give us more details on the mission.

"Elites, as you all know that Alvinor has now been destroyed by God. There is no need for it anymore. It was God's plan for the new angels to train there, and since the demons had learnt of its location, it had to be destroyed regardless. The command centre is now the grand citadel and that is all we need. That means that the demons have full control of the realm between heaven and earth. The demons stand between heaven and humanity, and it is becoming more difficult for angels to descend to earth, especially when some demons like to block our path. Demons in this realm like to block our aid to humanity. As commanded by God, we are to destroy Reynak, and the elites are to take control of the second heaven." Vintore stood there quietly, waiting for us to speak.

This time, Izralina spoke, and she didn't sound happy. "Vintore, are you aware that if we destroy Reynak, the demons will fall on earth? This will make things worse. They will retaliate by destroying humanity. We would only be helping them to do it quicker," she said, and I could hear the agitation in her voice.

"Izralina, I understand your hesitation, but this is a direct command from God. I have been assigned to this task, and I intend to see it through. God has only told me to assemble a team to lead this mission. He will continue to reveal more of his plan as we progress," said Vintore, trying to reassure Izralina. Everyone else remained quiet, and this time, I spoke.

"Vintore is right," I said. "When I was training on Alvinor, I had many encounters with Jesus in my visions. In one of the visions, he told me of this plan. He said that for him to descend on earth, Reynak must be cleared. Reynak must be destroyed. When I was in hell, Satan had revealed that he had already chosen his human vessel, the Antichrist," I said, and some memories of hell began to rush back in.

"That means the time is near," said Elandriel.

"Yes, my friend," replied Vintore.

"Since the fall of Satan, we have never been assigned to any mission such as this. Vintore, you know that I would never go against God's authority on this, but you know what this means and the risk that this entails?" asked Izralina, and she still seemed quite uneasy.

"What about you two?" Vintore faced Nikolai and Valiana.

Valiana nodded for Nikolai to speak. "While the mission that God has us on must remain our top priority, unless he says so otherwise, you can count on both of us to be a part of this," said Nikolai, and Vintore nodded in appreciation.

"Count me in," said Elandriel, and I nodded in agreement.

"Me too," said Quiff.

All eyes turned on Izralina.

"Izralina," said Vintore. "The time is here. All of creation has waited for this moment. For humanity to be reconciled to God forever. It is time to bring them home. Arden's testimony affirms this. Jesus has revealed the same plan to me. We all have a part to play in this. It is time to bring this to an end."

Izralina sighed and bowed her head. "I know full well what this means, Vintore. Alright, I will be a part of this."

"Thank you," said Vintore, acknowledging all of us.

"If this is one of the biggest missions in the history of the universe, then why is it that only a few of us have been assigned to this mission?" this time, Quiff asked.

"God has not revealed the entire plan to me, warriors," said Vintore. "I have been asked to choose a specific number of elites to lead this mission. I do know that legionnaires of elites will be required when the time comes to destroy Reynak and take control of the second heaven. This mission will take much preparation before the big battle takes place. For the moment, all of you are to focus on your own mission, and when I do require us to meet and speak about this mission, you will know," said Vintore.

"How?" asked Valiana.

"You will discern it when I summon you. You will know that it is me summoning you, and when I do, we are all to meet here, in this arena. If you are on earth, you must ascend to heaven," said Vintore.

"Understood," said Valiana.

"That will be all for now, thank you, elites," said Vintore. The rest of the elites orbed away, maybe on their classified mission, but I remained back in the arena with Vintore.

"I remember us talking about this in the observatory on Alvinor. I knew the time would come soon. Otherwise, Jesus would not have revealed it to us," I said.

"Yes, Arden. We must prepare, and we must expect that the demons will not sit back. They will fight back, and they will be swift. Speaking of the observatory, follow me. I have something to show you in the citadel."

I followed Vintore back to the citadel, and he led me upstairs that spiralled upward to a tower. We reached the top, and I grinned. I looked around and saw lots of books and scrolls sprawled around the tables in a big room with light gleaming through the stained windows. This reminded me of the observatory on Alvinor.

"I knew you would like this," said Vintore. "This room is filled with books and scrolls for the elites specifically. You can say this is an observatory for the elites in heaven of some sort. It has the Bible, the Book of Elohim, and other books that will be of interest to you. You can learn more here and catch up on some history."

I looked around, not knowing where to start.

"I'll leave you to it," Vintore chuckled.

"Thank you," I said, still looking all around the room and watching him walk away with another elite. I was now all alone in this observatory, wondering why I did not know of this room before. I picked up a scroll and opened it to see a plan of Reynak and a blueprint of the entire dominion. This was the same one I saw on Alvinor, only this one was much bigger. I saw the layout of camps set below the main citadel of the commanders and the old ruins of Reynak with a drawing of the dark lake.

I walked across the room, and I noticed a big book with the mark of the legion engraved on the cover. I pulled back the armour on my right arm and saw the gold carvings along my wrist. I began to think about when I received the mark. I had just been rescued from hell by Michael and I lost Zaphael. My attention came back to the book, and I began to flip through its pages. This was a combat guide for the elites. The book revealed the different types of weapons wielded by the elites and combat techniques to fight the demons. I stopped when I saw the bow.

"Archery: the elite who wields a bow can summon the arrows at will. The elite must wield this with caution and must not allow demons to take control of the bow."

I began to think about the last battle on earth and how Meridan broke my bow during our fight. Thankfully, Michael gave me a new one. I must never let it fall into the enemy's hands again. I read through the book and noticed that everything that Izralina had taught me about archery came from this book.

I opened a scroll and this one looked familiar too. It read, "The reveal of his son from the clouds will bring light on earth and destroy the darkness on the first realm and the realm between heaven and earth."

I remember reading this on Alvinor and thought about my vision on Alvinor. Jesus revealed that the elites must destroy Reynak for him to break through the clouds and descend on earth with the angels. I wonder why Izralina was hesitant about this mission. I wonder what will happen next. If God has commanded this, then I know that his plan will work. I must have faith in this mission. Speaking of missions, I began to think about my mission on earth. God has assigned me to Kitana. I sat down on the chair as the light beamed on my face through the windows and focused on earth and on Kitana. The vision pulled me in, and I saw Kitana walking around with books in her hand. Someone was following her, and his voice was all too familiar.

"What did you say your name was again?" Kitana asked the man. He turned around to face her and his red eyes gleamed.

"Zaphael," he said.

"I must say, your contact lenses are strange. I have never seen anyone wearing red lenses," she said, and I could sense she was feeling uncomfortable.

"It's the latest trend," said Zaphael.

What was Zaphael doing on earth with Kitana? I focused harder on the vision, and I observed where they were. I could see the Sydney Harbour Bridge through the window.

"How long have you been working here, Kitana?" asked Zaphael, focusing on her intently and walking closely behind her.

"I have been working in this library for a few years now. I also do some research work here."

"What kind of research?" asked Zaphael. He was in civilian clothing, and I could see the black trident on his arm as he reached to take the book from Kitana.

"Cool tattoo," said Kitana.

"It sure is." Zaphael smiled.

"Well, my focus is on Christianity. I also tutor university students in this library. What interests you about demonology?" asked Kitana, signalling to the book that Zaphael was holding.

"It's my favourite topic. Thank you for your help, Kitana. I hope to see you soon," he said and walked away.

Kitana stood there until Zaphael went out of sight. Another woman came up to Kitana and joined her.

"Who was that?" she asked.

"Some guy I have never seen before. He wanted to know about demonology."

"Strange," said the woman.

"Very strange," said Kitana.

I broke away from the vision and orbed out of the observatory and before God's palace. I opened the gold doors and saw God sitting on this throne. The rest of the palace was empty. I admired the beautiful jewels radiating across the palace as I walked toward God and bowed down before him.

"Lord, it is time. I saw Zaphael talking to Kitana when I was observing earth. He made contact with her in his angelic form. He didn't possess any other human to make contact with her."

"I know, I saw that too. Satan has assigned Zaphael to Kitana. I have assigned you to her. I am commanding you to go to earth and keep watch over her," commanded God. "Arden, I want you to be aware of the rules. I do not want you to interfere with her free will, and you are not to reveal your angelic self to Kitana. You are only to learn about her, observe her, protect her if demons try to lead her astray, and do not engage in combat with Zaphael. This is a time for you to get to know her, and as you do so, you will come to know why she is important to Satan, and to me."

I stood up and met his brown eyes that were piercing deeply into mine.

"Arden, I want you to focus on this mission, but I also want you to focus equally on the mission of destroying Reynak. My plan is unfolding perfectly, and it will not be revealed all at once. I must not overwhelm my angels. I am in control and in command, and I will carry this out with precision. Do not fear for what is to come. Trust in me, valiant warrior. I am with you every step of the way.

"Observe Kitana from the spirit realm. If I want you to engage with her in the physical realm, then I will command you to do so. Zaphael does it because the demons follow no rules and are ruthless. They have no regard for my cosmic laws. You must obey me and keep my command." There was authority in God's voice, and I bowed down again.

"Yes, Lord. I will do as you say, and I will not let you down," I said.

He smiled at me and beckoned me to descend. "Remember, Arden, I am always with you. You were created for a time such as this," said God.

I nodded and changed into my full armour. I summoned my bow in case I came across demons on earth.

I focused on Kitana and on earth, and I was surrounded by heavenly light. I channelled my energy toward earth, and I descended into the spirit realm on earth, on my new mission.

# CHAPTER 2

I stood in front of the library. The spirit realm was silent. All was still. There were no demons, and there were no elites nearby. I looked behind and saw the bridge and the harbour. Humans walked about in the physical realm. I went inside the library and found Kitana sitting in front of a group of people.

"Okay, class," she said. "This semester, we will focus on the armour of God. We will talk about spiritual warfare, and then one by one, we will cover the armour of God. Any questions about this?"

"Will there be an assessment for this, Kitana?"

"Not for this topic, Ed. This topic is open to this class as well as to the public. It is purely informational. I do hope it will help you all in your life, and I hope that with what you learn here, you will pass onto others. Any other questions?" asked Kitana.

"Why the armour of God?" I noticed the man who asked the question. It was Aaric.

"It is essential for every Christian to wear the armour of God. It keeps us protected from the wiles of the enemy. Wearing the armour ensures that we stand firm and that we continue to walk in obedience to God and do all that he has called us to do without hindrance. I will talk about this more next time, I hope to see you there." She smiled, and he reciprocated.

"Sure," he said.

"Alright, class dismissed," said Kitana. Everyone walked out except Aaric.

"I did not expect to see you here today," she said. He held her hand and kissed it.

"I thought I would surprise you, Kita," he said, and they embraced. "How was your day?" he asked.

"It has been good and productive. And yours?" she asked.

"Made a few arrests today, but other than that, the station has been quiet," he said. "But today is all about you, birthday girl." He kissed her, and they embraced.

"Twenty-five today," said Kitana.

"This is definitely the worst part, I just think this is all a little too cheesy, don't you think?" His voice was all too familiar. I turned around and saw Zaphael walking toward me. I summoned my bow and wielded an arrow toward him, ready to strike.

"Relax, Arden, I am not here to hurt you," he said comically. "I was wondering how long it would take for you to get here."

"What do you mean?" I asked.

"Satan has assigned me to Kitana here. She is very important to him. I knew you would be watching me from heaven, I just thought I would get you here a little sooner," he said. I looked toward Kitana and saw she was walking away with Aaric.

"Why?" I asked.

"It is all part of Satan's plan. I'm simply here to observe. I am not going to hurt her."

"You're a demon now, Zaphael, why would I trust you now?"

"I am not asking you to trust me. I am not here to hurt you, and I am not here to hurt her. I simply come and go as I please. Satan has me working on bigger missions than this," he said.

"Good for you!" I said, and he rolled his eyes.

"Sarcasm aside, how is heaven treating you?"

"You would have loved it there, Zaphael."

"No, thank you, I am quite enjoying my role as a commander. No rules on this side," he said, and I noticed that something else held his attention. He looked concerned, and he changed into his armour from his civilian clothing. "I am warning you, Arden. I have my orders, do not get in my way."

Before I could say anything, he ascended.

This was the first time I had seen him since the battle of the legions on earth. The angel I knew on Alvinor was no longer there.

15

He forfeited his grace and chose Satan. What did Satan want with Kitana? I realised that Zaphael was not going to reveal anything. I must focus on my mission and protect her. I focused on her again, and I saw her in her apartment with Aaric.

I orbed to her apartment and saw that she did not live too far away from the library. I looked around and studied the apartment. She lived in a penthouse with a view to the bridge and the Opera House. It was beautiful. Her home was tidy, and I could see that she liked warm colours. The sun was setting in Sydney, and I saw that there were less people walking along the street. Aaric was singing happy birthday to her, and Kitana was laughing.

"I love it!" she said. She blew out the candles and cut the cake. They began to dance, and they swirled around the apartment.

"I have never seen her so happy!" I gasped and saw another angel standing next to me in the spirit realm.

"Who are you?" I asked. She wore a long white robe, and she had long brown hair. Her eyes were the same as mine, gold mixed with blue. I had never seen her kind before on earth or in heaven, but I knew she was an angel.

"I am Yalina. I am Kitana's guardian angel. You are Arden, you are an elite assigned to protect her."

"Why couldn't I see you in the spirit realm before?" I asked.

"I understand your reaction to this. After all, this is the first time you have encountered a guardian angel. I have been assigned as her guardian angel since the time she was born. While there have been other elites assigned to protect her, they come and go, but I am with her all the time, and I will be with her until the end of time. I watch over her, guide her, and I protect her too. God told me that you are assigned to her."

"Then why did God not tell me about you?" I asked, feeling both curious and intrigued.

"Every guardian angel is assigned to a child of God. We, too, stand guard in the spirit realm, but we remain invisible to the demons and to the elites. We only reveal ourselves if we want to, otherwise, we remain hidden in the spirit realm. God has guardian angels shielded and protected in the spirit realm so no other angelic being can see us. It means we are protected from Satan and his demons."

"Then why did you choose to reveal yourself to me?" I asked.

"You are different from the rest of the elites I have seen and met. I also know that you are going to be with her for a long time. If God has assigned you to her especially during this season of her life, then I know you will need my help."

"Thank you," I said, and she nodded.

Kitana and Aaric continued to dance around the apartment as we watched.

"What makes you different from the rest of the angels?" I asked.

"Guardian angels are solely assigned to watch over humans. We do not engage in warfare with the demons. We stand by the humans and watch over them from the spirit realm. We do not fight with the demons. That is where the elites come in. Tell me about you," she asked.

I started to tell her about my time on Alvinor, my time with Satan in hell, and about Zaphael. She listened to me intently.

"Sounds like an adventure. You are truly a valiant warrior. I can see why God has assigned you to Kitana," she said.

"Zaphael has also been assigned to her. Do you know what Satan wants with her?" I asked.

"Arden, I have certain rules and restrictions of my own. I can only help you when I am commanded to. I am not to interfere in your mission but only help you to a certain extent, especially if she is targeted by demons," she said.

"I understand," I said. I thought about asking her for more information, but I decided not to. God has asked me to learn about Kitana and protect her. I must not disrupt Kitana's guardian angel. Yalina has her own mission, and I have my own.

"As an elite assigned to protect her, you are welcome to ascend to heaven anytime you like. You can stay in heaven, and you can descend at will. I have seen many elites do that, knowing that some elites have more than one mission. I won't interfere with your mission, but if you need me, you can simply say my name, and I will make myself known to you."

"Thank you, Yalina. I appreciate that," I said, and she nodded.

I felt a familiar chime ringing in my ears, and I knew I was being summoned back to heaven. "Speaking of ascending, it looks like I am needed in heaven," I said.

Yalina nodded again, and she veiled herself from me, disappearing into the spirit realm. I glanced at Kitana and Aaric one more time before ascending to heaven. I found myself standing in the arena, next to the grand citadel. It felt strange stepping out of time and into eternity. Pure light is constant in heaven, and I have grown to like watching the sunrise and the sunset on earth.

"Thank you for coming," said Vintore. Nikolai, Elandriel, Quiff, and Izralina joined after me. "Where is Valiana?" asked Vintore.

"She had to stay behind on earth for our mission. I will fill her in when I return," said Nikolai.

"Very well," said Vintore.

"Elites, as you are all well aware that we have a mission to destroy Reynak, I have learnt that there is a way we can bind the demons in Reynak so that when we destroy Reynak, instead of falling on earth, they will be permanently held in hell, unable to escape."

"How is that possible?" gasped Izralina. "Where did you get this intelligence from, Vintore?" she asked.

"From Michael. I have been working with him and Gabriel, and he was able to point me in the right direction. He said that there is a way we can bind up the demons in Reynak, and he said that to do that, we must find Cain."

"Cain, the human Cain?" said Elandriel. "How is Cain the key to binding up the demons?" he asked.

"The spirit of Cain. His mortal body no longer remains, but his spirit lingers on earth still," said Vintore. "And that is up to us to find out. Michael and Gabriel have their own missions on earth. I am grateful that they have guided me this far. We must learn all that we can and not go into this blindly."

"Where do you suggest we start?" asked Nikolai.

"Learn all that you can about Cain. He is the only lead we have at the moment. If you have anything vital, simply summon me, and I will be there."

"Understood," we all said together. I stayed behind in the arena while everyone else orbed away. I closed my eyes and focused on Kitana on earth. She was sleeping, and the spirit realm was quiet around her. I decided to go into the observatory in the citadel to see if I could find some information on Cain.

Izralina mentioned that Cain was a human. I decided to start with the Bible. The Spirit of God in me instructed me to start with the Genesis chapter. I thanked the Holy Spirit with my heart and started reading Genesis. I remember the first time I encountered the Spirit of God. I was in Reynak, held hostage by the commanders. The Holy Spirit's presence is strong, a blessing to both the angels and the humans on earth. I turned my attention away from my memories in Reynak and to the Bible. I only remember the creation of the universe, the angels, and the fall of Satan when God first created me and filled me with knowledge. I know that there is much to learn. Cain's name appeared in Genesis 4, and I began reading through the passage. "Adam made love to his wife, Eve, and she became pregnant and gave birth to Cain." Cain is the son of Adam and Eve, and he had a brother named Abel. Cain was angry with God because God favoured Abel. Cain killed his brother Abel, and so the Lord cursed Cain to be a restless wanderer on earth. God put a mark on Cain so that no one who found him would kill him. That must mean that Cain is an immortal on earth. I summoned Vintore, and he appeared.

"I see you have been doing a bit of reading, Arden. Good to see you focusing on this."

"Since Alvinor, I have been focusing more on the New Testament and the Book of Elohim than the Old Testament. The Spirit of God directed me to read Genesis to learn about Cain," I said, still holding the Bible.

Vintore sat across from me and grabbed another Bible. "I am well aware of the Genesis story. Though I must admit, I am finding it quite difficult to see any relation between Cain and Reynak," he said, flipping through the pages of the Bible.

"Vintore, God said that Cain will be a restless wanderer on earth. Cain cannot be killed since the time of Adam and Eve, before Jesus, he must still live. He must have died of natural causes, but his soul is immortal. His soul must still be wandering around earth. How can we find him though?" I asked.

"I am sure things will unravel as we do more research," he said reassuringly. "Should you not be on your mission right now?" he asked.

"I am assigned to observe a human. I have been keeping watch on her. In the meantime, I can travel between earth and heaven and focus on both missions."

"Anyone I know?" he asked, putting the Bible away.

"Yes actually, her name is Kitana."

Vintore did a double take and looked surprised. "Interesting," he said. "Well, I am sure you will enjoy this assignment. You can summon me if you need my help at all."

I thanked him, and he left the library.

Cain is the world's first murderer. How can the elites detect his soul? It would be impossible for his natural body to be sustained through thousands of years. Cain is immortal, but what does his immortality have to do with binding up the demons on Reynak, and how can Cain do this? Does he serve Satan? I decided to go to the one who could help me with this.

As I opened the palace doors, I saw that God was not alone. Michael and Gabriel were standing in front of God, adorned in their silver armour.

"That will be all for now Michael and Gabriel," said God, and they orbed out of the palace.

"Arden, I did not expect to see you back so soon. Is everything okay?" asked God.

"Yes, Lord. Everything is well on earth. I saw Zaphael. He said he has no intentions of harming Kitana and me. He is simply there to observe her and interact with her as he pleases. I have also met Yalina, Kitana's guardian angel, which has indeed been a new experience. I am glad that Kitana has that protection."

"As do all my children on earth. I shield the guardian angels in the spirit realm with my grace so that they remain unharmed from demons. They have orders too, as do the elites," said God. "There is something on your mind, and you want to ask me about it." He stood up from his throne and sat down on the steps, beckoning me to do the same.

"I will start with Kitana. I feel like there is more to her. It's like everyone knows something that I don't," I said.

"Arden, you must walk by faith and not by sight," said God. "If I tell you everything now, then you will miss the lessons I have for you to learn. There is a purpose for everything, and that is why I have asked you to observe and learn more about her. If I tell you everything all at once, then things will not move forward as I have planned. The future will be manipulated. You must take it step by step, walking in faith, with my guidance along the way."

"Okay," I said, knowing that it would be unwise to argue with God. I must have trust in him. "I have also been researching Cain for the mission with the other elites. I take it that I must also walk by faith and not by sight on this mission as well?" I asked God, and he smiled.

"Yes," he said. I sat silent for a while, and God sat there with me patiently. I had many questions for him, but I decided that today I would focus only on Cain. "Lord, what can you tell me about Cain?"

"I loved Cain very much. He was the firstborn of the first two humans I created on earth. He broke my heart when he murdered his brother, Abel."

I saw the sadness in God's eyes, but I remained quiet, waiting to hear more.

"Cain murdered his brother because of pride, hate, and jealousy, and so I cursed him to wander the earth forever. He would not die even if he wanted to. I cursed him to linger on earth until the final judgment."

"He is immortal?" I asked, and God nodded.

"Every human's soul is immortal. As for Cain, I was very angry at him for that is not how I intended humanity to progress since Adam and Eve's disobedience. Through my wrath, I cursed his soul to linger on earth. His natural body has withered away, but his soul lingers on earth. I have given a mark on him so that no human can ever kill him, not even Satan or the demons can harm him. He is to wander the earth until the end of this age. That is his punishment."

"Lord, we have learnt that in order to destroy Reynak, we must find Cain. Cain is the key to binding the demons in hell," I said.

"Yes, he is, and it is all part of the plan. The elites must work together to see this through. You do not need to fear, everything is under my control. Remember, you must walk by faith. The more you keep moving forward, the more things will unravel before you. Keep going."

I felt encouraged by God's words and knowing that no matter what, I must trust in him. At least I know that I am moving forward in the right direction. I bid him farewell and orbed down to earth to see Kitana.

A week had gone by since my last visit to Kitana. I had not seen Zaphael in a while, and Yalina remained hidden in the spirit realm. I sensed that Kitana was in the library and orbed there. She was teaching a class, and I noticed Zaphael sitting at the back in the physical realm. He noticed my presence, but his attention went back to Kitana.

"Today, we will talk about the armour of God. This topic is based on spiritual warfare and how we must stand firm against the enemy, who is the devil, by wearing each piece of the armour properly," said Kitana. "If you can all please turn to Ephesians chapter 6 and read from verse 10 to 17.

"Right then, the passage starts by asking us, the people of God, to be strong in him. It is God who gives us strength, and we are to trust in his power. By putting on the armour that is provided by God, we stand firm against the devil's schemes. Our struggle is not against humans, it is against the devil, the demons, and every kind of demonic powers and spiritual forces. Paul encourages us to stand. Notice that he is not speaking to people privately or individually. Paul is addressing the Ephesians as a group, as a community. This means that as Christians, we are to stand united because when we wear the armour and be part of a group, we stand stronger against a common enemy, who is the devil. If you stand alone, then it will be easy for the enemy to come with full force and weaken you and tempt you. If you are surrounded by people who belong to God, you are stronger to battle the enemy because you will always have help.

"Any questions so far?" asked Kitana, looking around the room.

"I have one!" said Zaphael.

"Yes, Zaphael."

"Verse 12 speaks of the spiritual forces of evil in the heavenly realms. What can you tell us about this heavenly realm?" asked Zaphael. I wonder what Zaphael could be up to. He already knew the answer to that question.

"I believe this heavenly realm that Paul speaks of refers to a spiritual realm between heaven and earth. The verse clearly says that there are spiritual forces of evil in the heavenly realms. I believe that there are demons residing in a realm above earth, a realm of its own. Satan's headquarters you could say," said Kitana, and the audience laughed.

"What are your thoughts on this, Zaphael?" asked Kitana.

"I think you are right. I would say that Satan and his demons rule the heavenly realms, or the second heaven as I like to call it. I believe that the demons on earth take their orders from demons who reside in the second heaven. The fallen angels have their own ranks."

"Interesting," said Kitana. "Thank you for sharing, Zaphael. I'm quite aware that you have an interest in demonology, so I do appreciate your input." Kitana picked up the Bible and continued to talk about the spiritual forces, and I could see that Zaphael was pleased with himself. He did not turn to me throughout the session but instead focused on Kitana. Surely he was not here for a lesson on spiritual warfare. There had to be more to this.

"We will stop here for now. Next week, we will begin talking about each piece of the armour, starting with the belt of truth, and we will go from there. But before you all go, I want to tell you about a debate that may be of interest to you so you can research about this in your own time. Some may agree to this, and some may not, while others believe that both sides are relevant and significant. I'll start with this question. Do we wear the armour of God against demonic powers, or do we wear it against human institutions who seek to oppress us? I will let you all think about this, and we can talk about this in our next class. See you all then." Everyone left except Zaphael.

"Zaphael, it is good to see you here again. I take it that you found this session interesting," said Kitana.

"I did. I was just here to return the book I borrowed. I do have a question for you though. What can you tell me about Nephilims?" asked Zaphael.

"Nephilims?" Zaphael nodded, and Kitana began flipping through the pages of the Bible. "Interesting question, Zaphael."

They sat down, and I saw Zaphael looking intently at her. Why was Zaphael asking Kitana about Nephilims?

"Let's see here," said Kitana. "Genesis 6 speaks of the Nephilims. I must say, that is something I rarely talk about in my research or at the library, but now that you have mentioned it, this does pique my interest. Verse 2 talks about the sons of God, whom I assume are the fallen angels. They saw that the daughters of humans were beautiful, so they married them. The Nephilims existed before the flood. We can only assume that the Nephilims are the offspring of human and the fallen angels. After that, the flood happened because God saw the wickedness in the heart of men."

"Do you think the Nephilims existed after the flood?" asked Zaphael.

"God chose only Noah and his family as the only humans to survive the flood. I cannot say if the Nephilims survived after the flood. It would be impossible to survive the flood. Unless the fallen angels mated with humans after the flood, then it is possible for the Nephilims to exist. But that is just my theory. The Bible rarely speaks of Nephilims. I'm curious, why do you ask about Nephilims, Zaphael?"

"I am intrigued about Nephilims. I want to learn more about it," he said.

Kitana studied Zaphael, and I could sense she was feeling uneasy around him. "What exactly do you do, Zaphael?" she asked.

"I am a writer. I am thinking about writing a novel on Nephilims. That is why I have taken an interest in them."

"Interesting, you do not look like a writer," she said.

"Appearances can be deceptive. I get that a lot," he said and smiled slyly. "But I would appreciate your help if you can help me with my book. I promise I won't intrude. Perhaps we can spend time talking about it after your class on spiritual warfare. I am usually free on this day."

"Sure, I can try to help you as much as I can," said Kitana. She picked up her books and walked away. As soon as she was out of sight, Zaphael stepped out of the physical realm and into the spirit realm.

"What do you think you are doing?" I asked.

"Researching," he laughed. It was a long time since I had seen him laugh like that. It reminded me of the Zaphael I knew on Alvinor. The Zaphael who had grace and hope. I realised that I could not allow my emotions to rule over me, so I focused on what Zaphael wanted with Kitana.

"Are you going to tell me what you want with her?" I asked.

"No," he said. "You have your orders, Arden, and I have mine. I have not hurt her, and I have not hurt you. I simply leave you alone. If I wanted to hurt you, I would have by now, yet here you stand."

"Why are you interested in Nephilims?" I asked.

"Well, that is for me to know and find out, and for you, well, to only find out."

He orbed away before I could ask him any more questions. Kitana was safe, and I am sure that Yalina is with her all the time. I decided to walk around Sydney and explore the city. The sun was about to set again. I enjoyed watching the sunset. The sunset today was different. The sky was filled with blushes of purple and pink, and I saw humans staring at it in wonder. Many took their phones out to take pictures of it. I orbed over to the top of the bridge where I once stood with Emrail. Watching Sydney from the top of the bridge became my favourite thing to do. I did this often after the last battle on earth between the demons and the elites. It would be dangerous for me to shift into the physical realm. I could not risk the humans seeing me in my armour. As night came, the city bustled to life, and the streets became more crowded than usual. Humans began gathering across the harbour, and they were dancing and having a good time interacting with each other. The spirit realm was quiet, and there were no demons in sight.

I focused on Kitana and saw that she was in her apartment with Aaric. I orbed down to her apartment and saw that she was upset with him. "You said you will come with me to church, Aaric. How can you change your plans so easily?"

Aaric sat next to her on the couch as Kitana grew more frustrated. "I told you how I feel about church. I was interested before, but not anymore. I am not interested in religion, Kita, and you will just have to accept that. I enjoy watching you speak at the library, and I am interested in what you do, but I am not interested in converting to Christianity," he said calmly.

"I just thought…" whispered Kitana, but this time, Aaric finished her sentence.

"You thought that you could save me," he said, and Kitana nodded.

"We have been through a lot together, Aaric, and you know how much I love you, and I do want to be with you. I had hoped that if you could come to church with me, you would see why I believe the things I do and that one day, you could give your heart to Jesus too, like I once did."

"Kita, I have never doubted your love. I am happy where I am, and I admire your faith, but for now, I want to stay away from religion. I do not have any intention of converting. I still want to marry you. I love you, but I need you to know that if you think you will change my mind after we get married, you will be disappointed. I don't want your expectations for me to ruin our marriage. If you want to be with someone who shares the same beliefs as you, then that is up to you." Aaric kissed her forehead and walked out of the apartment.

As soon as Aaric left, Kitana began to cry. I had never seen her so upset.

"Yalina."

She appeared to me in the spirit realm, in her long white gown, and she seemed to know why I had summoned her.

"I'll explain," she said.

# CHAPTER 3

Kitana was sleeping as we watched her from the spirit realm. "When I was on Alvinor, I saw them together. I saw Aaric proposing to her and saw how happy they were and are together. What can you tell me about them?" I asked Yalina.

"Kitana and Aaric have been together for many years. They fell in love when they were working together, and then they both started working in different places. Kitana got saved, she gave her life to Christ. She knew he was not a Christian, but she thought that one day he would be, and she still believes. It is dangerous being unequally yoked with nonbelievers. Is he good for her?" I asked, and Yalina looked at Kitana wistfully.

"Aaric is not the one for Kitana, he is not sent by God. I believe there is a man out there who is worthy of Kitana and who belongs to Christ. Aaric is not a bad person, but I believe he is holding her back from her true potential. God has much planned for her. She cannot move ahead until she truly decides what she wants. Deep down, I think she knows that it might not work out. She struggles because she has loved him for so long, it is hard for her to let go," she said.

"I wish I could talk to her," I said. "I am only commanded by God to observe and get to know her from the spirit realm. Zaphael, on the other hand, can do whatever he wants."

"Demons are ruthless, they do not adhere to divine commands. Angels are to obey every command of God. When God wants you to make contact with humans in the physical realm, he will let you do so in his timing, Arden. Have faith."

I heard Kitana scream, and I summoned my bow, ready to make a strike. I looked around and saw that there were no demons. The spirit realm was quiet.

"She just had a nightmare. It has been happening a lot," said Yalina.

"Do you think it is Satan?" I asked. "I have had visions where Satan would taunt and intimidate me."

"When humans dream, it is much different to a vision. I cannot discern the source of these dreams. It is difficult to say. I have heard her telling Aaric about her nightmares. She usually speaks of being surrounded by fire and darkness."

Kitana turned her bedroom light on and began to pray. "In peace, I will lie down and sleep. I will rest and lay my head down in the love of Lord Jesus Christ. I soak my entire being and my dreams with the precious blood of Lord Jesus Christ, and I declare that no weapon forged against me shall prosper. In Jesus's name, amen." Kitana bowed down and went back to sleep.

"There's a kind of strength to her," I said. "I can sense it in her, a peculiar form of power that I have never sensed in a human before. Something supernatural."

"She is powerful indeed," said Yalina. With another glance, Yalina shifted away from the spirit realm and into her own.

It was midnight on earth, and knowing that Kitana was safe, I orbed onto the top of the bridge overlooking the Sydney skyline. There were no humans around me. I checked again and shifted into the physical realm.

I liked being in the physical realm on earth. There is no sound or wind in the spirit realm. The wind blew across my face as I held onto the bars. Suddenly a light hovered over me, and Nikolai appeared. He stood next to me in the physical realm.

"I was not expecting to see you here, Nikolai. I thought you would be with Valiana on your mission."

"I am just checking to see if you are okay. Valiana is still on the mission. We usually take turns to go back to heaven or travel around to other places on earth," he said. He looked around the skyline and admired the view. "Is this your favourite place?" he asked.

"Yes."

"I like visiting New York, the city is never quiet," he said.

"I am also on a mission here," I said. "I have been assigned to a human, Kitana."

"I remember her. I was protecting her from demons on earth with Vintore and Valiana," he said.

"What do you think about the mission on Reynak?" I asked Nikolai, curious to know what he thought about destroying the second realm.

"I am actually excited about it. It means the end is near for Satan, and for the humans, the beginning of eternity. Isn't this what we are all waiting for?" he asked, and I nodded.

"I have actually found something on Cain. I have been researching in the observatory in heaven. I think it has to do something with the mark of Cain. The mark of Cain might be the key to binding up the demons in hell."

"Interesting," he said. "Arden, Valiana, and I don't really have time to research. The mission God has sent us on is very important. While we may be able to help in combat when the day comes, I don't think we can help at this stage. I am reconsidering this mission."

"That's okay, Nikolai, I understand, and I am sure Vintore will too," I said reassuringly.

"I must go now, Arden. Be safe." He admired the skyline again and orbed away.

I was still curious as to what mission Nikolai and Valiana were on, but I had to respect that the mission was classified. I focused on Kitana and saw in my vision that she was safe and the spirit realm was quiet around her.

I ascended to heaven and went back to the observatory to research more on Cain. I picked up the Bible and began reading through Genesis again. Cain worked the soil, yet when it came time to make an offering to God, God favoured Abel over Cain. Cain killed his brother, Abel, and so God cursed Cain to be a restless wanderer on earth. God said that no evil or man can touch him. He must still live on earth, but how can we all find him? I continued to read through the Genesis chapter, but then something caught my attention. *Nephilim.*

Genesis chapter 6, verse 4: the Nephilim were on the earth in those days—and also afterward, when the sons of God went to the daughters of humans and had children by them. They were the heroes of old, men of renown. What interest did Zaphael have in Nephilims, and what did it have to do with Kitana? The fallen angels mated with women on earth, and the offspring were called Nephilims.

"Thought I'd find you here." I looked up and saw Vintore walking toward me. "Just returned from an intelligence mission from Reynak," he explained.

"How is everything in Reynak? I have not been there for a long time," I said.

"The elites, including myself, are monitoring the commanders. Since our last invasion, there has been higher security. It is harder to gain intelligence, but we still try."

"I have already told the others, Nikolai and Valiana will not be part of the intelligence process for the Reynak mission. They will be part of the battle, but for now, they must focus on their own mission."

"That is fine. I have actually been doing a lot of learning and research. Cain must still wander on earth, but my question is, does he wander as a soul, or has his soul inhabited another body? It would be impossible for his natural body to exist in its natural state after thousands of years."

"Well thought out, Arden," said Vintore. "But we must be careful on how we approach this. If the elites are interested in Cain, then you can rest assured that the demons would be too."

"Understood," I said. I then decided to ask Vintore about Nephilims, and he looked surprised when I told him about Zaphael's interest in Kitana and Nephilims. "What can you tell me about the Nephilims, because I can't recall everything that God imparted to me when he first created me?" I asked Vintore.

"That is correct, Arden. God will only show you what he needs to. He did not want to overwhelm you. As a new warrior angel, he only showed you what you needed to know at the time. As for

Nephilims, I do not know why Zaphael would take an interest in Kitana and in Nephilims, but I believe God has endowed you with the grace to find out. He has assigned you to Kitana for a reason, and as you move forward, I am sure things will begin to unravel.

"I can tell you what I do know about the Nephilims, in the ancient times," he continued. "Before the flood, the fallen mated with women, which resulted in the Nephilims. The Nephilims were mortal."

"If angelic beings are spirit, then how can they mate with humans?" I asked.

"The fallen possessed men, willingly and unwillingly, and married the women. After the human body withered away, the fallen possessed another body. This made God angry. It was not the natural law, and the fallen, the demons, were distorting God's plan. God intended for a man and a woman to be together and procreate, not demons and humans. God wiped away the human race, all except for Noah and his family. After the earth was filled with people again and they flourished, the demons began to mate with women again. They were ruthless, and they mocked God. The numbers of Nephilims increased across the earth. Though mortal, they inherited some supernatural abilities from the fallen. God promised humanity that he will never wipe them away again. God saw that not all Nephilims were bad. There were some Nephilim that were good, who obeyed God and surrendered to him. And so God made a covenant with the Nephilim who obeyed him, that they will receive salvation and fight the fallen and the Nephilims who followed Satan.

"Should I continue or does this overwhelm you?" Vintore asked, but I encouraged him to keep telling me more. I found this very intriguing and perhaps this can help me understand Zaphael's curiosity with Kitana.

"Very well," said Vintore. "The Nephilims who were good were called the heroes of old, the men of renown. They lived a long human life, and after that, they ascended to heaven. The Nephilims who were bad, after their death, some were banished to hell, and some lingered on earth but in an immortal form. The good Nephilims, the heroes, were called the descendants, and the bad Nephilims were called the dominants. There was a large group that flourished during the reign of earth's biggest empire, the Roman Empire. The Nephilims lived alongside the Romans, but their identity remained a secret. Just as the elites battle with the demons, the descendants battled with the dominants. The dominants wanted to manipulate the natural law, they wanted immorality, and so they sought to find a solution that would give them immortality, just like the demons. They were not satisfied with having only half human traits. They saw it as their birthright to live a life of immortality."

"And did they find immortality?" I asked.

"Yes, but at a great cost. They had to complete a ritual, but before they could complete the ritual, the descendants intervened. Instead of attaining their full fallen nature, the dominants got turned into disembodied spirits. They are unable to assume demonic form, they linger as shadows. They are what you call evil spirits that taunt humanity. They, too, possess human bodies, causing them sickness and creating havoc in their lives. They serve and answer to Satan, they are a plague on earth."

"Can't we bind them in hell, just as we intend to do with the demons on Reynak?" I asked.

"I'm afraid not, Arden. Besides the ones in hell, the dominants are condemned to linger on earth until the final judgment."

"What about the descendants, what happened to them?" I asked.

"After the descendants destroyed the mortal form of the dominants, they were able to also make sure that no demon would ever mate with a woman again. They sacrificed their collective supernatural powers to make that happen, and they lived the rest of their lives as humans. Magic and sorcery were common during the ancient times. They did what they had to. It was a noble thing to do, and the covenant between God and the descendants remained strong.

"That is very interesting, I would have loved to witness that. Though it is a burden to know that we cannot do anything about the dominants that are on earth."

"The dominants, or evil spirits, get their orders from demons and Satan, so if we cast out demons and continue to disrupt their plans, then we are doing something about it. We both are witnesses of Jesus's plan for Reynak to be destroyed. We both know that the end is near. We can do it, the elites can do it. I have faith."

"Me too," I said, feeling hopeful.

"I am happy to see your progress, Arden. You are vital to this mission. Summon me if you learn anything new," he said, and I nodded.

I remained in the observatory, reading through the scrolls and the Bible and learning more about the creation of humanity and the events that happened after the fall. The angels in heaven are greater in numbers and in strength than the demons. The God of the universe is on our side, there is no greater power than God's power. I put the books aside and rested for a little while. I found myself being pulled into a vision. Something felt different about this vision; I did not have any control of it.

I was standing on top of a tower; I remembered this place when Satan held me captive. I was standing in Italy on earth, and it was dark. I turned around to see Satan walking toward me, wearing his black suit and a sly smile spreading across his face. I tried to break free from my vision, but I couldn't.

"It has been a long time. Arden. I must say, I do miss your company," he said.

"What do you want, Satan?" I asked, still trying to break free from the vision, but Satan had a strong hold over my mind.

"Why are you interested in Kitana Denali?" he asked.

"I could ask you the same, Satan."

"I want you to stay away from that human. She is mine," he snarled.

"No can do, Satan. All the more reason for me to protect her if she is of interest to you. She belongs to God," I said.

"I am warning you, Arden, stay away from this one. Otherwise, there will be consequences."

Before I could retort anything back, the vision ended, and I found myself back in the observatory. I sat up and saw Gelin sitting across from me.

"Are you alright?" he asked.

"How long have you been sitting here?" I asked.

"Long enough to know that something is not right. You want to tell me about it?" he asked.

"I just had a vision of Satan. He pulled me in while I was resting. I had no control over it. He wanted me to stay away from the human I am assigned to protect and watch over."

"Does this happen often?" he asked.

"It happened a few times when I was training on Alvinor. Ever since I ascended to heaven, this is the first time it has happened here. I don't understand how he can do this."

"Satan likes to play mind games and tricks, Arden. You were spiritually vulnerable when you were training on Alvinor. This allowed Satan to play mind tricks, lure you, and try to control you. Your strength diminished his deception. I believe he may have found some loophole so he can intimidate you. You must learn to shield your mind from him."

"How can I do that, Gelin?"

"It is simple. In your moment of weakness, you must find your strength in God. You must trust in God's saving power and call on God to help you. Do not engage with Satan when he tries to control your visions. Begin to pray, and call upon the name of the Lord.

"It can be easy, in a battle, to lose sight of God's presence and power and try to handle it on your own," he continued. "The more you do this, Arden, the stronger you will get in shielding your mind and visions from Satan. Practice makes perfect."

"You are right, Gelin. I will do that," I said.

"I will also be joining you in finding Cain. I volunteered to help on this mission since Nikolai and Valiana are unable to help for the moment. It is only a few of us elites who will be part of the intelligence gathering process, but when it comes to the final fight, the entire battalion will be a part of this. It will be grand. I can tell you that I am probably the most eager one to see Reynak destroyed," he said.

"I believe that," I said, and he chuckled.

"Remember what I taught you, Arden. You must shield your mind. Don't lose sight of God in the middle of trials."

I heard a familiar chime ringing in my ear, and I knew that God was calling me to the palace. I orbed to the front of the steps of the palace and opened the doors. God was seated on this throne, magnificent in all his glory. I bowed down in reverence. "You summoned me, my Lord?"

"Yes, my valiant warrior," he said. He stood up from his throne and sat down on the steps again and beckoned me to do the same.

I enjoyed sitting on the steps of the throne with God. I enjoyed spending time with him in his loving presence. I remember being here for a long time, learning from God, when I ascended from Alvinor and before I explored heaven.

"I like to spend time with each of my angels in heaven. I do the same with the humans on earth and who now live with me in heaven. I know you have a few missions, Arden, but I want you to know that you can always come and spend time with me too. It can be perplexing, especially when you have to deal with demons. You can find rest in me by spending time with me. Your entire being will be refreshed. Don't think you can do this alone because you are not alone."

"You are right, Lord. I have been very much occupied with my missions. The truth is, I have never thought of coming before your presence to rest. I don't like to stop, I like to keep going and moving forward and do everything I can," I said.

God looked at me lovingly and smiled. "I know that about you, which is why I summoned you here. It is okay to simply stop and spend time with me. It does not mean that you are behind on your missions. On the contrary, by resting in me and spending time with me, you will regain strength, and your spirit will become refreshed," he assured me, and I found myself letting go of all my tension. "Cast your burdens and anxieties all onto me, and I will sustain you, Arden," he said, but it also sounded like a command as well.

I nodded and changed from my armour and into a white gown.

"Tell me about Kitana. What have you learnt?" he asked.

"She is strong, and she is teaching the humans at the library about the armour of God, which I find very interesting. I liked the part when she was telling them to stand firm. She takes great interest in spiritual warfare."

"She is a valiant warrior, much like you, Arden," said God. "What did you learn about standing firm?"

"She said that the humans must wear the armour and stand firm as a collective. Standing alone leaves you with less protection against Satan, but being together with other Christians who also wear their armour is better. Humans are shielded and are stronger when they stand together and fight."

"I hope that you apply this to yourself too, Arden. My people must stand united. They are stronger together than they are alone. It does not mean they are weak if they are alone. I am with each and every one of my children. But if my people stand together by helping each other, praying for one another, they are shielded from every snare of the enemy. They are covered with a supernatural shield of protection. The same goes for the elites. Although most elites are assigned to one mission, they must stand together against Satan. The elites can always call upon other elites when they need help. The elites can also call upon me. I want to teach you, Arden, that you are never alone. You always have help all around you. For example, now, you are assigned to Kitana, but when in need, you can always call upon me. You can come before my presence, and you can summon other elites for help, at any time, for any reason. It is very important for you to remember this, Arden."

"Yes, Lord," I said, feeling encouraged by his words.

"I want you to keep learning about Kitana but also keep learning from her. Both of you are under my protection. Everything is going according to my plan, trust in me," said God, and he encouraged me to descend to earth.

I changed back into my armour and focused on Kitana. I descended on earth and found myself standing on a beach. It was evening on earth, and the sun was beginning to set. Kitana was standing there with Aaric. I moved in closer so I could hear what they were saying.

"I am glad we can talk about this, Kita," said Aaric.

"Me too, Aaric. I have missed you, missed us. I needed some time to think about all this," she said.

"I know, and I missed you too, Kita." Aaric held her close and they began to kiss.

She pulled back, and they sat down on the beach. "I'm sorry if I pushed you into converting to my faith. I said yes to marrying you because I loved you, and I will always love you. Yes, I hoped and still hope that you would give your heart to Christ, but I would never force you to do it. I love you for you, and I want to be with you for the rest of my life, Aaric," she said, and a tear escaped her eye.

Aaric wiped it away and kissed her forehead. "I love you, my Kita, and I want to be with you forever too. I am yours," he said, and he kissed her.

"Let's get married, let's elope," she said.

"Are you sure?" he asked.

"Yes, I don't want to wait any longer. We can go to Fiji next month!"

He studied her carefully and said yes. They embraced again and walked back to the city.

I continued to watch over Kitana over the months while she planned her elopement to Aaric and taught at the library. I had not seen Zaphael in the spirit realm in a long time, and I did not have any vision from Satan too. Everything was still, and I wondered how long this stillness would last for. I wondered if Aaric was the right man for her. Was Yalina right that there was someone better for Kitana, someone who loves God too, and someone who belongs to Christ? Was Kitana making a mistake by marrying the wrong man?

The day came for her to teach on the armour of God again. This time, I saw Zaphael sitting at the back again. He noticed my presence in the spirit realm, but he did not acknowledge me.

"Thank you for joining me today, everyone. We have been talking about standing firm and spiritual warfare. Last time, we talked about the armour protecting us from spiritual forces of evil as well as human institutions on earth and their persecution and oppression of the people of God. While that was a very lively discussion, I'd like us to move onto focusing on each armour of God. Today, I will briefly cover each part of the armour.

"Before I begin class, I want you to study this passage in your own time as well and understand it in its historical context, how it applies to the Christian community, and how it applies to you personally. You'll find that there can be differences when it comes to analysing this passage in its historical context and how it can be interpreted in contemporary Christian society in many different ways. I want you to think critically. Any questions so far?" she asked. No one answered, and they all seemed eager to learn.

"Alright, we will start with Ephesians 6, verse 14. You must wear the belt of truth buckled around your waist. The belt of truth is associated with integrity and honesty and trusting in God's truth. You must trust in God's faithfulness and in his truth, but you also must have integrity to walk the Christian faith in truth, without falling astray to the lies of Satan. You must also have the breastplate of righteousness in place. You must not allow Satan to attack your heart and fill it with impurity. You must put on the gospel of peace so you can stand firm every time Satan wants to disrupt the peace in your life and peace between others.

"Verse 16 states that you must take up the shield of faith so you can stand against Satan's arrows. Satan will try to confuse you and make you doubt in God and God's plans for you in your life. You must not allow him to do so. You must take up the shield of faith and fight the good fight of faith. You must take up the shield of faith by quoting Scriptures of faith from the Bible. Every time Satan tries to tempt you, confuse you, and utter lies to you, you must straight away declare Bible verses that empower you. You must speak out God's Word and have faith in God's salvation. This is just one facet of using the shield, which is exciting because there are many ways you can use the shield to defend yourself. Let us move to verse 17. You must wear the helmet of salvation, meaning that you must trust in God's salvation. Notice that the pieces that I have mentioned so far are only defensive. That means that the church, the Body of Christ, must stand united and stand firm in a defensive posture. Christ has already won the victory, and the people of God today must continue to declare their victory in Christ. The last piece of the armour is the sword of the spirit, and that is the Bible, the Word of God.

Notice that this is the only piece that is offensive. You must wear the armour of God effectively through defensive and offensive means. The armour is a gift of God, you must rely on God's strength and not on your own. You must wield the sword of the spirit and come into agreement with God's Word and declare his Word over your life so that all may go well with you. We will stop here for now, everyone."

Everyone went away except for Zaphael.

"Zaphael, it has been a long time since we last met."

"I'm sorry, Kitana. I had to travel for a while, but I'm back now, and I am hoping we can pick up where we left off."

"Sure, I can stay for a little while. I do have to leave a little early today. I will be meeting my fiancé soon."

"Certainly!" said Zaphael. "I have been doing some more reading on Nephilims so I can write about it in my book in detail. While I want my book to have some aspects that are historically accurate, I do want to leave room for my readers to indulge in the fantasy theme that my book has to offer. While I am sure I can easily do well in the fantasy part, I do need your help in understanding the historical part."

"I am not sure how much I can help you, Zaphael. The Bible offers very little information on Nephilims, and we have already made many assumptions and theories on the existence of Nephilims after the flood."

"My research has led me to conclude that there may be humans today who could have traits that Nephilims had. Perhaps they may come from the Nephilim bloodline, traits passed down to generations. Ordinary-looking humans but with unlimited supernatural potential." Zaphael implored her, but Kitana began to laugh.

"That does sound like a good storyline for your book, Zaphael, but that has no historical backup. If it is not in the Scripture, then we cannot assume it to be true. I have to leave now. I can no longer help you anymore on this. Good luck with your book, Zaphael." Kitana picked up her books and walked away.

The revelation hit me suddenly, and I stood right in front of Zaphael from the spirit realm. "We need to talk," I exclaimed.

# CHAPTER 4

"What are you playing at, Zaphael?"

"However do you mean?" he said playfully.

"You are saying that Kitana is a Nephilim!"

"No, I am saying that Kitana comes from a Nephilim bloodline, she has Nephilim traits, abilities that need to be unlocked."

"Is this what this has all been about? Satan warned me to stay away from Kitana because he wants to use her."

"Precisely," said Zaphael, and I began connecting the pieces of the puzzle. "She's a powerful human being, and we want her on our side," he said.

"I am assigned to protect her, Zaphael, so if you are going to get to her, you will have to go through me," I warned him.

"Your warning means nothing to me, but as a peace offering, I am willing to help you find Cain."

"How did you know about Cain?" I asked him. I did not expect him to know at all about Cain. How could he have found this information?

"You elites think you can outsmart us," he scoffed. "Demons keep watch over your activity too. We stumbled across some elites talking about Cain."

I studied Zaphael for a moment, and I did not believe that he was telling me this to make a peace offering. It was either a trap, or he was not telling me the whole truth. "What is your agenda, Zaphael? I don't believe that you are telling me the truth. Why do you want to help me, and why are you telling me this now? What do you want in return?"

Zaphael was quiet for a long time, and then he spoke. "You came to hell to rescue me, you wanted to save me, and you fought hard for me. Consider this a gift for your effort. Do not for a second think that I will ever return to God or help you again."

I did not reply. I stood there motionless for a while, finding it hard to believe that Zaphael wanted to help me in earnest. For a moment, I thought I saw the grace in Zaphael, but then I remembered the times we fought in the battle on earth. He has already given his allegiance to Satan, but it is hard to not have hope. He only gave me a name and a place before orbing away. "Adrian Galdon, Amsterdam."

I checked to see if Kitana was okay, and then I ascended to heaven. I stood in the arena, and I summoned Vintore, Gelin, Elandriel, and Izralina. They all appeared at once, and I told them about what happened on earth.

"It must be a trap. You can't expect a demon to help you willingly," said Izralina.

"It is the only lead we have on Cain, and it is the best one. It might undoubtedly be a trap, but we still have to try. I thought about Cain possessing a human body and that it turned out to be true. Cain, or his soul that is, is inhabiting the body of a human named Adrian Galdon. We must keep moving forward as things unfold, and we will stand firm, together, not alone," I encouraged them, and they all agreed.

"Here's the plan, elites. Izralina and Elandriel, you will stand guard in heaven and be on standby in case we need backup. Too many elites will be risky and may attract unwanted attention from demons. We also don't know how Cain will react when we question him. Gelin, you will keep watch from a few distance away. Arden and I will lead this task. If anything goes wrong, I want us all to ascend back to heaven," he ordered. "Is that clear?" he asked and we all nodded.

"Gelin, you will follow us in the spirit realm while Arden and I will walk in the physical realm," said Vintore.

Vintore and I changed into our civilian clothing and descended on earth. We walked through the streets of Amsterdam. The city was crowded, and it was dark.

"Where do we start?" I asked Vintore.

He looked around and saw a group of men sitting together near a bar. "Excuse me, gentlemen, we are new to Amsterdam, but we are looking for a man named Adrian Galdon. Do you by any chance know of him?" he asked.

They shook their heads, and we walked further into the city. Before I could say anything, Vintore answered my question. "I know what you might be thinking, Arden. It is like looking for a needle in a haystack as the humans say, but we still have to start from somewhere. If Zaphael told you just the name and the city, then perhaps he might be well-known, otherwise Zaphael could have given you more details on Cain."

We reached another bar and saw a group of men and women sitting outside and smoking. "Let's try here," I said, sensing that they might know Adrian Galdon.

"Hello, everyone," I said. They noticed us but went back to smoking except for one man. He stood up and approached me. "Hey, are you lost? I heard today that God is missing one of his angels?" he said playfully, and the others laughed hysterically.

"Nathaniel, is that the best you can do?" said one of the girls.

I saw Vintore trying to hide his smile. "We are looking for a man called Adrian Galdon."

"What do you want with him?" he asked.

"Our business is our own," I said, and he sat back down, ignoring me.

"Fifty-Four Lancaster Avenue," said one of the girls sitting next to Nathaniel. "That's where you'll find him."

We walked away, trying to find the street. We came upon a dark alley, and it was quiet. I led the way, and somehow, I knew we were walking in the right direction. We stopped when we found Fifty-Four Lancaster Avenue. We opened the door and saw two guards standing at the front, and we could hear music coming from below.

"We are looking for Adrian Galdon," said Vintore.

"Do you have a pass?" asked one of the guards. We saw a man entering the building behind us, and he showed one of the guards a gold wristband.

"No pass, no entry. This is a private club," said the guard.

"It's alright, Dave, they're with us."

I turned around and saw that it was Nathaniel and his group.

The guards nodded and opened the doors. "Thank you for getting us in," I said.

"Not a problem," he said and walked away with the rest of his group.

"This is a nightclub," said Vintore. I looked around and saw that below the level we were standing on, there was a big dance floor. People were dancing and drinking. There were private lounges all around the club where people sat and talked.

A grand chandelier hung from the top, and it reminded me of the citadel in Reynak.

"Follow me." We turned and saw Nathaniel beckoning us to follow him. He led us down the stairs and inside another set of doors. Two guards were guarding a large door. Nathaniel opened the doors and led us inside. A man sat on a couch, with two women at each side of him.

He gestured to Nathaniel to leave us alone with him. "Delilah, Martina, I will see you ladies later." He kissed them both, and they left us until we were alone with Adrian. He sat there, looking at us for a while, studying us, and he said something that I did not expect.

"I was wondering how long it would take for the angels to find me," he said.

"Am I talking to Cain or Adrian?" asked Vintore.

"That didn't take too long, I'm impressed," he said. "I am Cain, and the body that I am inhabiting belongs to Adrian Galdon, who is my host."

"How is that possible?" I asked.

"I am immortal, cursed to be a restless wanderer. I have been inhabiting human bodies for thousands of years. Mortals who practice sorcery and divination willingly open their bodies to be possessed by demons or any kind of spiritual entities. I am no demon, but I am a soul who can inhabit bodies who worship Satan. Adrian Galdon here practiced witchcraft. He opened his life to the supernatural realm, and I possessed him. I must say, I enjoy inhabiting the body of a nightclub owner and a drug dealer. Sin at its best! I'm going to hell anyway, might as well enjoy the ride."

"We need your help," said Vintore.

"You want my mark, the mark of Cain," he said, and Vintore remained quiet. "The demons want my mark too. They have been chasing me for a long time. They cannot hurt me though, nothing and no one can," he said wistfully.

"Then you know why it is important for us to get your mark," said Vintore.

"Yes, the demons want it to use it on you, and you want to use it to bind demons," he affirmed, and Vintore nodded. "Intriguing," whispered Cain. "And you believe that you would just find me and think I would easily give you my mark," he said.

"Which side are you on?" I asked.

"Neither," he said. "I'm merely wandering on earth until the final judgment. I enjoy my time living amongst humans in host bodies and knowing that no supernatural being can hurt me."

"You knew the angels would find you, you were expecting us. You allowed your workers to help us, you wanted the angels to find you," said Vintore, and I realised he was right. Nathaniel and the people with him worked for Cain. They led us straight to Cain, and if Cain did not want us to find him, then we would not have found him so easily.

"Do your workers know?" I asked.

"No, they believe they are serving a drug lord," he said.

"Cain, you wanted us to find you. If you are not willing to give us the mark, then what do you want with us?" asked Vintore.

Cain was silent for a while. He stood up and began to study me and walked around me, looking at me with a curious gaze.

"I'm harmless." He smiled. "I want to know more about the angels. I want to know more about you. These are my conditions—if you want to have a chance at getting my mark, then I want to get a chance to know you," he said, gesturing at me. "Is this a chance you are willing to take?" he implored. "I will leave you here to talk about it, and when you have your answer, you can meet me outside."

"This just keeps getting interesting," I said to Vintore, and he agreed.

"Arden, you don't have to agree to his conditions." I thought about this and realised that there was no other way. The mark of Cain was the only way to bind the demons, and if the demons want him to get to us, then we must get his mark first. If there's a chance that Cain can help the angels, then I must accept his conditions.

"Vintore, I will do it. He cannot hurt me, and I don't believe it is a trap. I think Zaphael gave me his location so if we have the mark, they can steal it from us. He said he is bound to go to hell, what does he have to lose?"

"I'm still suspicious," said a familiar voice. I turned out and saw Gelin standing behind me. He shifted from the spirit realm and into the physical realm.

"It's all clear, there's no demons nearby in the spirit realm," he assured us.

"We all know how important time is. If we have any chance at getting the mark of Cain, then this is the only way. We have to protect and guard it from the demons. He said he wants to get to know the angels, to know me, what is the harm in that? Vintore," I said, knowing that he would understand, "I told you to trust me when you had to let me go in hell. Trust me now, this feels right."

Vintore and Gelin exchanged glances, and Vintore nodded.

"I know." Vintore smiled. "Summon us if you need us," he said, and he orbed out of the room.

With one last glance, Gelin orbed too.

I walked outside of the room and saw Cain sitting on the other side of the dance floor, before the bar. I sat next to him, watching him drink and gesturing to the person serving to get me a drink, but I declined.

"I'm a spiritual being, I do not need to eat or drink, and I am not fond of alcohol," I said to Cain, and he politely nodded.

"I take it you have agreed to meet my conditions?" he asked, and I nodded. "Excellent!" he said and asked the man at the bar to pour him some more drink.

"What exactly do you want with me?" I asked.

"I want to know more about you."

"But surely there has to be more?"

"Yes, but all in good time." He grinned.

"Okay what do you want to know?" I asked.

"Oh, straight to business, I like it! How did you actually find me?" he asked.

"It started with Michael, the archangel, and then after doing some research on you, I was able to learn of your location through a demon, Zaphael."

"Ahh interesting, yes, Zaphael came to visit me many weeks ago. He wanted my mark, but I told him no. I got sick of the demons, so I considered going into hiding, but I'm having so much fun with the life of Adrian. It's hard to let go," he said and ordered another drink. "Okay next question, what is happening in heaven now, between the angels and the demons?" he asked.

"Angels and demons are in constant battle in the spirit realm. Demons always plot to conquer humankind. Ceaseless warfare."

"If the demons and the angels want my mark, then the end is near. I can sense it, I can feel it. Tell me, when is the final descent of Jesus? Has God decided on a time?"

"I can only tell you that the time is near, nothing more. Only God knows when Jesus descends on earth for the second and final time," I said, and he looked disappointed. "I don't understand. You said you are bound to go to hell, and you look disappointed that you do not know the exact time. It is as if you want the end to happen now."

The man at the bar offered him another drink, but this time Cain declined. "If you did your research on me, then you are well aware that I am cursed. It can get a little boring when you've been a restless wanderer for thousands of years. Everyone I have ever loved has gone to dust. I have watched all my family die, one by one, and there was nothing I could do. Though I enjoy this sinful life, sometimes I grow weary. Cursed to be a wandering, restless soul."

I was about to ask him some more questions, but something else took my attention. I could feel that Kitana was in distress. I focused on her and saw that she was in her apartment crying. I phased out of the vision and saw Cain was watching me in fascination.

"I must go!" I said.

"You know where to find me," he said.

I walked outside of the club and made sure that there were no other humans around. I shifted into the spirit realm and orbed straight to Kitana's apartment. I saw that she was surrounded by demons in the spirit realm. They were whispering things to her, and they were taunting her. Kitana was screaming, and she was asking God to help her. I summoned my bow and attacked the two demons that were surrounding her. I did not recognise any of them.

"Lord, help me! Make these thoughts stop!" Kitana cried out. "Lord, send down the angels that you have assigned to me. I pray that they surround me with a hedge of protection and heavenly fire. May they cast away the evil and darkness near me. Help me, Father!"

I continued to block myself from their attacks. Two of the demons had swords, and one held me to the ground while the other pointed his sword to my neck.

"The famous Arden of heaven," said one of the demons. "I'm disappointed. After all the talk going around, I thought you would be stronger. Yet here you are, right under my very sword."

"Satan will be pleased," said the demon standing next to him.

I lifted up my right hand and held it up. I began to pray to God, and the demons began to laugh. "She's a fool like this mortal here."

"Help me, Lord," I declared out loud.

As soon as I did, I saw a lance pierce the demon holding his sword against me and vanish into black smoke. It was Gelin. The other demon orbed away when he saw that Gelin was about to attack him. He lay back down on the floor in relief. I was not expecting to confront demons, especially after this very eventful night on earth.

"I'm glad you prayed for help," said Gelin, holding out his hand to help me up.

"I didn't expect to find demons. I have had a lot on my mind and have been busy."

"So I've noticed," he said. I checked on Kitana and saw she was lying on her bed, feeling at ease, and she appeared to be much calmer.

"Expect the unexpected," Gelin reminded me.

"Thank you, Gelin." He made sure I was okay and then ascended back to heaven.

I made sure that the spirit realm was clear and then summoned Yalina. She appeared from the spirit realm and appeared concerned.

"The demons have taken interest in her since she gave her life to Christ. I see them tormenting her from time to time," she said solemnly. Before I could say what I wanted to, she answered my question for me. "That's why there are elites, Arden. I am not here to fight the demons."

I understood. "They appeared out of nowhere. I am trying to learn more about her, protect her, and I am also trying to stay focused on my other missions."

"You are overwhelmed," said Yalina, and I nodded.

"Arden, it is okay for angels to be overwhelmed. We have will, emotions, and intellect too. Where do you find rest? What gives you peace the most?" she asked, and I knew what she was trying to tell me. I thanked her, and I ascended to heaven before God's throne. He was sitting on the steps before his throne, as if he was expecting me. I joined him, and realising that I was still holding my bow, I summoned it away.

"I am pleased, my valiant warrior," he said. "Yalina is right. I am happy that you came to me. I am your source of rest, your source of peace and your strength," said God, and I smiled at him. It was true, the overwhelming feeling that I felt on earth was gone, and I found myself to be in perfect peace when I was with God. The cloud of darkness and scattered thoughts disappeared when I was in his presence.

We both sat quietly in the palace, and I was shrouded in peace as the light of heaven filled the palace. I felt ready to speak, and I noticed that God was still patient and full of love and kindness.

"I did not expect that my missions would be two of the most important missions ordained by you in the end times. I am not ungrateful, and I do not ever have any intention of making any complaints Lord, but sometimes, it feels like I am walking in the dark.

Why not reveal everything about Cain and Kitana to me right now rather than me having to discover it for myself step-by-step?"

I thought God would get annoyed, but his demeanour never changed. He was still very much patient, and his eyes showed love and understanding. "It would be easy if I gave you all the answers, Arden. If I did that, then I would not have the need to create new warrior angels in the end times. I have specifically created you, Nikolai, and Valiana for my end time plan. You all had to go through many trials and tribulations, and you passed. All but one. Zaphael made his choice, and you made yours. I require my people to walk by faith and not by sight. Faith brings an atmosphere of miracles, doubt kills miracles. I have ordained events to happen in a time and place, and if you walk toward it with faith, then it will unfold as I have intended. If you doubt and question my authority, then it will fall apart, and that is where confusion comes in. If I tell you everything about Cain, his mark, and what this means for the end times, you will fail to understand the significance of my end times plan and purpose for both the angels and humanity. As you continue to walk by faith, you become stronger, and everything that I have purposed will continue to unfold before you effortlessly. There are some things that you must discover for yourself so you can become the warrior I have created you to be. I would have easily used the other elites and assigned them to Kitana and to Cain, but I have chosen you and set you apart for the final part of my plan." He stopped and waited for me to speak, but I stayed quiet, wanting to know more. He smiled and continued to talk.

"Arden, look how far you have come. From your days of training on Alvinor and to destroying Reynak, you have grown so strong. If something was not going according to my plan, you would know it by now. I ask that you trust me and walk by faith. It is okay and perfectly acceptable to be overwhelmed. What you are doing is no small feat. You are right in saying that you are leading two of the most important missions in the end times. For that is why I have created you, have I not?" I nodded, and he smiled again.

"Call upon me like you did just now, and I will intervene. Remember, there is no power greater than mine. I am God of the universe, and I can see everything that happens. I ask that you trust in your calling. Come to me, and find rest, and you'll find that your spirit will be refreshed. You are on the right path, Arden, keep going."

He was right. The doubts and worries I had disappeared, and I felt my spirit refreshed and stronger. "Yes, Lord," I said. I sat together with God in the palace in silence, enjoying his presence, and I felt my spirit at peace before his presence. There was no need to speak anymore. I realised that words did not matter anymore when full understanding was perfect. God knew how I felt, and God can see everything that I do on earth, and I have full faith that I was and am never alone. He has declared many times to me that he is always with me and I must trust him on that. I know I can succeed on these two missions. God was right. If something was not happening according to his plan, then I would know it by now. I believe that I am on the right path. I believe that I am going in the right direction with Cain and with Kitana too. There is a plan and purpose for everything that God ordains. I bowed down to God in reverence and descended back to earth.

Once I made sure that Kitana was okay, I orbed to Amsterdam. I was in the spirit realm as I walked around the club, trying to find Cain. I went to a corner and shifted into the physical realm, making sure that no human saw me. I noticed Nathaniel sitting on a couch, sitting with a group of women. "You're back. Good to see you again."

"I am here to see Adrian."

"I had hoped you'd come to see me," he said and winked. "I take it that business went well with him last time?" I nodded, and he gestured to the door that he led us in last time.

"I was beginning to wonder if you would ever come back. I am pleased to see you here. How rude of me! I don't even know your name."

"Arden."

"Arden. Beautiful name, like yourself," he said. "Let us walk outside."

I did not know what to expect with Cain, but I knew that God was with me, and so far, I knew I was going in the right direction. We walked along the cobbled streets of the dark alleyways until we came to a larger city centre where there were more people. It was evening in Amsterdam, and the city was full of life.

"I love Amsterdam," said Cain. "It is different from all the other cities I have lived in. I feel much more free here. Adrian Galdon has an amazing life."

"How long do you inhabit the body of a host?" I asked, feeling curious about the first and only immortal human I have met.

"Being a sinner that I am, I can only inhabit the body of a sinner. I cannot influence those who have received salvation. I only inhabit a human body for a decade, and then I change to another host. It would be unfair for me to steal all of their life."

"But you do have morals," I said.

"Yes." He smiled.

We came across another city centre, and I saw that we were surrounded by many gothic structures and cathedrals.

"In the thousands of years I have lived on earth, I must say, Amsterdam is the most wonderful city I have lived in. Magnificent," he said, admiring the buildings and the city. "Now tell me all about you. I want to know more about you, Arden."

I did not know where to start, and knowing that I only met Cain, I became cautious. I told him about my time on Alvinor and battling with the demons. Cain listened intently.

"Your friend, Zaphael, he came to see me," he said, and I nodded.

"Former friend, and yes, that is how we were able to find you in the first place. He gave us your location."

"We both know the demons want to trap you somehow. He is using you to get my mark. I suspect they will attempt to somehow get it from you, if I do decide to give you my mark," he said.

"We are well aware, Cain, but we have something or rather someone that they don't."

He arched an eyebrow, waiting for me to answer.

"God and his power." Cain didn't say anything, and he stayed quiet for a long time.

"Cain…what will exactly happen if the demons do get your mark? I know that nothing can harm you as long as you are on earth, but if you decide to give your mark to the demons, what will happen?"

He sat on a bench, and I joined him. "The demons want my mark to use it against the angels. You want it to eliminate the demons from the realm between heaven and earth, to make way for the Son of God. If the demons have the mark, they can use it as a shield so no angel can come down from heaven down to earth. The mark will act as a shield so the demons can do anything they want in the second heavens and on earth without the intervention of angels."

I looked at him, feeling a little shocked, and he continued.

"The demons have been pestering me for thousands of years. They cannot harm me, but they do like to intimidate me. I have grown quite weary of their presence to be honest. That is why I do not give them my mark, and I like my life on earth. I have watched humanity in all their glory and in all their doom and destruction."

"Cain, if you wanted to give your mark to the demons, you would have given it to them by now. Why are you willing to take a chance on the angels? Why are you considering helping us?" I implored him.

"Because for the first time in my entire existence, I want to do something right."

## CHAPTER 5

"Oh, don't look so hopeful, I still haven't made up my mind." He chuckled. "You look a little bewildered," he said, and I could not help but smile.

"I just did not expect our meeting to go this way. I did not expect you to be so civilised," I said.

"You did not expect the world's first murderer to behave so civilised," he said. "Believe it or not, Arden, but a lot of things have changed in my thousands of years of existence. I am immortal not by choice, this is a punishment. It was a mistake killing my brother, Abel, and though it is too late for me to repent, I do take responsibility for my actions. I am condemned to go to hell, Arden, and I accept it."

"But now you want to make it right. You want to make it right with God?" I asked.

"I did say I enjoy my time on earth, but sometimes, I do want this all to end. I have grown weary of the demons harassing me. I have grown weary of wandering around waiting for the end. I want the end to come sooner rather than later. This is all part of God's plan, Arden. God will not interfere with my free will. It is up to me to decide."

"What will happen when you do give your mark? Your mark grants you immortality, so when you give your mark, you will cease to exist?" I asked.

"Giving you my mark means that I will have to sacrifice myself. Rather than waiting for the final judgment, I will go to hell sooner." He looked amused.

"You are perfectly at ease going to hell before the appointed time?" I asked, not knowing how I should navigate this conversation.

"Like I said, I accept my punishment for murdering my brother. Pride, envy, and jealousy overtook me, and I did not like how God favoured Abel. It has taken thousands upon thousands of years for me to grasp the magnitude and consequences of my sin."

"Yet you continue to commit sin through sinners?" I asked.

"After my natural body withered away and I died, my soul was raised up through the mark given to me by God, and I have been wandering around earth ever since. If I walk around as a soul, I can see the spirit realm, but if I inhabit the body of a human, I can walk among humans in the physical. I grew tired of demons chasing me in the spirit realm, so I decided to choose host bodies."

"What could you see in the spirit realm?" I asked, finding Cain more fascinating.

"The spirit realm was dark, a void, empty. Demons only chose to reveal themselves if they wanted to, otherwise, I merely just walked alone through the void, no one to talk to and with nothing to do. I like my time with the humans, but if what I'm sensing is true, then the end is nearer than I thought. God has asked me to play a part in it, through you, and I must decide if I want to, or not."

"What is stopping you?" I asked.

"Precious time," he whispered to himself, and I wondered what he was talking about. "I will consider giving you the mark, only under one condition."

I stayed quiet, waiting for him to tell me more about his condition. He grew sad and looked at the people having fun and laughing in the city centre.

"Once I go to hell, I will be alone for eternity, separated from every soul that is there. I will see people I have known suffering in hell, and I will suffer too. My wife is in hell, Arden. She rejected God's salvation. I loved her with all my heart. We both lived in disobedience. Though I was condemned, my wife was not. She did not repent, and she lived her life on earth outside the will of God. Her soul is in hell, in torment. When I go to hell, I know Satan will torture and torment me, separate me from her for eternity. I yearn to see her, speak to her, Arden. I want you to take me to hell, Arden. I want to see my wife one last time if I am to give you my mark."

"A mortal cannot survive hell. Adrian Galdon's body cannot survive hell," I exclaimed.

"I take it you don't fancy another trip to hell?"

"I'm not very fond of all that happens there, Cain," I said. I did not expect this to be his condition.

"I'm going to hell anyway, Arden. I want to see my wife, Awan. I trust the angels to see this through. I don't trust the demons to help me. They will trap me in hell, even if they can't harm me. I want you to take me to hell to see my wife and bring me back to earth. If you do this, then I will give you my mark. I will go as a soul and leave this body. You will see my soul in the spirit realm."

"You are thinking if you should trust me, that I might be working with the demons to trap the angels?" he asked. I considered this but my spirit knew that he was telling me the truth, even if it sounded very absurd. "I must speak with the other angels, Cain. This is a decision that I must make with the others. It is not a matter of trust. You said so yourself, Cain, the time is near, and time is precious."

He stood up calmly and smiled. "You know where to find me." He walked away without looking back, and I remained sitting in the seat.

This was big. How can we possibly go into hell with Cain, and where would we begin looking for his wife? Hell had many tunnels, it was endless, and how can we be shielded from the demons in hell? I needed to talk about this with the others. I walked into an alley where there were no humans, and I shifted into the spirit realm. I ascended to heaven and stood in the middle of heaven, in front of God's palace. I saw Vintore and Gelin walking out of the palace, and they stood still when they saw me.

"You have news," said Gelin, and I nodded. We walked toward the grand citadel, and I told them about Cain's offer.

"That is absurd and dangerous," said Gelin.

Vintore remained quiet throughout the walk and listened intently. "What do you think about all this, Arden?" he asked.

I turned to Vintore and we all now stood before the grand citadel steps. "This is all happening more quickly than I thought. I thought it would take a little more convincing for Cain to give us his mark. He is willing to sacrifice his immortality for this plan. We need to move forward with caution," I said, and they both agreed.

"How do we go into hell this time?" I asked. "I cannot go alone with Cain. I will need backup."

"Arden, you are not alone. We are all in this together. Cain has chosen you to reveal all this to you. Gelin and I will go through the strategic details. You have done so much, I need you to take a break," said Vintore, and I knew he was right. "Leave this to us. We will summon you once we get more details. I will speak to Michael myself. For now, rest in heaven." They left me outside the citadel, and I thought about what I would do. Kitana is safe on earth, Cain is waiting for my answer, and Nikolai and Kitana are on some secret mission. I decided to go down to my quarters and rest.

I lay down on my bed and closed my eyes. It has been a long time since I have been in my quarters. I suddenly got pulled into a vision, and I found myself sitting by a lake. I was on earth, and I didn't recognise where I was. The lake stretched on, and behind me, there were dozens of trees. It was midafternoon, and I felt that I was not alone in this vision.

"We meet again."

I turned around and saw that Satan was sitting next to me on the bench. I tried to shield my mind and get out of the vision, but he was strong.

"Stop resisting. I only want to talk," he said, looking amused.

"What do you want, Satan?"

"I know the angels want the mark of Cain, and I know that he is cooperating with you. Once you get the mark, I want you to give me the mark. If you don't give me the mark, I will kill Kitana, the human you have been assigned to protect."

"You can't kill, Kitana. She belongs to God. You don't have any say in her life. Empty threats don't really look good on you, Satan," I said, and I tried to shift out of the vision. "Lord, get me out of here," I declared out loud, and I focused on getting out of the vision. I saw

Satan glaring at me one last time before I found myself back in my quarters. It worked! This took a lot of strength, and I must rely on God's strength to protect myself from Satan's schemes. I knew where I needed to go next. I went out of my quarters, and instead of orbing into the palace, I walked to God's throne. He was sitting alone, on the steps, as if he knew I was coming to see him.

"You've been expecting me." I smiled.

"Yes," said God and held out his hand so I could sit next to him before his throne.

"It is good to see you learning to shield yourself against Satan," he said.

I relaxed in his presence, and I took comfort in him. "All it takes is to call upon you and not believe Satan's lies," I said, realising that Satan was intimidating me and that he is intimidated by what he is threatened by.

"Tell me about your progress," he said.

I began to tell him about my encounters with Cain, observing Kitana, and my time with the other elites. God listened patiently and intently. There was something in my spirit that was bothering me, and I knew I could not keep it to myself.

"Cain is willing to help the angels gain the upper hand and sacrifice himself and go to hell before the appointed time. Can he not be redeemed?" I asked God.

"My decision and authority is final, Arden. When I make my judgment, I do not turn back. Cain accepts his judgment, and I will not interfere with his will. The mark I gave him is a supernatural mark, it has divine power. The mark of Cain is just one powerful cosmic power, and if he does not want to give his mark, there would be other ways for my plan to work. My plan will move forward regardless of Cain."

"Cain has asked me to take him to hell to see his wife. That is his condition. If I take him into hell and take him out, his soul that is, then he will give us his mark," I told God, but he waited patiently for me to speak more. "I can do it, Lord, but I need your grace to shield us, make us invisible to the demons. But in my vision, Satan said that he will kill Kitana if I do not give him the mark of Cain when Cain does hand it to me."

"And you believe him?" asked God.

"I believe that he is unpredictable and that he can do anything without remorse."

"Arden, Satan is a liar. He is intimidated by you, and he has seen how much you are capable of. There is no power greater than mine. You did the right thing by calling upon me for help. You relied on me and my power, and I gave you the strength to overcome his schemes. That does not mean you are weak. You are a powerful angel. It is your humility and obedience to me that helps you stand firm against Satan. I am in control of the universe, not Satan."

I sat quietly for a while and admired the crystals around the palace. I found so much peace with God before his throne. I enjoyed resting in his presence. I began to think about Cain and his request, wondering how it would ever come to pass.

"I admire your courage to go to hell again," said God. "I will allow you, Cain, and another elite to go to hell. My grace will shield you. However, it will only be for a limited time. Light does not belong in darkness, therefore, good cannot survive in evil. It will be like last time. You will all have an hour, and when you will find time closing, you will feel it. You must all ascend back to earth before the portal closes. My grace will shield you from the demons, but you will remain visible to the souls there."

"Thank you, Lord. You are most gracious and kind." I bowed my head in reverence.

"I believe in you, Arden, and I believe in this plan. Trust in me, valiant warrior."

"Yes, Lord." I went out of the palace to find Vintore and Gelin. I found them inside the observatory looking through scrolls. I began to tell them about Cain's conditions as well as God's.

"I spoke to God, and he said he will shield us with his grace, though he said it will be Cain, myself, and one other elite," I said, looking between Vintore and Gelin.

"I'd like to volunteer," said Gelin.

Vintore nodded, and Gelin looked excited.

"Arden, you will be leading this mission. When you are ready, you may summon us. Michael will open the doorway to hell," said Vintore. "I have every confidence in you." He smiled.

"Thank you, Vintore. I must go to earth and tell Cain," I said.

I descended to earth, and as I was focusing on Amsterdam, I felt my spirit churning uncomfortably, and I felt something was wrong with Kitana. I focused on descending to Sydney instead and found myself in Kitana's apartment in the spirit realm. She was not alone. She was angry, and I felt a powerful surge rising in her. I have never felt that in a human. She was yelling at Aaric, yet he appeared to be quiet and calm.

"How can you do this to me, Aaric? How can you do this to us?"

"Look, Kita, nothing happened after that. It meant nothing, and it was a mistake," said Aaric.

"I saw you kissing another woman, Aaric, a month before our wedding!" she yelled.

"We were drunk, Kita. It was a work party. She kissed me," said Aaric, trying to console her, but she signalled him to stop where he was.

"And I saw you kissing her back, passionately!"

I summoned Yalina, and she appeared. "I thought you would need me for this," she said.

"I could sense her distress. I needed to make sure she is safe," I said, thinking about that powerful surge of energy I felt in Kitana. "What happened?" I asked Yalina.

"Kitana was in distress last night. It wasn't demons, it was a nightmare. It was the worst one yet. She needed to find Aaric, and she knew he was at a work party just down the street at the bar. Everyone was very drunk at the party. Kitana found Aaric and another woman kissing and getting intimate. I have never seen her so heartbroken. The woman made advances toward him, and he reciprocated because of his drunkenness."

I looked back between Aaric and Kitana, and I knew that whatever came next would not be good. Kitana took off her engagement ring and gave it back to Aaric.

He fell down to his knees. "Don't do this, Kita. Give me another chance. I was drunk, I'm so sorry, please forgive me." He started crying, but she was still very angry.

"We have been through so much together, Aaric, and we have fought hard for our relationship, but I am done fighting. Sober or not, if you loved me, you would have never reciprocated. I have accepted many of your vices, but what happened last night, I can never accept that."

"I love you, Kitana," whispered Aaric, staring down at the ring.

She faced away from him and stared out to the harbour. "I need you to go now, Aaric."

Aaric looked defeated. He gave her one final glance and walked out of her apartment. Kitana fell on the floor crying again, and Yalina sat down next to her.

"Lord, give her comfort. Bless her with peace that surpasses all understanding," Yalina prayed. "She is strong, she will be okay," said Yalina.

"Yalina, I have to go on an important mission, and I don't know when exactly I will be back. I know I am assigned to protect Kitana. I also know that Satan has taken great interest in her," I said, trying to reassure Yalina, but I think it was more to reassure myself. I know I had much more to learn about Kitana and her identity, but the mission to hell was more important now.

"Arden, Kitana will be okay. Let God's plan unfold as it is meant to."

I nodded in acknowledgement and orbed to Amsterdam. I stepped into the club, and the security guards recognised me. They did not stop me this time. I found Cain sitting in a lounge with Nathaniel.

"Ahh, Arden, good to see you back," said Cain. "Nathaniel, let us be."

I sat next to Cain as Nathaniel joined others on the dance floor.

"I take it the angels have made a decision?" asked Cain, and I nodded.

"We have agreed to your terms, Cain. We will take you to hell, and after we bring you back to earth, you will give us your mark."

"We?" he asked.

"If you want to see your wife, you must be invisible. That includes us angels too. Demons are sprawling around hell. If they see us, we will be trapped. God has allowed you, myself, and another angel to help, and his grace will keep us invisible in hell for an hour of your earth's time. We will be invisible to the demons, but not to the souls, so we must be careful, and you must follow my instructions when you are with us."

"What will happen if we don't make it out in the hour?" he asked, looking concerned.

"We will be trapped. Remember, we are entering their dominion. If we don't find your wife in hell in time, we must get out."

"Understood," he said. He looked around the club solemnly and began to smoke his cigar.

# CHAPTER 6

S tanding in Cain's room, I could see he was starting to get anxious. "What is it like there?" he asked.

"It is unlike anything you have ever experienced. I must warn you, Cain, you will see much pain in hell."

He began to pace back and forth.

"Cain…you don't have to do this. No one will interfere with your free will. We can stop this right now," I said.

He stood still for a moment and gazed at me silently. "No, I will not let fear take a hold of me. I will stand by my word. I'm ready," he said. "I will need you to shift into the spirit realm. I will meet you there," he said with a command.

I nodded, and I shifted into the spirit realm. I summoned Vintore and Gelin to earth, and they descended immediately.

"I take it that Cain is ready?" asked Vintore, gazing at Cain in the spirit realm. "This is progressing well," he said, and Gelin nodded.

I looked around us in the spirit realm, and there were no demons near us.

Cain rested on his bed and closed his eyes. There was a surge of energy coming from the physical realm and into the spirit realm. Cain's soul emerged from Adrian's body, and he was standing before us.

I looked down at Adrian's body and saw that he was still. As if reading my mind, Cain followed my gaze to Adrian.

"He will awaken in a few hours, as if nothing has happened. He will continue on as Adrian Galdon, drug lord and club owner. He will have no memories of the things I did while I was in his body. It will be as if he had awakened from a long, deep sleep."

My attention now returned back to Cain, and for the first time, I saw his true self. His soul reflected his form when he was human. His black hair fell to his shoulders, he was youthful, and his brown eyes scanned around the spirit realm.

"I thought we would be surrounded by demons any moment now," he said.

"We are protected by God's grace for this mission. They cannot detect us," said Vintore.

"What now?" asked Cain.

"We are going to need some altitude," said Gelin.

"Meet us at the top of Mount Fuji. Michael will be waiting for us there," ordered Vintore, and he orbed instantly. Gelin joined him.

I held out my arm to Cain and beckoned him to hold on. As soon as he did, I focused on Mount Fuji and began to ascend, and we found ourselves standing at the top of the mountain.

"Ahh, Japan. It's been decades since my last visit here," said Cain wistfully.

I saw Michael standing at the peak, in his silver armour and holding his sword.

Cain looked at Michael in awe. "You don't have to tell me who that is," said Cain, looking at Michael in admiration.

We joined the others at the peak and stood in a circle.

"Son of Adam," said Michael, acknowledging Cain.

"Let's strategise," said Gelin, waiting for me to take the lead.

"We have one hour according to earth's time to find Cain's wife, Awan, her soul that is, and get back to earth before the portal closes. This is much like the mission that Vintore and I went to, when we went to find Zaphael." I started having flashbacks of my last time in hell. I regained my focus and saw others were patiently waiting for me to speak further.

"The souls in hell will be able to see us, but through God's grace, no demon will be able to detect us. We will be shielded for an hour. We will be trapped if we don't get out. We will know when it is time to leave."

This time, I turned to Cain. "Cain, you will have your time with your wife, but when it is time, we will need to leave, and you will give your mark to us as agreed."

He nodded his head.

"I will stand guard from up here. As long as the door to hell is open, I can see all that happens," said Vintore.

Michael thundered his sword to the ground, and the portal to hell opened. "Be on your guard," commanded Michael. "And, elites, let's not make a habit of this." Michael stood there, waiting for us to jump into the portal.

Gelin jumped in first. Cain stood there, looking inside the portal.

I signalled him to descend, and with a final glance around us, he jumped in, and I followed him.

The descent to hell was quick, and the smell of the sulphur burnt into my nostrils. "Everyone okay?" I asked.

"This place is hideous," said Gelin, looking around the tunnels. I noticed that this time, we were standing between deep tunnels, and I could hear howling and screams echoing toward us. Cain was looking anxious, waiting for my command.

"Where do we even start?" said Gelin.

"I think I know," I said. I commanded Gelin and Cain to walk behind me as I tried to remember the tunnel where Idora was at. As we walked through the tunnels, the souls looked at us solemnly, reaching their hands out to us.

"Help me," one woman cried out.

"Take me with you," said a man, banging against the bars.

"We are getting some unwanted attention, Arden. Where exactly are you taking us?" asked Gelin.

"I'm taking you to a fallen angel I met here last time. Her name is Idora. She has been condemned by God."

"I know Idora from our time in heaven when God first created the heavens," said Gelin.

We came across the middle of hell, and I could see the lake of fire in the distance.

"Eerie," said Gelin, glaring at the lake.

I could feel tension radiating from Cain, and I encouraged them to keep following my lead. I saw the stairs that led up to Satan's lair and remembered where Idora was from here. I turned to the tunnels to the right and walked deeper in.

"I believe we are here," I said, scanning through the tunnels.

"Welcome back, never thought I would see you again." I noticed Idora's voice. Her chains rattled as she walked toward the bars. "And I see you have brought some company," she whispered and glared at Cain and Gelin. "Cain." She smiled. "Unusual circumstances, I see you have chosen to give your mark to the angels. Noble decision," said Idora. "It has been a long time, Gelin," she said, and I could hear the agony in her voice.

"Idora," said Gelin. She was waiting for him to speak but he retreated back and stood guard. She signed and bowed her head.

"Cain, my Cain, is that you?" a voice whispered from down the tunnel.

"Awan!" Cain ran down the tunnel and held onto the bars.

Gelin followed him and stood guard. I remained with Idora.

I could hear Awan crying and Cain trying to console her. "Why are you here again, Arden?" Idora looked at me intently.

I told her everything that happened the last time I saw her.

"The demons want the mark of Cain to use it on the angels," said Idora, and I nodded. "We are aware."

"There has been some talk of a Nephilim on earth, a descendant. Have you found her?" she asked. Sensing my surprise, she smiled. "I'm glad you did. The Nephilim is on Satan's agenda. Keep the descendant safe from Satan's grasp."

This caught my attention, and I saw that Cain was still talking to Awan. "What can you tell me about this?" I asked her.

"I only know that you must protect the descendant at all cost. If the Nephilim is led astray by Satan, there will be much damage," she said. "The end is near, much nearer that you think, Arden. Be on your guard," she said and walked to the back of the cage.

I joined Cain and Gelin.

"Awan, my love, I am content now that I have seen you again," said Cain.

"You did not have to make the sacrifice, my Cain, you could have more time on earth. It is agony in hell, why did you do this?" she cried.

"So I could have this moment with you. Now that I do, I can bring this to an end. I will gladly give my mark to the angels rather than the demons. Awan, my love, the end of all things is near. God has asked me to play a part, and I have decided. I will not retreat. My time on earth is over."

I began to feel uneasy and noticed that Gelin was frowning. We both knew it was time to get out of here.

"Cain, it is time, we must go," I said.

"Cain, the longer we stay here, the weaker our shield gets. We can easily get detected by demons. We need to leave now," I commanded, and Cain nodded.

"Goodbye, my love. I love you for eternity," said Cain, and Awan began to weep.

We came out of the tunnel and saw demons hurling down souls to the lake of fire. Gelin looked at them in disgust.

One of the demons signalled the other demons to be quiet and looked around. "Do you feel that?" he asked the others.

"Can they sense us?" asked Cain, and I signalled him to be quiet. I signalled the others to follow my lead back to the doorway. The demons could sense us, that means our shield is becoming weaker.

Suddenly, a force pulled us into the middle of hell, and we found ourselves pinned to the ground. The screams coming from the lake of fire grew louder, and I could see that the souls were trying to climb out, only to be pulled back again.

I tried to get up, but the force was still pinning me to the ground. The demons across the lake looked at us, and I immediately knew that we were no longer shielded.

"Fancy seeing you here!" I noticed that familiar voice. I saw Meridan walking toward us, and we were now surrounded by demons.

I could no longer feel the force pinning me down and stood up. "I see that you have done the easy work for us, bringing Cain right down to our doorstep. Well done," she said, smiling wickedly.

"I will never give my mark to the likes of you, demon filth," said Cain.

"You are in no position to make demands, Cain. You're in our territory now," she snarled. "And you, I'm stuck here because you cast me away," she said.

Before I could say anything else, Meridan and the demons around us shifted into a beast form. They were no longer in their angelic form. Their claws clicked together, ready to attack, and they snarled with their long, deformed teeth.

"You are hauntingly hideous," said Gelin, summoning his lance, and Meridan leapt toward him.

"This was never part of the plan, Gelin," I said, trying to protect Cain from the other demons. I summoned my bow and began to attack the demons.

Gelin looked like he was having fun battling with Meridan. Knowing that the portal might close anytime now, I raised my right hand and began to pray. "Father, help us."

There was thunder, and the ground beneath us began to tremble. Light broke through, and elites began to descend. I noticed Vintore, standing ready with his blades.

"I brought reinforcements." He smiled and moved me aside to attack the demon that was coming from behind.

More demons began to surround us, and the elites were attacking them, trying to shield Cain and me. I saw Azarey helping Gelin fight Meridan.

I looked around and saw that the demons were beginning to overpower us.

"Arden!" screamed Cain, and I saw a demon trying to pull Cain into the lake. My arrow hit the demon, and it sprawled back to the lake. I pulled Cain back up. "We need to take this fight to the surface," he said, and I agreed.

"Vintore, we must ascend," I said.

Vintore commanded the elites to ascend. We all raised our right hand up and began to ascend. I held out my arm to Cain and ordered him to hold on.

We found ourselves in the spirit realm on earth. We were standing on an open field, on a desert in the northern part of the world. The demons followed us to the surface, and the battle continued.

"Didn't go according to plan, but I'm glad we brought the fight to the surface before the portal closed," said Vintore, and before I could reply, he began to help Azarey with a demon.

I felt Cain tugging my arm. "Arden, I must flee. I can't give my mark here to you. The demons are distracting us. I need to go, you must trust me," said Cain. I thought about this for a moment and knew he was right. "I give you my word, Arden, when the time is right, we will meet again, and I will give you my mark. I must go," he said reassuringly.

"Okay," I said. I saw him disappear into the physical realm, perhaps inhabiting the body of another human.

I noticed an elite lying on the battlefield and a demon pointing his blade to his neck. It was Gelin, and I saw that he was wounded. White light was beaming from the claw marks that were on his arm. I charged toward the demon, but he saw me coming. He grabbed me by my arm and hurled me down next to Gelin. He changed back into his angelic form, and I saw that it was Spirion. He attacked me with his blade, but I quickly shielded myself with my bow. His foot pressed my arm, and I couldn't move.

"Not so tough now are you, angel!" he said and began laughing. He was about to attack again but then stopped midway. The other demons changed to their angelic form from their beast form. One by one, they began to burst into black smoke. I sat up and looked around. Only the elites remained; some were lying on the ground, also wounded.

"What was that about?" said Gelin, struggling to get up. I helped him get up, but he was still unsteady. I saw the other elites helping the wounded, and they ascended to heaven.

"I don't know," I said. "I'm glad it's over though."

Light beamed from Gelin's wound, and I struggled to keep him steady. Vintore came and helped me keep Gelin steady. "Let's ascend now to the grand citadel. We are taking the wounded elites there to be healed," said Vintore.

I focused on the grand citadel, and the three of us ascended to heaven.

Elites walked about carrying the wounded in the grand citadel. "Here, let's take Gelin into that healing room," said Vintore, leading the way to the back corner of the citadel.

I opened the door and saw another elite. She had long blonde hair, and she was also wearing an armour just like us. She gestured to us to help Gelin sit on the bed.

"Arden, I will leave you here with Gelin and Freydah. Freyda is an elite and also a healer. I must go and attend to some things," said Vintore.

Gelin began to shift uncomfortably.

"Be still," said Freydah. She hovered her hand over Gelin's wound and closed her eyes. As she did, light began to illuminate from her hand, and Gelin's wound began to close. Gelin's wound disappeared, and he looked like he was no longer in pain. He looked down his shoulder and smiled.

"Thank you, Freydah. Thanks, Arden," he said, and I nodded.

"What happened this time?" asked Freydah.

"Angels being angels, and demons being demons," Gelin said, and Freydah laughed.

"Gelin, I advise you to take some time to rest before going on any mission. That wound was very deep," said Freydah, looking concerned.

"I shall," said Gelin. "Arden, I will see you later." He walked out the door, leaving Freydah and I alone.

"I have been eager to meet you, Arden. I have heard of your many braveries." She gestured to me to sit on the chair as she sat on the one across from me. The room was warm and peaceful, and I could see the arena through the window.

"There's many elites I have not met. I have to say, seeing you heal Gelin was remarkable."

"Thank you," she said. "All the elites can heal. I have been especially assigned to heal the elites that are wounded during battles. I also heal humans on earth. That is what God has commanded me and assigned me to do, and I enjoy it. I can teach you how to heal if you like. I do understand that you have much to learn than the other angels. I can feel the Spirit of God nudging me to teach you healing."

"Yes, I would really like that," I said. Before I could ask any more questions, she began to frown.

"You'll have to forgive me, Arden, I am being called on earth."

I nodded, and she orbed from the room immediately. I began to feel excited about learning to heal. I could heal humans, and I could heal other elites too. Freydah was right, I do have much to learn, but I have already come so far since my time on Alvinor.

I saw Azarey and Quiff in combat in the arena and decided to join them.

Azarey hurled Quiff to the ground, and Quiff began to roar with laughter.

"That technique is horrible, I can easily break free, Azarey," he said.

Azarey hurled him up and summoned her bow. Quiff also summoned his staff, and they began to combat. Quiff was stronger in weaponry than Azarey, and Azarey was stronger in physical combat.

"Ahh, Arden, good to see you. You were great on the battlefield. I don't know what happened with the demons, but I'm glad they disappeared," said Quiff, blocking another attack from Azarey.

"I admit that was very strange, but I won't worry about that. I see you two have been busy," I said.

"Just helping with each other's weaknesses." Quiff chuckled and blocked another attack from Azarey's bow. "Azarey is helping me in physical combat, and I am helping her in weaponry. All this time together since the fall, and we still have much to learn."

"Maybe I can help," I said.

"Oh?" said Azarey in surprise, and they both stopped where they were.

"When I was observing you two, I could see your techniques easily. Quiff, you spend more time defending your opponent rather than attacking. You need to find a balance and focus on the weak spots of your opponent and use that momentum to be on the offensive. Notice the moments your opponent gets caught off guard, and use that time to attack them. Azarey, you are great with your bow when it comes to the offensive, but as you can see, Quiff is strong in blocking offensive attacks with his staff. You will gain more advantage if you learn to do the same, by using your bow to block your opponent's weapons."

"The student becomes the teacher. Well done, Arden, you have a good eye," said Quiff.

Azarey used her bow to attack Quiff, but he quickly diverted it away, and her bow fell to the other side of the arena.

"Perhaps some more practice," he teased her, and she rolled her eyes. She picked up her bow, and they began to combat again, and other elites came to watch them on the sidelines, cheering for both of them.

I stayed for a little bit longer, and suddenly I heard a familiar chime ringing in my ears. God was calling me to his throne.

I left the arena, and rather than walking to the palace, I orbed up and stood before the palace doors. I opened the grand doors of the palace and saw God sitting on his throne. God's glory filled the palace, and I admired the jewels glistening from the walls as I walked toward him. I bowed down in reverence.

"You summoned me, my Lord?"

"Yes, Arden," he said. "Tell me what happened?"

I stood back up, and I saw God holding his gold staff with his right hand. His beautiful brown eyes gazed down at me, and his grace radiated throughout the palace.

"A lot has happened since our venture in hell. Cain was able to meet his wife in hell, but we ended up getting caught by demons, and there was a battle. We led the demons to the surface, and they burst into black smoke suddenly and unexpectedly. It was too dangerous for Cain to give me his mark during the battle. He fled, but he gave me his word that he will give me his mark. Some of the elites got wounded, Gelin being one of them. Freyda healed him, and she has offered to train me in healing."

God remained silent for a moment and smiled. "This does not overwhelm you?"

"What do you mean, Lord?"

"My valiant warrior, how fearfully and wonderfully I have created you. Even some of the elites can get overwhelmed with all the tasks they've been assigned to, but you, warrior, are standing firmly.

You speak with confidence, and you have grown a lot since your time on Alvinor. I summoned you here so you can simply be still and know how incredible you truly are. You are the only angel since the fall to have ventured to hell twice. You have led battles, overcome many of Satan's attempts to lead you astray, and you have continued to stand strong in me. I want you to know how important you are in this war. I want you to know how truly precious you are to me. Your humility to help your friends, your love for humanity, your aversion to evil, your thirst for righteousness, and your obedience to me, I adore you, my chosen one. Yet here you stand, unshaken and power-ful, like a tree on earth, planted firmly, and you are being continually watered by my grace and guidance."

I bowed in reverence again, not knowing what to say. I did not expect God to shower me with these words of encouragement.

"You assumed that I would assign you more missions?" he asked.

"I have been so busy, Lord, with many things, and you are right, I have not stopped. And I don't like to stop, Lord. I like to soar, and I know I have much to do."

"You need to hear my words, Arden. My words have power, and it refreshes your spirit. When I summon you here, it is not always to give you more tasks. I like to spend time with my angels too, to uplift and encourage them. I want you to know how proud I am of you, Arden. You are doing well. You did the right thing to let Cain go. I want you to keep moving forward. I know you have many tasks ahead of you, but never forget, you can always ask for help. You are never alone, remember this, always."

"Yes, Lord, amen."

I walked out of the palace. I didn't feel weary from the battle, and my spirit felt light and refreshed. Suddenly, the Spirit of God in me began to churn, and he whispered, "Kitana." It dawned upon me that I have been so busy with Cain, hell, the demons, and the other elites that for a moment, I forgot about Kitana. I focused on Kitana, and I could not feel her presence on earth. Something was wrong.

"Go down to earth now," said the Spirit of God, and I didn't hesitate.

# CHAPTER 7

I descended to Kitana's apartment, and she was not there. I orbed down to the library where she worked, and she was not there either. I closed my eyes so I could focus, but I could not feel her presence anywhere on earth. How could I have been so foolish? Weeks have passed by on earth since my last visit to Kitana. There was no way I could summon Yalina; she would be with Kitana, and I could not detect Kitana at all.

"Zaphael!" I summoned him in the spirit realm as I scanned across the library. I waited, and I could feel his presence.

"You called?" he said.

"You know why I have summoned you here, Zaphael, where is she?" I asked, and he was smirking. "She has been under my watch, and I know she has been under yours as well. Now where is she?"

"I am not at liberty to say anything. If she is under your watch, then it is up to you to find her. Goodbye, Arden, I have more important things to attend to," he said, and he ascended before I could say anything else.

I looked around the library, hoping I could find Kitana, but she was not there. The other elites are busy with other missions, I would not want to hassle them. Aaric! If something was wrong, then Aaric would know where she is. I closed my eyes and focused on Aaric. I could see him outside of the central police station on duty. I orbed down behind the alleyway, making sure there was no human nearby. I changed from my armour and summoned human clothing, my usual blue jeans and black top. I saw him opening his car door.

"Aaric."

He turned back in surprise. "I'm sorry, do I know you?" he said.

"I am a friend of Kitana. I can't find her, and I was hoping you would know where she is."

"I've never met you before?" He studied me curiously.

"I'm actually visiting from Europe. We actually met in the Netherlands when Kitana travelled around. I didn't tell her I was coming, and I was hoping to surprise her."

"Ah okay. I am on my way to the hospital to see her. I received a call from her work not too long ago. She collapsed, and she hasn't been waking up. She is at the Orion Hospital. I can take you there too, if you want."

"That would be great," I said, walking toward the passenger side and sitting beside him in the car.

He was quiet as he began to drive toward the city. After a few moments of silence, he finally spoke.

"I am still surprised that she has not mentioned you before, and you know me and know where I work," he said.

"We met in summer school at Utrecht in the Netherlands, and we became really good friends, and we have kept in touch. She has talked about you and that you are a police officer. I came to the closest police station I could find near her address, and here you are."

"The timing is great," he said, still looking at me suspiciously.

"Yes, definitely," I said, thinking about Kitana. "What else can you tell me about what happened?" I asked.

"Her work friend called me and told me to go to the hospital. All I know is that she collapsed and is not waking up. I don't get it, she was well and healthy the last time I saw her."

I could hear the sadness in his voice. He didn't bring up his and Kitana's break up, and I didn't ask any more questions. We stayed silent throughout the entire way to the hospital.

Aaric pulled up to the front of the hospital, and the staff directed us toward the reception. "Hi, we are here to see Kitana Denali," said Aaric.

"How do you both know her?" asked the receptionist.

"I am her partner, and this is Kitana's friend. She has no other family," said Aaric.

After scanning through her computer screen, she gave us two passes and directed us to Kitana's room.

"Room 21B, here we are," he said. He led me inside, and we saw a doctor standing by Kitana's bed.

"Hello, I'm Dr. Lana Lordel. You must be Kitana's partner." Aaric nodded, and he walked to Kitana, holding her hand.

"How is she?" he asked, stroking her hair. I stood at the edge of her bed while Dr. Lana grabbed the report from the bedside table.

"Kitana is in a coma. I have never come across a case where a patient is perfectly healthy and is in a coma. Kitana's vitals are good, there is nothing internally wrong with her. She may have hit her head when she fell, but that alone is not enough to send someone into a coma. This is one of the strangest cases I have ever come across."

Aaric looked like he was deep in thought. This time, I spoke. "What can we do in the meantime, Doctor?" I asked.

"Wait," she said. "We will keep monitoring her and will keep you informed if there are any changes."

"Mr. Rashid, as her emergency contact and partner, I will need you to fill in some paperwork, when you are ready of course. I will meet you at reception," she said, leaving us alone.

Aaric kissed Kitana's hand and closed his eyes.

"I don't understand," he whispered.

"She will be okay," I said.

"I'll do the paperwork now. Would you like some coffee?" he asked, and I shook my head.

As soon as Aaric left, I shifted into the spirit realm, and I summoned Yalina.

"I'm here," said Yalina, appearing behind me.

"What happened?" I asked, scanning around the spirit realm, but we were alone, and there were no demons.

"Whatever this is, it is supernatural. When she fell, there were no demons in the spirit realm. There is nothing wrong with Kitana in the natural. There is a darker power at hand."

"Can you not see further into this?" I asked.

"My vision is being blocked. I can't see any further than this, Arden."

"I should have kept a closer look on Kitana, this is my fault," I said.

"This is not your fault, Arden," said Yalina.

"Kitana has been on Satan's agenda for a while and I should have prioritised her."

"Arden, I'm sure that all your other missions are just as important. Like I said, this is beyond my control. I watch over her soul, and I am always by her side," said Yalina, trying to reassure me.

"That's it!" I said, and Yalina looked surprised. "Only Satan would do something like this. This explains all the other things," I said, already planning about my next step.

"Whatever happens from here, Arden, be careful, and stay on your guard. If Satan is behind this, he is using very dark power," warned Yalina.

The door shut, and we saw Aaric come back. He looked around, no doubt wondering where I was. He walked to Kitana and sat beside her, holding her hand.

"I'm sorry, Kita, I love you," he whispered, holding his head down.

"He still cares very deeply for her," I said.

"He does, but he is not the one for her," said Yalina. We stood there, watching them both from the spirit realm for a while.

"I must go now. I think I know where to begin," I said. I ascended from the hospital, and I orbed to the top of the Sydney Harbour Bridge. It was twilight, and the city skyline was beautiful, just as I had remembered it. I shifted out of the spirit realm and into the physical. The wind was strong, and the air was cool. I needed to get this right. God had assigned me to protect Kitana, and it was my duty to watch over her, especially knowing that she is of interest to Satan too. Zaphael didn't prove to be useful the last time we met. This time, I had to try something a little more radical. I closed my eyes, focusing on the one who could hopefully help.

"Thinking about switching sides?" he said.

"Emrail," I said, acknowledging his presence. He stood next to me on the bridge, admiring the bridge.

"I remember bringing you here. Don't worry, we can share our favourite place," he said and smiled wickedly. "You know, Arden, usually I don't answer when an elite summons, but when I saw you, I just couldn't resist."

"I called you here because I need your help, Emrail," I said.

"Oh? And what makes you think I would help you?" he asked.

"You are less intimidating than the rest of the commanders," I said.

"I'm actually hurt that you said that, Arden," he said playfully. "What do you want?" he said, his playfulness disappearing instantly, and his face grew serious.

"What can you tell me about Kitana Denali? She is in a coma, and I know that Satan is behind this."

Emrail was quiet for a long time, and he faced away from me, looking down to the humans dancing in the club below us.

"Satan has her soul, hence, the coma. If you want to find her, you will have to find Satan," he finally said, looking at me curiously.

I thought about his words for a moment. Satan has her soul trapped. This sounds like a trap, and I did not expect Emrail to help me, yet he did. Is this another trap? Zaphael didn't help, yet Emrail has been very willing.

Emrail snapped his fingers, and my attention returned to him.

"Satan doesn't have the authority to trap living souls in hell, therefore, he can't be in hell and neither in the second realm. He is on earth," I said, trying to put the pieces of the puzzle together.

"Very good," said Emrail.

There could be a million places where Satan could be on earth.

"Let me give you a hint, elite. Think back to when you were touring the earth with Satan. Is there anywhere specific that he took you that was pure evil, evil at its best?"

I thought about my time with Satan, and there were many places he took me to. I remember being at the Vatican where Satan showed me his human followers worshipping him. Satan said the Vatican was the centre of his dominion on earth.

"Ah, there it is, I can see it in your eyes," said Emrail.

"I know. Thank you," I said, and he nodded.

Emrail was about to ascend, but before he could, I stopped him. "Wait."

He stopped, keeping his back toward me. "Why did I help?" he said, turning his head to the side but still keeping his back toward me.

"Yes," I said.

"Because I can," he said, and he ascended.

I closed my eyes, and I focused on the Vatican. There was no time to waste. I orbed instantly to the Vatican and found myself standing on top of the building in the spirit realm. It was midafternoon in the physical realm. People were scattered about on the streets. They walked along the cobblestones, and the sun was at its peak. The spirit realm was quiet, and I was alone. I remembered the way in from the last time that Satan took me here.

I walked downstairs, and I saw a figure sitting in darkness. She sat, kneeling in the middle of the room, and I recognised her soul. Her brown hair fell to her face, and she looked scared. She was alone.

"Kitana."

She looked up at me. She looked weary, and I saw that she could not speak. She wanted to say something, but she couldn't.

"She can see, she can hear, but she can't speak in the spirit realm." I recognised that familiar voice, and Satan emerged from the shadows and stood in front of us. "You look well, Arden."

"What have you done, Satan!" I summoned my bow, ready to attack.

"You elites need to relax. I'm not here to fight," he laughed. His eyes were fiery red, and he wore his usual black suit.

"What do you want, Satan?" I asked again.

"It's simple actually. I want the mark of Cain. I saw the battle in hell and on earth, and I was not pleased. If he gave you the mark, I would know it by now," he said, circling us, and I stood close to Kitana, shielding her.

"That was you. You made the demons disappear during the battle," I said, realising that Satan had something to do with that.

"Meridan and the others were banished to hell for eternity after our last...conflict. You look surprised," he said and smiled menacingly.

"They were fighting us for infiltrating hell," I said, curious as to why Satan would throw his own into the lake.

"I ordered them never to ascend to earth, and they disobeyed me. Why are we even talking about this!" he scoffed.

I looked around to see if there were any demons lurking around us.

"We're alone," said Satan.

Kitana began to writhe, and she looked between us, wanting to speak.

"Satan, you don't have the authority to trap a human soul."

"Ah, but you see, she's not fully human. She's a descendant, the last remaining descendant of the Nephilim bloodline. I want her all to myself. There's a darkness within her, and I can use that darkness for much greater purposes. You could have been my treasure, but I have found someone much better," he said, holding up Kitana's chin.

"Don't touch her, Satan!" I stood between Satan and Kitana.

"I see that your God has failed to tell you of her significance?" I stayed silent, and he laughed. "Ah the old free will and him wanting you to discover it for yourself, pathetic! Well then, I'll be transparent with you, Arden. In my kingdom, there are no secrets. I tell it like it is." He held up his hands as if mocking God.

"That doesn't answer my question, Satan. Why have you trapped Kitana's soul?"

"Hmmm...because she is special. In the ancient times, after the flood, the fallen continued to mate with the women on earth. This produced some supernatural traits in their offspring. The Nephilims. These Nephilims were both angelic in nature and human too. They had supernatural abilities. They flourished during the rule of the Roman Empire. The traits passed down from generation to generation. Some Nephilims, called the dominants, served me, worshipped me. I prolonged their human life, and in return, they served me by leading humans astray. They wanted more. They wanted to have eternal life on earth, they wanted immortality, until the final judgment. There were other Nephilims, they called themselves descendants. They served your God and worshipped him. The dominants and the descendants were in constant battle, much like the demons and angels. Before the dominants could attain immortality, the descendants intervened and sacrificed their collective power to stop the dominants. The ritual was not complete, and rather than attaining immortality in human form, they turned into spirits, immortal, plaguing humankind, which I must say, I don't mind at all."

He stopped, waiting for me to speak, but I didn't say anything. I already knew this much.

"It seems there must have been some kind of loophole, but after that, there should not have been any Nephilim. But here we are, the last remaining Nephilim on earth," he continued. "I have been keeping an eye on this one for a long time. I thought she was mine, but when she gave her heart to your God, I became convinced that she was different from the rest. Your God kept her hidden in darkness, and for a time, she was mine. Your God has great plans for her, but so do I."

"How do you plan on using her?" I asked.

"I plan to use her in partnership with my vessel." He smirked. "And that is all you need to know for now."

"Release her now, Satan. You have crossed your boundaries," I demanded.

"Okay." He snapped his fingers, and Kitana's soul disappeared.

"Enough with your mind games, Satan. What are you up to?"

"All in good time, all in good time," he said. "Oh and, Arden, bring me the mark of Cain. Otherwise, there will be consequences."

"I tire of your empty threats, Satan," I said, and he scowled.

He was about to say something, but something grabbed his attention. He gave me one last glance before disappearing into the spirit realm.

I ascended from the Vatican, and I orbed back to the hospital where Kitana was. Aaric was still with her, holding her hand. He was asleep with his head resting next to her shoulders.

I summoned Yalina in the spirit realm, and I told her everything that Satan told me.

"That explains a lot of things, Arden. Thank you for letting me know," she said and looked at Kitana in relief.

"You didn't know all this, about her Nephilim bloodline?" I asked.

"I knew Kitana has always been special, but no, I did not know about the Nephilim bloodline. I believe that God would have revealed this to me when the timing was right. It seems like Satan is trying to hurry this up." Yalina gazed down at Kitana curiously. "I must seek the Lord, but I will also keep an eye on her," she said, and she ascended to heaven.

The hospital monitors began to rattle, and I saw Kitana open her eyes. She opened her eyes, and it appeared that she was in shock. Did she remember what happened in the spirit realm? I observed her from the spirit realm, and she began to move her hands. Aaric woke up and looked at her in surprise.

"Kita, you're awake!" He was about to get up, but Kitana held him back.

"No, don't," she whispered. "What happened?" she asked.

"You don't remember?" Aaric asked.

"I remember being at the library, and suddenly I felt very weak. It's as if I have woken up from a horrible nightmare," she said, looking around the room.

"You're safe, you're back," said Aaric, trying to reassure her and calm her.

"How long have I been out?" she asked.

"Only a day," said Aaric, giving her some water to drink. "Given what the doctors were saying, it seemed like you would be in a coma for a while. This is unexplainable, but a miracle," he said, holding her hand.

She was about to say something, but then she stopped and looked around. "Are we alone?" she said, looking around the room. "It's as if there is someone else here."

"No, we are alone, Kita. I mean, there was a friend who came with me to see you. I didn't even get her name. I was too worried about you, but she had long black hair, olive skin. She said she was from the Netherlands, you met her in summer school," he said. "She disappeared though. No one has seen her. I can look into this more," he asked, and Kitana shook her head.

"No, it's fine, don't," she said.

"Are you sure? She didn't look harmful, but I have my suspicions," he said.

"Yes, let it be," said Kitana.

Aaric stood quietly and began to look around the room too. "I'll get the doctor now," he said, and she nodded.

She could feel my presence. How is that possible? She looked around the room again as if sensing that there was someone else there with her. Yalina was right; she is special. God wanted me to find this out in his perfect timing; it seems that Satan wanted me to know this much quicker. He has plans for Kitana, and I can't allow this to happen. Kitana is a descendant, the last remaining descendant of the Nephilim bloodline. I only know about the Nephilims through a little research, and from what Vintore and Satan have told me, I need to know more. I need to protect Kitana.

I needed answers, and I could not wait any more. I ascended to heaven and found myself standing before heaven's doors. What would I say to God? Where would I start? I contemplated turning back and going back to the grand citadel, but the doors opened before me, and I could feel God's presence. He was sitting on this throne, dressed in white, and he was holding his gold staff in his right hand. I walked up to him, my mind filled with many thoughts. I bowed down before him and stood up, meeting his gaze. I could not read his gaze, but God was silent for a long time.

"You wanted me to find out about Kitana myself," I said.

"Yes, but not this soon," he said. "Satan has crossed the line, and he has sped up the process."

"What do you mean, my Lord?"

"I intended for Kitana to discover about her special heritage on her own, in my perfect timing, and when she would be truly ready. Satan has meddled too soon," said God. "Satan is trying to set a challenge. After all this time, he still fails to grasp that his tricks don't work on me. I saw everything that happened at the Vatican. And yes, Arden, I allowed this to happen. I did this to protect Kitana's mind. If I meddled in that moment, Kitana's mind would have collapsed, and Satan knew this. Kitana is still very much human. By exposing Kitana's soul to the spirit realm, Satan has unlocked her abilities much sooner than I planned."

"That is why she could sense me in the room. She knew she wasn't alone," I said, and God nodded. "What happens to her now, Lord?" I asked.

"Kitana's mind is like Pandora's box, to use a human analogy. Pandora's box was to be kept shut to protect its contents from the rest of humanity. Much like the truth about Kitana's Nephilim heritage was supposed to be kept locked to protect her mind from being overwhelmed. Satan has gone ahead and has unleashed Kitana's Pandora's box all at once.

"Satan underestimates her, Kitana's spirit is strong. She is more than a conqueror, and she will not break," he said and placed his staff beside his chair. He stepped up from his throne and sat on the steps, beckoning me to do the same.

"Arden, I want you to continue to watch over Kitana. Learn about her, protect her, and guard her."

"Yes, Lord."

"I admire your courage and tenacity, Arden, but you ran ahead of me," said God, but he spoke with love.

"I know I took matters into my own hands, Lord, but I did what I had to do, and Kitana is now safe," I said.

"Yes, she is," he said, but I knew God had much more to say. "You thought you were alone in this. Yes, there is much that is happening, but you must remember, Arden, that you are never alone in this war. I have put my spirit in you to guide you. Just as I have poured out my spirit into my people on earth, I have done the same for my angels, whom I have created. It is the spirit in you that has given you strength during those trials."

I began to think about the time I was held captive in Reynak and the Spirit of God was at work in me, helping me, strengthening and encouraging me.

"Arden, it can be very easy to get distracted, especially when you have many missions. You must discern carefully, especially when liaising with demons."

"Are you not pleased, Lord?"

"I am most pleased, my valiant warrior," he said, smiling, and his grace radiated throughout the palace. "I am not condemning you. I am teaching you. There is much to learn. There is a certain vulnerability when it comes to being a new creation in me. Satan is aware of your strengths and of your valour, and he will continue to play tricks and lure you away. I want you to be wise, use discernment, be careful when it comes to interacting with demons, and above all, know you are not alone. Help is always here, you simply need to ask."

"Yes, Lord."

"Know that while there are some things that I want you to discover and learn for yourself, that does not mean you should hold yourself back from wanting to know more, especially things of long ago." God was right; there is one thing that I wanted to know, and only God alone could reveal this to me.

"Yes, Lord, I wanted you to tell me about the Nephilims."

# CHAPTER 8

"Vintore and Satan have only told you so much, but I am delighted to tell you everything about the Nephilims. This knowledge will help you in the wars that are to come ahead on earth. This knowledge will prepare you when it comes to protecting Kitana and working alongside her."

I thought about God's words as we sat together before his throne, and the revelation dawned on me slowly but powerfully.

"She will have the ability to see the spirit realm. She is going to lead an army," I said.

"Yes, I have created you both for a purpose. Satan will want to lead her astray, but she will have you. It is important for you to know the history so that you can be equipped to fight the good fight both now and in all the things that are to come ahead, in heaven and on earth, and the realm in between."

We sat in silence for a few moments as I dwelled on God's words and his revelation. I met God's eyes, and as I did, my worries and doubts went away, and I sat still before his presence.

"Let me show you," he said. He waved his hand across my face, and I began to have visions.

"The creation of Nephilims was Satan's strategy to create a mortal army on earth who could do his bidding and serve him, both in the natural realm and the spiritual realm."

As God spoke, I delved deeper into the vision, as if I was right there, in that time, yet still aware that God was sitting right next to me.

I was in the spirit realm, and I could see demons inhabiting the bodies of mortal men and seducing the women on earth.

"Demons inhabited the bodies of the unrighteous, and in that time, there were many unrighteous. The Nephilims became a plague on earth, evil prevailed, and darkness spread across the earth. My plan for humanity was not to indulge in sin, murder, lust, hatred, and evil. I decided to wipe the earth. The Nephilims were out of control, they used their powers for evil, to lure the minds of humans so they may not know me. But in the midst of such evil, I saw hope. That hope was Noah. He was a righteous man and a man after my own heart. His heart was pure, and he stood firm and had hope against all hope. He walked by faith, just like Abraham, the father of many nations."

I saw the flood spreading across earth and humans falling into the depths. I saw Noah and his family in the ark and a rainbow emerging from the heavens as Noah and his family stepped out of the ark and saw daylight.

"But the fallen didn't stop," I said, and I heard the soft whisper of God saying, "Yes."

My visions changed, and I saw billions of humans across earth. I saw myself standing in the midst of a particular civilization. I saw a man standing on top of a chariot with guards leading him through the streets. The people stood on each side of the streets venerating him, bowing down to him.

"Satan's schemes didn't end with the flood. The fallen continued to inhabit mortal men. Men whose hearts were far away from mine. This resulted in the creation of a new generation of Nephilims. But something happened that Satan did not intend."

As God spoke, I could see two people in a forest. The man wore clothes that were similar to the other men who were standing in the streets, but the woman appeared as if she was royalty. She wore a long purple robe made of silk, and she wore a silver crown on top of her head.

"I am filling in the missing pieces of the puzzles. You already know about the dominants and the descendants during the rule of the Roman Empire. You are looking at Ephesus, the home city of the last generation of Nephilims. The people you are looking at are the last descendants. That man is a descendant, his name is Darius. The woman is the emperor's daughter, a human. Her name is Idrina.

They both served me. They were good, and they received salvation. Darius's parents were leaders of the descendants. They sacrificed their collective power to foil the plans of the dominants, this much you know," said God, and I nodded while looking at the two humans.

"The dominants sought ancient rituals to become immortals on earth. This came at a cost, an exchange. The descendants could not let this happen. The descendants sacrificed their collective power to disrupt the ritual. Two things happened. First, rather than becoming immortal humans in the physical realm, the dominants turned into spirits, shadows, roaming in the spiritual realm, unable to assume human form. They can only do so by taking a human host, causing them sickness and many kinds of ailments. Second, the descendants' intervention bound the fallen so that no fallen could ever procreate with a human again. This ended the Nephilim bloodline.

"Kitana comes from the bloodline of Darius and Idrina. When the descendants foiled the plans of the dominants, their act of sacrifice unleashed a force that Satan did not intend. Darius's mother, Nyla, was the leader of the descendants. She was gifted, a prophet, and she could see well ahead into the future. She saw the plans of Satan. She saw the darkness and the birth of evil in the last days. She pleaded with me that the descendants would sacrifice their collective power, their supernatural abilities, but she wanted the last remaining descendant of their bloodline to take their mantle. The children of Darius and Idrina, their children, and their children's children lived a full mortal life. Their Nephilim abilities were suppressed and passed down from generation to generation, only for it to be awakened at the right moment.

"I hid Kitana's heritage from Satan until the opportune time. Kitana comes from a powerful bloodline of descendants. She is human, yes, but she has suppressed Nephilim abilities that Satan has unlocked, and it is now being unleashed, like waters being unleashed from a dam that has been overflowing for far too long."

My visions faded, and I was back in the throne room, sitting with God.

"The last remaining descendant of their bloodline. Kitana is the last. There will be no more after Kitana. That means Jesus's descent will happen in Kitana's lifetime," I said.

"Yes," said God.

"Kitana is no ordinary human being, and Satan is now aware of her special lineage. He will do all that he can to sway her, tempt her, and lure her. I have assigned you to her for a purpose, and for all that is to happen on earth, you will need to be by her side, both in the physical realm and in the spirit realm. She will need you," he said. "It is a lot to process, Arden, but this is war, and you can do all things through Christ who gives you strength, you can do all things through me. I am your rampart, your shield, your fortress," he said, his peace radiating through my entire being.

Suddenly, a bright light hovered in front of us, and Michael descended. He held his sword in a battle position. Not long after, Gabriel descended too, standing beside Michael. They bowed before God, and I knew it was time for me to leave.

"Thank you, Lord." God sat before the throne, and the glory of the Lord radiated throughout the palace. I stood outside the palace doors, and I looked around heaven. The grand citadel sat majestically above the hills. I could see the other elites walking about. I checked to see if Kitana was okay. I saw her in her home, resting alone. She was safe, and there were no demons around her.

So much has happened in such a short time. We still have to find Cain and get his mark as he had promised. Reynak has to be destroyed. Kitana is a Nephilim, the last descendant, and Satan is after her. I walked toward the farthest corner of heaven and found myself in a familiar place. A place of my own, a place of peace.

The light of heaven shone down on the meadow, and the trees enveloped me as I sat down on the fields and closed my eyes.

Time didn't matter in heaven, and it seemed like I have been sitting here in the meadow for eternity. I stopped thinking about the missions, and my spirit quietened within me.

"Ah, I see this is your favourite place too." I turned around and saw Freydah walking toward me. She was wearing her armour. "May I join you?" she asked, and I nodded.

She sat silently for a long time, admiring the flowers on the field. "I like to come here after coming from a battle on earth. This is my favourite corner of heaven. I like to rest here," she said solemnly.

We sat in the meadow for a very long time. It is as if we were being healed from our worries and all that we saw on earth.

"It is not easy," said Freydah. "Since the fall of Lucifer, there was much war, it has never stopped. But in these last days, everything has become much more complex. Even we angels can get weary. We also need rest."

She crossed her hands and began to glow. Her armour disappeared, and she was now wearing a long white robe.

"Will you show me how to heal?" I asked.

"Gladly," she said. "It is quite simple really. I heal both angels and humans. Our physiology is different to that of humans. Humans are flesh and blood, whereas we angels are pure spirits. We are light. The healing technique is the same. We use our grace and channel it toward the injured. For example, if I am healing a human, I heal them from the spirit realm. I hold out my hand, and I channel my grace and love toward the human, and they are healed. I only heal humans if demons are the cause of their suffering or if God has called me to. With angels, I have the free will to heal angels anytime for any reason. I cannot interfere with a human's free will."

She held out her right hand, and her palm began to glow. "I am channelling my grace, and if I direct it toward a wound, that wound will heal. When you heal, you must focus on healing alone. Do not allow yourself to be distracted," she said. "When I see wars happening on earth, I see many humans wounded. Even though I want to intervene and interfere, I cannot. That is the hardest part. When it comes to human affairs, I can only intervene only if God has allowed me to. I can never go against God's authority. You will understand when it is time for you to do so, but do consider this a warning, Arden. Never disobey God, no matter how much you want to intervene in human affairs."

"Thank you, Freydah," I said.

"Anytime," she said. Her face grew serious, and she began to frown. "I have to go to earth," she said. She changed to her armour and descended to earth instantly.

My spirit began to churn, and Kitana appeared in my vision. I descended at once and found myself inside her apartment on earth. She faced the window, and Aaric stood behind her. I observed them both from the spirit realm.

"You need to accept that we are not going to happen, Aaric," she said. "Look, you have been wonderful taking care of me ever since I left the hospital. You have been amazing in these last few weeks especially, but I need it to end right here, right now."

"Kita, I love you. I made one mistake. We have been through too much together to end this now." Aaric held Kitana's face with his palms, and she began to cry. "We both love each other," he whispered.

Kitana sighed and pushed him back. "No, Aaric. I need space, I think it is best that you leave now."

Aaric walked toward her, holding out his hand, but she stepped back. He stopped and dropped his head. "It's always going to be you, Kita," he said. He walked out of the apartment without a second glance.

Kita sat on the floor crying. The sun was beginning to set in Sydney, and the rays were beaming through her apartment windows. I walked up to her, kneeling down to face her as she continued to cry.

"You are meant for so much more, Kitana. You are special," I whispered to her from the spirit realm. As I did, she stopped crying and looked around. She then looked directly toward me, and I wondered if she could see me. She then shook her head and walked into her bedroom.

"This is the turning point." Yalina emerged from the hidden realm. "He was holding her back. Things are now being set into motion," she said.

"What will happen to her now?" I asked.

"We don't know what Satan has done with her mind when her soul was held captive. Nothing like this has ever happened in human history, nor in ours. Kitana's Nephilim abilities have been suppressed, and we are talking about hundreds of supernatural powers being unleashed down through generations, and it all falls down to Kitana. God confirmed Kitana's heritage to me very recently too. I always knew she was special, and I sensed a different energy in her, something different to the rest of other humans. God's timing is perfect. Though Satan meddled, God is in control," said Yalina.

"I'll keep watch," I said.

Yalina nodded and retreated into her own realm.

I need to learn more about Nephilims, but where do I begin?

The air around me shifted, and I felt Nikolai calling my name. I could sense that he needed my help. I closed my eyes and concentrated on where he was. I could see a dark dungeon; there were cages that circled the interior of the building. There were five men, wearing long black coats. This was the physical realm. I concentrated and focused on the spirit realm and saw Valiana and Nikolai surrounded by demons. They were in America. I focused harder and pinpointed their location, Thirty-Three Myrtle Street, Florida. I orbed and descended right in the middle of a battle. I didn't recognise any of the demons. I saw one demon holding Nikolai down on the ground with his blade. I summoned my bow and shot the demon. He burst into black smoke and disappeared. The other demons noticed and surrounded me. There were four of them.

All of them wielded a gold staff. Nikolai went to help Valiana. I saw her struggling to get up, but I knew she would be okay.

"You elites think you can stop what is to come," scoffed one of the demons. "You are wasting your time," he said.

I blocked my bow from his attack, and I felt a sharp pain in my leg as another demon's staff hit me, and I fell to the ground. Nikolai summoned his sword and charged toward the two demons holding me to the ground. They vanished into smoke. Nikolai helped me up, and we each attacked the last two demons. Before I cast out the demon standing near Valiana, he orbed away. Nikolai cast out the other demon swiftly, and he summoned his sword away.

"Are you both okay?" I said, studying the dungeons. The cages were empty, and the room was damp and dark. There were small lamps with candles flickering around the dungeon.

"Thank you for helping us," said Nikolai. It didn't take me long to realise where we were.

"This is your classified mission."

"Unclassified now." Nikolai smiled, and he gestured to the men standing around the table. "This is the first time we have encountered demons in our mission. I take it they do not want us to meddle. Now that you are here, it would be good for us to tell you," he said.

"They serve Satan, this much I know," I said, sensing the darkness in them.

"The man with the brown hair, falling down to his shoulders," said Valiana, gesturing to the man standing quietly while the others talked. He had olive skin, and his eyes were blue. Though silent, his energy was the strongest, and I could feel it emanating from the physical and into the spiritual realm.

"I can sense it," I said. "Dark power, unlike I have ever sensed in a human."

"His name is Johann Vandel. He is Satan's vessel," said Nikolai.

I stared back at Johann in surprise. Though I could sense evil in him, his face and demeanour appeared to be innocent.

"An unlikely candidate, from the surface," said Nikolai as if reading my mind.

"Ow!" Valiana let out a painful gasp.

"I see no entry wound," said Nikolai. "One of the demon's staff hit my shoulder really hard, and the pain is not going away," she said.

"I'll have to take you to the grand citadel now," he said.

"Arden, will you be alright to wait here for me? I will be back."

I nodded, and they both ascended.

My gaze shifted back to Johann and the other men.

"We have tried our best to destabilise the south, yet the people are becoming more disruptive," said the man standing next to Johann.

"Johann, what do you think?"

"That is not Satan's plan, Henrik. Though Satan is pleased with your efforts to disrupt the politics in the south, it only plays a small part in the grand scheme of things. Once I come to power, we must win the hearts and minds of the people, twist their psychology, and bend their will to my authority."

"All hail Satan," said the men together, but Johann remained quiet. The rest of the men walked out of the dungeon, but Johann remained behind. He sat on the chair, and he appeared to be lost in his thoughts.

Nikolai descended and stood next to me. "It took a little longer than I expected," he said, and he followed my gaze to Johann.

I studied Johann, and I could see pain in his eyes, though the evil in him powered through to the spirit realm.

"Tell me about him," I said, watching him sitting silently.

"Not here, let's go somewhere else," said Nikolai.

We stepped out of the dark dungeon and found ourselves outside on the lively streets of Florida. People walked about, and there was a festival near the river.

We shifted out of the spirit realm and into the physical realm, making sure there were no humans around us. We changed from our armour and into human clothes. Nikolai wore blue jeans and a black shirt. I decided to change into jeans as well and wore a green top with sleeves that covered the mark of the legion on my wrist. It would look strange if people saw that we both had the same gold matching tattoos. Humans usually had black tattoos, and it would be best to not stand out.

"Let us sit down in that bar," said Nikolai, gesturing to a small bar that appeared to be very busy.

"Is that wise?" I asked.

"It is safer to be among humans right now in the physical realm," he said and led me toward the bar.

"I like to walk around in the physical realm," he said, and we both sat at a table with a view of the big Ferris wheel at the festival. The lights glowed under the night sky.

"Can I get you both anything?" A waitress held her pen ready to take our orders.

"Not at the moment, thanks," said Nikolai.

She was fixated on the mark of the legion on his wrist, and he followed her gaze to his wrist too.

"Cool tattoo," she said, blushing. "Well, let me know if you guys need anything."

Music echoed across the bar, and people talked and laughed.

"Are you uncomfortable?" said Nikolai, looking concerned, and I shook my head.

"Not at all. This is just something I don't do a lot often."

"Okay."

"Nikolai, when I was with Satan, he said that he had already chosen his vessel. How did you come to know about Johann Vandel?"

"God told us directly, and he sent us to study Johann. We are ordered to never intervene, but only to observe. This is the first time demons have attacked us. It might be a message from Satan to stay away," he said.

"Johann Vandel. Like you, I was surprised when I first saw Johann. At first glance, he would appear to be the most unlikely candidate for Satan. There's an allure to him that I can't put my finger on," I said.

"Indeed," said Nikolai and leaned forward. "Arden, the more you observe, the more you will learn. Johann Vandel has lived his life without hurting anyone. He has committed no murder, no adultery, he has never stolen anything, and he has never wronged anyone in his life."

"Then what makes him the Antichrist?" I said.

"He used to be a child of God, he followed Jesus as a child. But over time, his heart became hardened. He endured unimaginable abuse in many ways since his childhood. No one listened, no one helped. Though he continued to do no wrong, over time, he dedicated his heart to Satan. Satan has chosen him because Johann's heart is filled with hatred toward God and toward humanity. That hatred has only grown stronger, and no intervention can ever lead Johann back to God, this much I know. It is the deep hatred for God and humanity that Satan has chosen Johann as his vessel."

"Johann knows he is Satan's vessel," I said, and he nodded. "I am intrigued."

"I understand that you would be. I encourage you to observe and learn about Johann in between your missions," said Nikolai.

"How long are you and Valiana assigned to this mission?"

"For as long as it takes," he said. "This is the only mission Valiana and I are assigned to. This is important. What about you, Arden? How are you?"

I told Nikolai about Kitana and her Nephilim heritage, and he listened intently.

"That is interesting. I can see why Satan wants her on his side," he said. "What about Cain?" he asked.

"I have been busy with Kitana, and I have not heard from Cain. It was the right thing to do to let him leave during the battle. The fallen cannot have the mark. If they do, then they will have the upper hand. They can use the mark against us and destroy humanity."

"So what do we do?" he asked.

I thought about this and knew that it would be fruitless searching for Cain. He could be anywhere and in anyone. "The only thing we can do right now. We wait. One thing I am sure of though, Nikolai. When we do get the mark of Cain, we must move fast. The demons are watching our move as we are watching theirs. Once they know we have the mark, we must gather the legion and use it."

"How do we use it?"

"I'm hoping that Cain will tell me once I meet him again," I said.

"Arden, I know that we are both busy on missions, but just like I called you for help today, you can always call me and Valiana too. That includes the other elites. We are all in this together."

"I know."

I smiled and sighed as I gazed out to the festival. Fireworks erupted, and it lit the sky. The people around the bar cheered and stared out in awe. Nikolai did the same.

The spirit of God stirred within, and he whispered to my heart. "You are on the right track, keep going."

# CHAPTER 9

After walking around on the streets of Florida, Nikolai ascended to heaven, and I decided to orb to Amsterdam.

I found Adrian Galdon's club, curious to know if he remembered anything.

The guards at the door noticed me, but they didn't stop me. They led me inside, and I saw the usual crowd dancing on the dancefloor.

I saw Adrian sitting at the bar. "Adrian."

He turned around and looked confused. "I'm sorry, do we know each other?" he said.

The barman offered me a drink, and I declined.

It seemed like he did not remember anything, and it was as if nothing had changed for him, just as Cain had said.

"Oh, I'm sorry, there seems to be some confusion," I said, retreating before he could say anything else. Adrian's part in this war was over. I had to find Cain, but where do I begin?

I began to make a list of things in my mind that I had to focus on. First, there was Kitana, Cain, and now Johann Vandel. The impending war ahead began to make me anxious.

I orbed to my favourite place on earth and stood on top of the Sydney Harbour Bridge in the physical realm. It was midnight, and the city was quiet. I could see Kitana's apartment on the right. I could sense that she was safe.

The breeze brushed across my face, and it began to rain. I shifted into the spirit realm to avoid getting wet. The spirit realm was quiet, and there was no demonic activity around me in Sydney. I needed to learn more about Johann Vandel. I closed my eyes and focused on his energy signature.

He was still in Florida. I could see him in his home, he was in his living room, sitting on his chair by the fireplace. I orbed from the bridge and into his living room. His home stood on the edge of a cliff overlooking the ocean. A grand chandelier erupted from the high ceiling; it reminded me of Reynak. Johann was sitting quietly, drinking what appeared to be whiskey. I assumed Nikolai and Valiana would be here, but it looked like they only observed Johann when he was with someone. I will need to ask Nikolai about this later. At the moment, there was no threat around me.

"It's rude when a guest enters unannounced, even ruder when they don't make conversation even in company," he said.

I looked around, but there was no one around. I stood in front of the fireplace across the room, facing him.

His eyes met mine, and he smiled. It was not a menacing smile though, as demons usually do. It was warm and inviting, and I shivered. He can see me.

"You look alarmed," he said.

"You can see me?" I asked, feeling alarmed.

"I can." He continued to drink his whiskey. "Do you mind shifting away from the fireplace? You're blocking the warmth."

I retreated to the side, feeling confused and more intrigued.

"Thank you," he said, and he slid back further on his seat.

I was lost for words. How could a mortal see directly into the spirit realm?

"You must have many questions, but let me just say, I have been looking forward to meeting you, Arden. Satan has told me all about you, I am quite intrigued."

"Likewise," I said, still surprised. "If you can see me, then you must have seen the other angels watching you. You would have seen the battle."

"I am aware the angels have been watching me, but that doesn't bother me. I can't be harmed, and yes, I did see you and your friends watching me in that dungeon."

"How?"

"Satan has gifted me with extraordinary abilities. I can see all that happens and so much more. I will not hurt you, Arden," he said softly.

"Your attempt to lure me to your side will not work. Satan has already tried that, and it did not work," I said.

"Oh, I have no interest in that at all," he said, putting his glass on the table. He stood up and walked to the windows, gazing out at the ocean. "Our paths will collide in the future, and I wanted to meet the elite I am going to be up against."

He faced me, and I could now see his blue eyes directly, piercing into mine.

"What do you want with me?" I asked.

"I want you to get to know me personally. I want your friends to stop watching me from the spirit realm. Do this, and the fallen will not attack them any further."

I thought this might be a trap or a trick, but I did want to know more about him. I needed to talk about this with the others.

"I understand that you might want to discuss this with your friends. You can return to me when you have your answer," he said and sat back down.

I ascended to heaven without saying anything. I found myself standing in the middle of the arena and summoned the other elites.

Nikolai, Valiana, Vintore, and Gelin orbed to the forest and surrounded me.

"We saw everything that happened on earth. That was quite a meeting," said Vintore.

"I thought both of you kept watch over Johann all the time?" I asked, and they exchanged glances.

"Only when he is with others. We rarely keep watch when he is home alone. This gives us space to return to heaven," said Valiana.

"Arden, I understand that this may be happening a little too quickly. He is the Antichrist after all," said Gelin.

"I did not expect him to be the way he is right now, and I do want to know more," I said.

"God sent us to observe and learn, but if there is a chance that Arden could learn more and stop the demons from attacking us, then that can be best for all of us. This would give an opportunity for Valiana and I to search for Cain," said Nikolai.

"You can say no, Arden," said Vintore reassuringly. "Johann Vandel is working with Satan, and there is no telling what they can do." The air around us was heavy and mixed with anticipation.

"All he wants is to share his story. He wants to tell me all that has happened. I'm his opponent, and if I am to face him in the future, then he wants me to get to know him. He wants me to be a worthy opponent."

Everyone around me kept silent.

"Arden, you know what you need to do," said Vintore. "Just know that you have us to guide and guard you."

"I know," I said. I orbed down and stood before the palace doors. The doors opened before me, and I saw God walking out to greet me.

"I thought I would meet you instead." He smiled. "Let us walk," he said.

He held his gold staff with this right hand as we walked in heaven. We walked toward the grand citadel, and I told him about my meeting with Johann and the elites.

"There is much going on, Arden, and you don't know where to begin," he said calmly. We walked past the arena and deeper into the forest. "There is a lesson to be learnt here, Arden. You don't have to do everything all at once. You can't be everywhere at the same time. You are a new angel I have formed from my own hands and with my own spirit. That means you have my strength and wisdom. Tell me what you have planned or are planning to do."

"Johann, Kitana, and Cain are all important missions right now. I am connected to all of them. All three missions will lead to war between the elites and the fallen, now and in the future. I need to be strategic. We must find Cain and get his mark. Kitana is on Satan's agenda, and she will need guidance learning about her Nephilim abilities. Even I have much to learn about Nephilims. All this points to Satan and Johann and the war that is to come. Everything is connected, and I am at the centre of it all."

"You are overwhelmed?" he asked.

"Yes."

"Arden, I want you to know that even angels have free will. Even when I do assign missions to you, you do have the free will to say no. Communication goes both ways. I give my angels missions knowing that they have the power and my grace to carry it through. I only give what they can handle, and it is the same for humans as well.

"You are an end-time warrior angel that I have created. You have a special purpose, and everything that I have purposed for you will come to pass. You must have perseverance."

We came to the end of the forest and sat down on a bench.

"You are an elite. You will need to strategise and remember one thing, you are not alone. Everything will fall into place as you keep moving forward. The steps ahead will unravel before you as you keep conquering the wiles of Satan. You are on the right track," he said and placed his gold staff next to the bench.

"There is much more clarity when I spend time with you, Lord, thank you. I know what I need to do," I said. I knew I had to balance my missions. I will need to keep watch over Kitana, I must learn more about Johann, and I need to find Cain too. Spending time with God has given me strength.

"I believe I know where to help you begin when it comes to understanding Kitana's special heritage," said God. We walked back toward the centre of heaven, only this time, he was leading me toward the souls who dwelled in heaven. I could see Daisy's home sitting on the corner. Mansions were sitting on each side of the path, and there were people walking about. They were happy and admired God as we walked deeper into the path.

"Here," said God. We stopped in front of a small cottage. The garden was filled with red roses, and the door of the cottage was open.

A woman stepped out of the cottage, and she was tall and wearing a purple robe. Her long black hair fell down her shoulders, and her smile was warm and inviting. She bowed before God.

"I have been wondering when I would finally get to meet you, Arden," she said.

"Nyla, I will leave Arden with you. It is time for her to know about Kitana's heritage," he said and walked away toward his palace.

"Welcome to my home, Arden. Come, let us go inside."

She led me inside her cottage and into her living room. Her home was not modern like the others I have seen in heaven. It was cosy and warm, and it reminded me of houses I saw in my vision in Ephesus.

"Come, let us sit."

"You can see all that happens on earth from here too?" I asked.

"I can, Arden. I can see all that happens in the spirit realm on earth and the physical too. I am excited for Kitana to learn about her heritage, even though Satan has tampered with her mind."

"You are Darius's mother," I said, and she nodded. Her eyes reminded me of Darius. I remembered his eyes from when God was showing me the vision of Darius and Idrina.

"I am one of the descendants, yes."

I thought about Darius and Idrina, wondering if they were somewhere in heaven.

"I'm sure you will meet them one day, Arden, but God has led you to me for a purpose," she said as if reading my mind. "In time, you will guide Kitana and help her with her Nephilim abilities, both in the physical realm and the spirit realm. Both of you must be in sync. You will both face Satan and the Antichrist in the wars ahead. Johann Vandel is interested in you because he is interested in Kitana. It would be wise for you to not tell anything about Kitana. You can learn about him, but I would advise you to keep Kitana's abilities to yourself."

"I'm ready," I said. "Tell me everything I need to know."

She poised herself, and her green eyes glimmered with excitement. "Kitana is the last descendant of Darius and Idrina. Darius, my son, and Idrina, his wife. I am aware of all that you already know about our history. Darius's children and his children didn't have any Nephilim abilities. It has been suppressed for generations, and so they were protected from Satan. Satan thought the line of the descendant ended after the sacrifice. But what he failed to see was my alliance with God. The dominants had to be stopped, and

I saw the plans of Satan and the Antichrist. I knew that humanity still needed the descendants. I prayed to God that in return for our sacrifice, to sacrifice our Nephilim abilities to stop the ritual of the dominants, that he would suppress the supernatural abilities of our descendants but awaken it for one, the last descendant of our bloodline. He granted my request. Not many knew about this alliance, only my family. And now, Satan knows too, and he will come after Kitana. You were created for this very purpose, Arden, to walk alongside Kitana and to guide her and to prepare her for all that is to come ahead. Humanity will face wars and unimaginable evil. They need a leader to rally them, a leader who is a child of God with supernatural abilities. Satan wants to use Kitana's ability to lead humans astray. We cannot let that happen."

"What abilities will Kitana have?"

"She will have the ability to see clearly into the spirit realm, just like Johann Vandel, the Antichrist. She will have the ability to cast out evil spirits, the dominants, from people just by touching them. She will do this effortlessly. She is still mortal, and she will have the same life span as other humans. She will raise the dead. She will heal people from spiritual and physical diseases. She will have the ability to discern Satan's plans with ease. She will be steps ahead of Satan, and Satan cannot allow this. Satan has unlocked and unleashed these abilities all at once. God's plan was to unlock these ability slowly, one by one, so Kitana could adapt. She will need an elite's help to help her stay on the right path and to remain in obedience to God. Satan will not stop with his deception and torment. Kitana will need help to overcome this and fight the good fight."

I was finally beginning to understand why Kitana has been experiencing nightmares and taunts from Satan.

"What must I do?" I asked Nyla.

"Kitana needs to be trained in the physical realm and in the spirit realm. She needs to know who she is. She needs wisdom and knowledge, and you need to protect her from Satan and mortals that Satan will send her way to distract her and who want to stop her from reaching her full potential. You will know when the time is right to reveal yourself as an elite to Kitana," she said, sounding hopeful. "As you keep walking forward, Arden, the path before you will continue to unveil, and the spirit of God will guide you."

"Thank you, Nyla."

"I have been waiting a long time for this, and now the time is here. All of heaven has been waiting for this. You will lead this war, Arden, with Kitana."

After sitting with Nyla for a little while longer, I descended to earth.

It was sunrise in Sydney, and I sensed that Kitana was in the library. I watched her from the spirit realm as she talked with others.

Suddenly her eyes averted, and it met mine. Could she see me in the spirit realm?

She looked confused, but then she directed her gaze back to the woman she was talking to.

I walked out of the library, instead of orbing out. If she saw me orb, she could be more confused. This was not the right time to talk to her in the physical realm.

I orbed to Florida and saw Johann standing in front of his pool that was perched on the edge of the cliff. He was holding his whiskey, and he was deep in thought.

"Welcome back," he said.

I shifted from the spirit realm and into the physical. The ocean breeze was strong, and the waves crashed against the rocks at the bottom of the cliff.

"The other angels will not be watching you, Johann. I agree to learn more about you," I said.

"I'm glad you have decided to do that, Arden. Of course, you must know by now that we both have a common interest. Kitana. I am already aware of her heritage, but I am more intrigued by you, this you already know," he said.

"Why has Satan chosen you?" I asked.

"It's quite simple, Arden. I have a deep hatred for God and everything he stands for. Where was God when I needed him the most? Where was God when I needed answers?"

"Perhaps your faith was weak," I said.

"My faith was just fine," he said. He was not angry, and his demeanour remained the same, calm and composed. Yet I could sense evil in him, a kind of evil energy that I have never sensed in a human before. "I have never hurt a human, and I have led a good, honest life. I am the director of the security council in this country, respected and honoured."

"But you get your men to destabilise foreign countries. How is that a good, honest life?" I asked, thinking about his meeting with the other men in the dungeon.

"Ah, you are referring to the meeting you saw with Henrik, my advisor, and the other men? That is all part of the trade. The plan is to destabilise foreign nations, for people to lose hope in their country and on their leaders. People will have no hope, nothing to live for. There will be war and calamity. People will lose faith. When the time comes for me to rise to power, to lead this country, the entire world will be at my feet. I will bring peace, people will worship me, they will not need to worship your God."

"So that is your plan?" I said.

"A small part of what Satan has planned," he said, standing proudly.

"When did you surrender to Satan?"

"After enduring much abuse in many forms since I was a child, I cried out to your God, and he never answered. But Satan did. I worked hard to get to where I am today, and Satan gave me supernatural abilities to discern other people's ways and thoughts. I could converse with the demons in the spirit realm. I wasn't alone anymore. God stayed silent in my darkest moment, but Satan didn't. Satan is the saviour of mankind, not your God. People must and should bow down to Satan. I will never bow down to your God. He sits on his throne, with all his power, and he does nothing to help. People are suffering all around the world, but he sits on his lofty throne, without remorse. I have nothing but pure hatred for him. People need to see the truth, that the God they are worshipping is a joke. Humankind needs to see that there is a God who will listen to them, grant them power and eternal life, and that god is Satan, the king. All will see and all will know that Satan is lord. I will do everything in my power to make this happen. It is a great honour to be a vessel for Satan."

This was the most absurd thing I heard, but I dared not to argue with Johann. I knew God and the other elites were watching this. I decided to simply listen. "What will you get out of me listening to your story?" I asked.

"Like I said, our paths will collide in the future, and I want to be a worthy adversary. Satan has said that you are a new angel created by your God. I would hope in time, you will see what I see too, by your own volition. I will never interfere with your free will, but you need to see that everything I will do is to save humankind from your treacherous God. There is no other God than Satan, the true God and saviour of humankind. Your God has brainwashed humankind with his nonsense."

"I think we shall end our meeting here, Johann. I have seen and heard all that I need. Yes, our paths will collide in the future, but everything that you stand for is a lie. I serve a mighty God, and you are on the losing side of this war."

He smiled at me and then looked up to the sky. "As you wish," he said. "Until we meet again."

I could not hear any more of his story. He was clearly brainwashed by Satan, but one thing I knew with certainty, he will serve Satan to the very end.

I ascended to heaven and found myself sitting in my quarters. I lay on my bed and closed my eyes. I found myself getting pulled into a vision.

I was in the spirit realm, and I could not pull out of the vision. I felt his presence before I could see him.

"We were just getting started," he said, standing next to me.

We were observing a young boy sitting in his room from the spirit realm. He was curled up and crying on the floor. I could see bruises on his arms. Another man entered his room, and he was holding a belt. He started hitting the little boy.

"Father, please stop," said the boy screaming.

"What is this? Why are you showing me this?"

Satan laughed and waved his hand. The scenery changed, and we were now standing in the middle of a dark alleyway.

There were two men standing in the corner of the alley. I recognised his blue eyes. It was Johann. I did not recognise the other man.

"You promised me a job. I have done everything you asked me to. I am still waiting for my first month's wage," said Johann.

The other man began to punch Johann to the ground. He stole Johann's bag and ran away.

Johann began to scream to God for help.

"Abuse, torture, rejection, heartache," said Satan, gesturing to Johann. "Where was your God then?"

Satan was showing me Johann's past. "You have taught him lies, Satan," I said, and he smiled wickedly.

"He is the perfect vessel. I needed someone who could see that your God is a lie, and Johann, out of his own free will, chose to serve me. I have given him freedom, prolonged his lifespan, supernatural abilities, and fame."

"I am aware of his plans, and I also know that he will never surrender to God. Again, why are you showing me this, Satan?"

He gestured to Johann, who was weeping and screaming for help in the alley.

"I enjoy showing others your God's failure and lack of power," he said. "Until we meet again, Arden," he said and snapped his fingers.

I got pulled out of the vision and found myself back in my quarters in heaven.

The spirit of God stirred within, and I felt peace. "He has no power over you. You are stronger than his lies," said the Holy Spirit.

# CHAPTER 10

I looked through the scrolls in the grand citadel. I found another observatory on the lower levels of the citadel. Weeks have passed by on earth. Kitana continued to teach at the library. Nothing strange or out of the ordinary has happened since Satan meddled with her mind. Nikolai and Valiana were no longer observing Johann's activities and were pulled out of the mission. The elites kept watch on Johann from heaven. Wars and disasters ravaged across earth, and the demons continued to control the human leaders from the spirit realm.

"There you are!"

I saw Nyla coming through the corridors and into the observatory.

"I have been looking for you," she said.

We sat down near the table overlooking the rest of heaven. The palace stood gloriously in the middle.

"I have been observing Kitana from heaven. You should know that the awakening will begin to happen soon, Arden."

"What do you mean by the awakening, Nyla?"

"The awakening is when a descendant begins to experience their Nephilim abilities. This experience is unique for every Nephilim. Kitana is special. She is the last Nephilim of the descendant bloodline. Abilities have been passed down from generation to the next. Suppressed but now unleashed. I know all has been still on earth for Kitana, but I can sense her abilities will now start to awaken. You need to keep a closer eye on her."

"What will happen first?" I asked.

"First, she will begin to see clearly into the spirit realm. She will be able to see you. She will begin to see everything with clarity."

"God has not given me orders to reveal myself to her. What must I do so she is not confused or scared?" I asked.

"God's spirit in you will make it known to you. I recommend that you should start observing her from the physical realm when necessary and only when she is in public places. You can easily watch over her from heaven every other time."

"Thank you for this, Nyla. I will be careful."

"I'm glad the Lord has chosen you to guard Kitana. You were made for such a time as this. I see that you have also met Johann Vandel?" she asked, and I nodded, not knowing how to explain my last encounter to Nyla. "I have seen visions of Johann Vandel when I was on earth during my age. Do not be fooled by his calm demeanour. His heart is filled with malice. His allegiance is with Satan. Nothing can shake his loyalty for Satan."

"He has been wanting to speak directly to me. Our last encounter did not go so well. I grew tired of his arrogance," I said, and Nyla found this amusing.

"This is just the beginning, Arden. Once he grows to power, it will all be a facade, and then evil will grow and spread across earth. He will then become a host to Satan, and many will bow before him. Satan's pride will never cease. Johann is not interested in you. He is interested in the one that you are close to, the one under your protection," she said.

"Kitana."

"Yes," she said. "Kitana is Johann's counterpart. Satan, through Johann, will do all that he can to undermine her faith and supernatural abilities. The people will need her in a time of great suffering that is to come. She will guide others to faith. You will not only need to protect Kitana from demons in the spirit realm, you will also need to encourage her and help her to stand firm against evil."

I nodded and gazed out at the palace, contemplating the wars to come and Kitana's part in it.

"Remember, Arden, I'm here to help," she said and left me alone in the observatory. I began to think about Cain. There has been no sign of him since the last time I saw him at the battle. I must be prepared; I know that demons will swarm around us once Cain is ready to give me his mark. I wondered what the mark looked like. It could be in any form. I felt Vintore calling me to the arena, and I orbed down to meet others.

"Welcome, Arden," said Vintore. He was in his armour, and it looked like he just came from a battle.

"Demons disrupting the northern sphere of earth," he said, discerning my thoughts. Soon, Nikolai, Valiana, and Gelin descended. After a few moments, Izralina and Elandriel descended too.

Izralina summoned her bow away. "I could not reach earth this time. Ilthezar had my path blocked. I was surrounded by demons, and I could not get past them. They were too strong," she said. "Arden, any news of Cain? We need to get the mark as soon as we can," she asked, and I shook my head.

"That is why we are all here," said Vintore. "It has been a long time since we have gathered together like this. I need us to strategize for all that is ahead and discuss our priorities."

"Elandriel and I have been keeping watch over activities in Reynak. Nothing extraordinary, demons continue to disrupt the political realm on earth and take spiritual territories. However, they are growing stronger in blocking my path to earth from the second realm. It is very difficult for me to protect the humans I am assigned to," said Izralina.

"This is the same for me," said Elandriel.

"Which now brings us to you, Arden. What news of Cain?" asked Vintore.

"There has been no sighting of Cain since the battle. It was good for him to disappear. Otherwise, the demons could have captured him. He has given me his word that he will give us his mark. We met his condition by taking him to hell, that is all he asked for. I am certain that when the time is right, he will reveal himself, but I do believe we should all be prepared for instant war. As soon as he gives me his mark, the demons will intervene and try to take the mark or stop the transition from happening," I said.

"I agree with Arden," said Nikolai. "Valiana and myself have tried to gather intelligence, but to no avail."

"Gelin?" asked Vintore.

"I have been helping the other elites with their missions. I don't have any specific missions assigned to me by God," he said.

"Thank you, everyone," said Vintore. "I can confirm that with Johann Vandel, we can observe him from heaven, but not on earth. There is no telling what Satan can do to attack the elites if we do intervene. Let us stay focused on our current mission. I believe all will fall into place once we get the mark of Cain," said Vintore, and we all agreed.

"That being said, we need a battle strategy because we don't know when or where the hour will come. We must be prepared at all times. Arden, Cain will want to meet with you alone, and as soon as he gives you his mark, you must summon us immediately. We will descend without delay. If demons surround you before Cain gives you his mark, then you will still need to summon us. We can help you by distracting the demons, giving you and Cain time."

"It's a good plan, Vintore," I said, and everyone else nodded.

We all talked about the battle strategy and plan of attack, and then the others went back to their duties, except for Gelin and me. We stood in the middle of the arena.

"You need training," he said, smiling.

"I need training," I said, summoning my bow. "Can you discern my thoughts so easily?"

"You and I are very alike, Arden, and you won't need your weapon," he replied.

I summoned my weapon away and stood in a battle stance.

"If Cain is in the process of giving you the mark, and if you are surrounded by demons, it would be unwise for you to wield your weapon and focus on the mark too. We will protect and shield you during the transition, but there is always risk and uncertainty during any battle."

"You need to learn defensive and evasive battle maneuvers, and you will need to be quick, Arden."

"We will fight without weapons. I will attack, and you will need to evade my offensive tactics," he commanded.

He began to attack, aiming at my hands, and I mirrored his movements by blocking his attacks. We were in sync.

"Very good! We are in sync, but if you want to gain victory and to avoid wasting time, you need to be quicker," he said. "Rather than focusing on my attacks, I want you to think about what you can do during battle to distract your enemy. As you are fighting, start using your mind, and think of clever ways to either cast the demons or paralyse them."

"It's just a matter of perspective, Arden. You need to be ten steps ahead in battle, especially if it is with a fallen, or more so, one of the commanders."

"Would I have the time to summon my weapon even if a demon is with or without a weapon?" I asked. "Gelin, Cain has not revealed what his mark looks like. I don't know how it would look like or how long it would take. I will need cover," I said, thinking about the battle that is to come.

"Again, Arden, no matter what the scenario is, you will need to be quick, in every single possible way."

"Understood."

He stepped back, and I knew our training was over.

"No further training is necessary from here, Arden. You are very strong, and you have learnt quickly," he said, and I felt encouraged. "The only thing you need to be and to do is to be quick in battle. As you are fighting, use your mind along with your physical abilities, master your weapon to your advantage, and keep thinking about clever ways to disarm your enemy. Once you master this, it will go well for you."

He walked back toward the grand citadel, and I was now alone in the arena.

It has been a long time since my last visit to earth. I closed my eyes and checked how Kitana was doing.

She was in the library, and I saw she was not alone. She was talking to Zaphael.

I descended immediately into the spirit realm. Zaphael glanced toward my direction, and I knew he felt my presence. He turned his attention back to Kitana. The library was busy.

Kitana looked toward my direction, and she looked confused. She shook her head and began talking to Zaphael again.

I remembered Nyla's words and thought that it would not be a good idea to observe Kitana from the spirit realm and in my armour. I went to the corner of the bookshelf where it was quiet and changed into my human clothes, this time, wearing blue jeans and a white top. I remember a human wearing something like this on the streets. This felt comfortable. I shifted into the physical realm, and I could feel the cool breeze coming through the windows. I had no time to waste; I could not let Zaphael get closer to Kitana. This would be the first time I would talk to Kitana in the physical realm.

They were both standing against the bookshelf on the other side of the library.

"Zaphael!" I said, disrupting their conversation. I saw Kitana gazing at me, as if she recognised me.

"Arden, what are you doing here?"

"I needed help with some information, and one of the people working here directed me to Kitana here," I said and glanced toward Kitana. She gazed at me curiously.

"I'm sorry, do you two know each other?" asked Kitana, and Zaphael scoffed.

"Arden and I are old friends. We used to go to this school together, a heavenly place, but through time, we drifted apart," he said. "And here you are," he said, not sounding pleased.

"Here I am," I said, smiling, knowing that Zaphael was not expecting this at all. I needed to make a bold move and get to know Kitana. I knew that I would have to talk to her sooner or later in the physical realm. I could not allow Zaphael to get closer to Kitana.

"How about I let you two catch up. I will be over there if you need me," said Kitana.

"What do you think you are doing?" said Zaphael.

"I think it's about time I get to know Kitana," I said, and he rolled his eyes.

"You would know by now of her special heritage," he said, and I stayed silent.

"Why are you assigned to Kitana, Zaphael?" I asked.

"Satan has awakened her abilities. I'm here to teach her, help her harness her powers," he said.

"And keep her on your side," I said.

"Essentially." He gave me one last smirk and walked out of the library.

I thought he would have more to say and try to stop me from talking to Kitana. Kitana was sitting on her bench, overlooking the harbour. I joined her and gazed out to the harbour.

"Have we met before?" she asked, looking at me curiously. "I feel like I have seen you before, but…it's crazy, you were wearing some kind of unusual clothes, almost angelic."

She wasn't that wrong, but I could not reveal my identity. This was not the right time.

"I guess I have one of those familiar faces," I said.

"Huh." She shrugged and sipped on her coffee.

"I should warn you about Zaphael. It would be best for you to stay away from him. He can be trouble," I said. I could not allow Kitana any closer to Zaphael; he would lead her astray.

"I do feel a little uneasy around him, but he has been helping me with some research I have been curious about."

"What research?"

"Nephilims." She was getting closer to the truth. "This may sound strange, but I feel like I can tell you anything, even a total stranger. Arden, isn't it?"

"Yes, my name is Arden," I said.

"Arden…the Garden of Eden, the meaning of your name is unique," she said. "What do you do, Arden?"

"Still trying to figure out that part, but at the moment, I like to write."

"What do you like to write about?"

She was more curious about me than I was with her. I wondered if she could feel my angelic presence. Surely Yalina would be watching us from the spirit realm.

"Christian spirituality, angels and demons, heaven and earth."

She appeared to be more fascinated. "We have much in common then. I research in those areas here at the library, and my teaching centres around those topics. I love Jesus, isn't he just amazing?" She was in a daze, and I could see her love for Christ in her eyes.

"Kitana, what interests you about Nephilims?"

Her face grew dark, and she looked a little uncomfortable. "I have had some strange experiences, and I feel drawn to learn about Nephilims."

I didn't want to trigger anything, so I stopped asking any more questions.

"It's funny," she said. "There's something about you and Zaphael that is different. With him, I can sense a little darkness, but not danger. With you, there's just light but a little bit of rebelliousness within."

"Your gift of discernment is strong," I said, and she smiled.

She broke out of the daze and laughed, looking a little embarrassed. "You must forgive me, I have been having some strange couple of days."

"No, it is fine, Kitana."

"Kita, you can call me Kita," she said, and I smiled.

"Kita, we need you here." I saw one of the staff at the library waving at her.

"I'm sure we could talk for hours, Arden, and I hope to get to know you more, but I have to go now," she said.

"Likewise, Kita," I said, and she left.

That was a very brief meeting, and I had many things that I wanted to talk to her about. How much did she know about Nephilims, and what was Zaphael teaching her?

It would be unwise to watch over her from the spirit realm.

The air changed around me, and I could feel a shift both in the physical realm and the spirit realm.

I got pulled into a vision. This vision was different, and I could feel the spirit of God stirring within me. I suspected the vision might be from Satan again, but I knew this was from God as soon as I entered the vision. There was peace in the vision, and I could see everything around me clearly.

The vision led me to the northern sphere of the earth. There was a fort and water around the fort. The architecture was beautiful, a hidden gem on earth. I could see people walking on uneven paths made of cobblestones. I have never been to this part of earth before.

The vision changed, and I was on top of the island, inside an abbey. I could feel the sacred power emanating from the abbey in the vision.

It was empty, except for an old man sitting on the bench. He was looking ahead toward the front of the abbey, as if in a contemplative prayer. Who was this man? Why was God showing me this man?

His eyes met mine in the vision, and I was back in the library.

I knew that I had to orb there as soon as possible. I have never had a vision like this before from God. This had to be important.

I could see Kitana was with her colleagues, and they appeared to be helping students. Yalina would be watching over her. I was being called to an important mission.

I walked out of the library and to an alleyway. I was alone. I shifted into the spirit realm and tried to discern the location from the vision. I concentrated deeper and focused on the abbey. Mont Saint-Michel, France.

I orbed and descended onto the corner of the fort in a garden. I shifted into the physical realm. There were no humans around me. I walked to the edge of the fort and saw the mainland far ahead. The water was shallow, and the sun was beginning to set.

I needed to explore more of the earth; this place was beautiful and holy. This was a cathedral.

At the top, I could see a statue of Michael the archangel. I found a staircase leading to the abbey. I reached the top and saw the abbey. I could feel God's presence around me. The abbey was filled with people, and I could see the evening light dimming through the windows.

I looked around and saw someone who caught my eye. He sat on a bench at the front of the abbey.

It was the same man from the vision. His grey hair and blue eyes stared toward the front, just like he did in the vision. He didn't notice me staring at him. I sat next to him, and he didn't move away. It was as if he was waiting for me. We both gazed toward the front of the abbey, and there was peace. All was still.

"I asked God to give you a vision of my location, and here you are. I gave you my word, remember," he said. The way he spoke was familiar, and it didn't take me long to realise it was Cain. "We don't have much time, Arden. The spirit realm will be swarming with demons soon."

"How does the mark work, Cain?"

"The mark that God gave me is a supernatural force, Arden, mystical energy that connects the physical and the spiritual. A force I can transfer to you when I place my hands on you in the spirit realm," he said.

"The transfer has to be made in the spirit realm, that means we will be surrounded by demons instantly. They will feel this energy," I said, realizing that the exchange had to be fast, and he nodded.

"Exactly," he said.

"Cain, how can I use the mark against the demons?"

He shifted and looked directly at me.

"Arden, you will need to use the energy, the mark, when you are in the second heavens. You will need to exert the force across the realms, with all your will and your spirit. You must channel it with a force that I know that only you can do, that is why I have chosen you. I could sense it in you the moment I laid my eyes on you. Extraordinary power, justice, and good," he said. "Once you release the energy in the second heavens, it will act as a force field, a shield. The darkness in the second heavens will be destroyed, and the demons can no longer block the angels from descending onto earth. The angels gain control. There will be a strong force, and the heavens will shake. Demons will be cast into hell."

"And if the demons had this mark, they could use it as a shield against the angels," I said, and he nodded.

"You must remember, Arden, the demons have been wanting this mark from me for thousands of years. They will put up a good fight. We need to be ready."

"Everything is happening quickly," I said.

"That is a good thing," he said reassuringly.

"Cain, thank you."

His smile faded, and he looked at me solemnly. He stared toward the front of the abbey again. "There is a season for everything, Arden. Satan has stolen salvation from me, and by giving you the mark, the angels will be closer to victory against the demons. Satan's time is short, but now it will be much shorter. I accept an eternity in hell, and I accept my punishment. I wanted to see my wife, and you have given me the chance to."

I realised that the abbey was quiet, and it was just us two sitting. I knew the time was close.

"When you are ready to, Arden, place your hand on my shoulder, and shift us both into the spirit realm," he ordered.

"And what of this man?" I asked.

"It will be as if he was in a long dream. He lives near here. I have only been with him for a short time. Life will go on for him. He will be safe after we shift into the spirit realm."

I placed my hand on his left shoulder and sighed. I had to be ready. I only had a moment to strategise. I was about to shift us both into the spirit realm when he signalled me to stop.

"One more thing," he said, and I listened intently. "The Nephilim you are protecting, keep her on the right path. Do not allow the demons to lead her astray. She has a mighty destiny ahead. Keep her safe, Arden. She knows more than you think."

I suddenly had more questions, but I realised Cain had nothing more to say. I nodded, and I knew he was ready.

I knew the elites were watching me from heaven.

I placed my hand on his shoulder again, and I focused on the spirit realm.

"Ready?" I asked.

"More than ever," he said.

I pushed us both from the physical realm and into the spirit realm. There was a powerful surge, and I could feel a supernatural power in the spirit realm that I have never felt before. I could see Cain, his soul standing beside me, and I kept my hand on his shoulder. His soul was tangible in the spirit realm.

I changed into my armour, and I held my right hand up to heaven. I had to be quick because I knew what was coming next.

The spirit realm trembled, and the heavens opened. Thousands of elites descended around us in their armour, with their weapons ready. As they did, the demons appeared too.

# CHAPTER 11

The elites circled us, protecting us from the demons that stood in front of the elites.

For a moment, all was still. This gave me a small window to study the battleground.

I saw Vintore, Izralina, Gelin, Quiff, and Azarey leading the elites on my right. On the left, I saw Nikolai, Valiana, and Elandriel leading the others.

I saw the commanders leading the demons. I recognised Carinz, Demiriz, Emrail, and Balnor. I also recognised Ilthezar.

The demons engaged with the elites as soon as they saw Cain and I standing in the middle.

I could see the man who was host to Cain was no longer in the abbey. The physical realm was quiet.

Cain's shout brought me back to the spirit realm. I could see Ilthezar charging toward me, but Vintore got to him quickly and shielded his attack.

"Whatever you need to do, do it now," Vintore ordered.

The spirit realm was roaring with sounds of weapons and shouts from the demons and the elites.

"Focus, Arden," said Cain. He was standing across from me, and he put both of his hands on my head

"For Awan," he whispered.

"Stop them!" I heard one of the demons shouting, but I tried to block the noise from the war and focus on Cain.

"Focus, Arden," he said again. He pressed his hands deeper into my head, and he closed his eyes.

I felt a burst of energy and it merged with my spirit. I could feel the power as Cain transferred the mark. I screamed as the energy melded with my being. The pain grew stronger, and I screamed louder. The intensity of the power was building up, and it emanated across the battleground. There was another burst of energy that thundered around us, and I could see the demons flying back through the burst.

I felt the pain disappear, and I could feel another power in me. The power was heavy, and I felt strong, a kind of strength that I have never felt before.

I opened my eyes, and Cain was not there anymore. I looked around the spirit and the physical realm, but he was not there. This was his sacrifice. This was the cost of the merge.

The battle didn't stop between the elites and the demons. The demons were still trying to get to me, but the elites were still guarding me. My eyes met with Emrail. He was standing away from the battle, but I could still see him clearly. He kept his gaze on me and nodded. I wondered why he was not fighting with the others. I didn't take my eyes off him and locked my gaze with his. He smiled and then orbed away.

I saw Balnor charging toward Quiff as the demons were holding Quiff captive. Quiff was trying to escape, but the demons were holding his hands from each side, and he was struggling to break free. I summoned my bow and aimed toward the demon standing on Quiff's right. The demon saw my arrow, and he blocked it with his lance.

Balnor was about to attack Quiff, but I was quicker. I orbed between Balnor and Quiff and stood as a shield between them.

I could feel Balnor hitting against me, and there was another burst of energy. He flew back to the other side of the battleground. This gave me the chance to attack the other two demons holding Quiff. I pushed the demon standing on the right with the same force, and he flew back. The other demon was about to attack me with his sword, but I blocked it with my bow. I dug the edge of my bow into his armour and pushed him back. I didn't wait. I aimed my arrow at his neck and cast him to hell.

"How did you do that?" said Quiff as if in a daze.

A demon was charging toward him, but he cast her out with his staff.

"It's Cain's mark," I said, realising that the surges were coming from this new power running through my spirit.

"We got it?" he said, and he looked excited. I had never seen Quiff so excited.

"We got it," I affirmed, and his strength grew. He cheered and went to help the other elites.

"You got the mark!" I saw Vintore standing next to me, looking at me triumphantly. "Now what?"

"We need to get to Reynak now," I commanded. I knew we had to be quick. I didn't wait and began to ascend. I saw Vintore ordering the elites to ascend to Reynak.

I was orbing from earth and up to the second heavens, and I felt a sharp pain cutting deep through my armour and through my entire being. I saw the gold spear cutting through me, and I felt pain.

I recognised this spear.

I felt my power weakening, and I fell onto the ground. I screamed and tried to pull the spear from my body.

This was an ambush. I was growing weaker by the moment.

I looked around me, and all was dark. I could see dark trees ahead and noticed that my vision was growing weaker too. What was happening to me?

"Here, let me help you." I knew that voice too well. Zaphael pulled his spear out of me, and I screamed again. White light appeared from my wound, and I lost my strength. I looked around me and saw that we were alone.

"Don't worry, we're alone," he said, bending down, summoning away his spear. "Didn't see me coming, didn't you!"

I struggled to speak.

"We are at the farthest corner of Reynak, where no one can find us." He gazed up in triumph as if taunting God. "Did you really think we could allow you to have the mark?" he sneered. "We knew we had to be one step ahead. You would need to use the mark from Reynak, and you would have to orb your way here. It would be impossible for Cain to travel here. And here I stand, victorious! Victory is ours alone!" he shouted up toward heaven.

I sighed slowly and felt my spirit becoming weaker. I tried to ascend, but I lost all strength. I didn't have any strength to call the other elites for help.

"Still think you can save me?" he laughed. "I can't take the mark out of you, it's part of you now. The only way to destroy it is to destroy you."

He summoned his spear again and raised it up.

"For what it's worth, Arden, this is for your good," he whispered. He aimed at the open wound again, and I felt another sharp pain cutting through my entire being, and I lost consciousness.

Peace. I could feel peace. The pain I felt was gone, and my entire being was being resurrected.

I wanted to open my eyes, but I hesitated.

"You are safe in me. You can open your eyes, my valiant warrior." I recognised God's voice, soothing, powerful, healing.

I expected to be before his throne, but I was still floating. I was pure spirit, and I could feel God's presence carrying me across the heavens.

"Where am I?"

"You are a part of me," he said. I could feel my spirit healing, but I still felt weak.

"You are an eternal being, pure spirit, part of me. Angels don't die, Arden."

I looked around me, and all was pure light. I could not see God, but I could feel his presence and his grace. I was a part of him.

"You are safe my special warrior, you are healing."

I felt every part of my spirit being reignited by God's power. I could remember what Zaphael did, but I could not remember the pain of his spear cutting deep into me. I remember his gaze, and he didn't hesitate when he attacked me. He was truly gone.

"Yes, Arden, he will never come back. It is time to let him go," said God, discerning my thoughts. "You still have the mark of Cain in you," he said, reassuring me. "Satan and his demons believe that you have been destroyed, truly, he should know better. I am in control."

"What about the elites?"

"The battle in the spirit realm is over, Arden. You have been healing in me for a long time. To you, it may feel like nothing has passed. I have made it known to the elites that you are healing. Rest, warrior."

I closed my eyes, and God's power enveloped me. This was the closest I have been to God. The last time I was feeling like this was when he created me, before he sent me to Alvinor. This is who God is. There is no evil or deceit in God. No malice, no lie, and no sin.

God is pure, God is love, pure love, unconditional everlasting love. God is mercy, God is eternal, God is good, God's grace and power channelled through me, and I felt my spirit gaining strength every moment. I could feel another power at work in me. A new power, the mark of Cain.

It was as if eternity was passing by and the former was gone. God is doing something new.

I saw the light fading around me, and I saw stars glimmering above me. I was floating across the universe, and it was beautiful.

I saw galaxies spread across the universe. God was showing me his creation.

"I created all that was, all that is, and all that will be. I created the stars. I am the maker of the universe and everything that is in it," said God.

He was guiding me and showing me the heavens.

The black canvas that was the universe was coming to life with billions of stars, nebulas, and the cosmos.

"First, there was me, then I created the universe and the heavens. I rolled out a blank canvas, and I created. I created and perfected. I birthed every star, every galaxy, every planet, the sun, and the moon. Then I created my spirits. My eternal companions."

I hovered in space, and then God brought me to another realm. I could see earth floating beneath. It stood gloriously in the universe.

"My treasure," said God. "My greatest work." I could feel God's joy as he showed me earth. "You see, Arden, in my entire existence, I have loved everything that I ever created. Earth is my most loved. Every human I have carved in my image, every human I have weaved myself. I have known every human before they were born. I have called them and have planned for each of them, a mighty destiny.

"I have set a time, and you know it is soon. You are vital for such a time as this, my valiant warrior. It is time to bring my people home, for I long to be with them eternally. There will be no more evil, no more pain, no more suffering, and no more of Satan's schemes. It is time to bring my children home to me. Together, with my angels and my creation, I will be with them, with you all, forever and ever, for that is all I have yearned for."

I felt God taking me into another realm, and I was descending onto levelled ground. I was clothed in a long white robe.

"What happens now, Lord?" I looked around me, and I was surrounded by white light.

"You may call this a waiting room. You can rest here for a little while longer, and then I will release you when you are ready," he said.

The light began to fade away, and I could see that I was looking over earth. This place reminded me of Alvinor.

The sky around me was dark blue, and the stars glimmered around me. An open cathedral stood in the middle of the city. I could see jewels glimmering from the walls from here.

This city was smaller than Alvinor, but it was just as magnificent. I looked down to admire the earth again.

"I see I have some company."

I turned around again and saw an angel walking toward me.

Her long blonde hair fell down her shoulders, and she was also wearing a white robe. "Arden," she said. I admired her beauty, and her presence was very powerful, and it grew stronger as she came toward me. "I have seen your adventures on earth from here. I am honoured to meet you. I am Reinaya."

I recognised that name. She was captured and imprisoned in Reynak. I remember Emrail telling me that he destroyed her.

"You must have questions," she said, smiling. Her power radiated across the city.

"I know that you are an elite and that Emrail destroyed you."

"Oh yes, I remember him mentioning that to you on Reynak. I am now an archangel, Arden. I was in training to be an archangel, though Emrail nor the other demons knew that. I stood with Michael and Gabriel, leading the battalion, until I was captured."

I looked at her in awe. This explained her powerful presence; it reminded me of Michael and Gabriel's power.

"You can see all that happens from here?" I asked, and she nodded.

"Indeed. Just like you did on Alvinor, you can also observe all that happens on earth and in the second heavens too."

"Where are we?" I asked.

"A waiting room, but in a realm of its own. Alvinor was between earth and the highest heavens. We are between the second heavens and the highest heaven. Do not fear, we are safe. No demons can get to us here."

"You have been here all this time?" I asked, and she nodded again.

"Perhaps I like it here too much. After Emrail attacked me, God was healing me, just like he did to you. God was ready to release me back to heaven, but I did not feel ready to go back to all that was. I needed more time to be alone with God, and so he created this city. Another home for me, until I am ready to go back." She looked at me solemnly and then looked down to earth. "Beautiful, isn't it?"

"Yes," I said.

"This realm has become a sanctuary for me. I pray and intercede for humanity from here. I talk with God here, and I rest here." She beckoned me to sit down. "Your healing has been long. It is good to see you healed and to have you here," she said encouragingly. "I'm sorry about Zaphael," she said gently.

"I have been blaming myself for a long time, I thought I could bring him back. All the blame and guilt I felt went away when I looked into his eyes before he attacked me. I feel released and free," I said, and she smiled.

"Though it took all that experience to feel this freedom, I'm glad that you have found peace with yourself, Arden."

"Have you come across others here, Reinaya?"

"Just you."

I looked at her in surprise, and she chuckled.

"No other angel has been severely wounded as much as we have. If an elite has been wounded in battle, they can be easily healed by other angels. I was brought here not only because of my wounds but because my spirit was crushed. I didn't want to move forward. I lost the will to move forward. It is here that God healed me and restored me."

I listened intently to Reinaya, and I knew she was about to tell me her story.

"I led many battles alongside Michael and Gabriel and with the elites too. Those were the glorious times, and there was a revival on earth where many humans were giving their hearts to Jesus. We were foiling Satan's plans before it even had a chance to come into fruition. We guided humans into their God-given destinies and led them from glory to glory and then home to us."

"What happened?" I asked. I didn't think it would be possible for an archangel to be wounded like she had been. I have faced Emrail in battle, and I defeated him.

"Exactly what happened to you," she said. "I was assigned on a mission to get the mark of Cain hundreds of years ago on earth's time that is. You see, Cain was very arrogant then, and he refused to surrender his mark. He had to surrender it to the angels by will. I would have used the shield to destroy Reynak once and for all. I was getting close to retrieving it, and the demons did not like it. A battle ensued, and I got captured by the commanders in Reynak. I was a threat to them."

"How long were you imprisoned in those dungeons?"

"A long time," she said and sighed. "The commanders wanted me to sacrifice my grace in exchange for my freedom and to be loyal to them. Emrail tortured me mercilessly, but I didn't give up my grace, and I stayed loyal to God. When the commanders finally realised that I was not going to give up my grace, they sought to destroy me. I stayed loyal to heaven until the end, only I realised it was not the end. Beyond time and space, God healed me in him. I was a part of him, just as you were a part of him. I gained wisdom and revelation of my time spent on Reynak, and I am now stronger than I have ever been."

"Then why have you not joined the others in heaven?" I asked.

"God has deemed me ready, but I am not, and he never interferes with my will. The battalion is strong. I will return soon." Her words encouraged me. "Arden, your will is strong, and know that God has created you for these challenges. You are unique, you passed the test on Alvinor, and since then, you have continued to grow stronger in will and power. Getting the mark of Cain and protecting the Nephilim is destined for you. You are stronger than you think."

*Nephilim.* I gazed down to earth and observed Kitana. She was safe, and she was in the library.

"She is safe. God has assigned elites to her, and they never leave her side. Once you are healed completely, you will be able to go back to her," said Reinaya. "Now that you are here, perhaps I can train you and prepare you for what is to come."

We stood up and walked to the middle of the city. Facing each other, she summoned her weapon, and I saw that she also wielded a bow.

"Are we going to fight?" I asked.

"No, and there is no need to change into your armour. I will show you how to use the mark of Cain. I will teach you wisdom."

She raised her silver bow and studied it. The archangels all wielded silver weapons, signifying their rank. I studied her bow in awe. It was bigger than mine, and it was carved in silver markings.

"Right now, your spirit is merged with the mark of Cain. You have supernatural energy, mystical power, running through your entire spirit. When you release the shield from Reynak, you will need to channel all that energy through a focal point. You will need to use your weapon to channel all that energy." She swirled her bow and hit it against the ground. "You will need to use your will, put your attention on what you want to use the mark for, and channel the force that drives you. Is it power, is it love, is it justice?"

I could feel the strange energy running through my entire being. I felt powerful, but this power was also a burden, and I felt heavy. It needed to be released. I thought about Reinaya's words. I was chosen to use the mark of Cain, and Cain had chosen me. The elites have a big part to play in this war. Using the shield would destroy Reynak, and it would clear the way for Jesus to descend, without resistance from the demons in the second heavens.

Reinaya walked around me, still carrying her bow and swirling it around.

"I stand for all that is good and pure. I stand for justice," I said.

Reinaya wanted me to reflect on why I was doing what I was doing. "It is good, Arden, to step back and remind yourself of your purpose. Purpose drives you, helps you stand firm and to push harder. I can see it, we are very near, and Satan will do all that he can to steal every soul on earth."

"Using the mark of Cain would be a setback for him and the demons," I said, and she nodded.

"Every time a demon tries to taunt you or make you question your allegiance, remember your purpose. Remember that God has created you for a specific purpose. You are set apart, Arden. Now, wield your bow," she commanded, and I did. "I have observed you. You are strong in weaponry and combat, which is why there is no need for me to train you in those areas. When the time comes for you to use the mark of Cain against the demons, I want you to be swift. Channel all that energy, and use your bow as a focal point. It will be as if you are transferring all that energy to your bow, and you will know when you are ready to release it. When the time comes, I want you to hit your bow against the ground on Reynak. Do not be distracted. Hitting your bow against the ground will release all that mystical energy, and it will instantly vaporise every evil near you. It will cast out demons to hell and destroy Reynak. You will see it for yourself, and it will be glorious."

"Will the demons be destroyed?" I asked.

"I suspect some will flee down to earth and others will be cast to hell. Demons are eternal beings, they cannot die. When the final judgment is here, they will then meet their fate. It is actually that simple really," she said encouragingly. "The hard part is done. You have the mark. It is just a matter of using it at the right time. Any questions?" she asked.

"Once the shield is released from Reynak, or in the second heavens, will the demons be able to steal it and use it for themselves?"

"No," she said firmly. "The mark of Cain can only be used once. What will happen though is that demons will cause more havoc on earth as revenge. They will regroup on earth in the spirit realm, and the war will only escalate, but that is to be expected. The demons will no longer be blocking the elites from the second heavens."

"I remember Izralina talking about that. Can you tell me more about this?"

We sat down again and looked down to earth.

"Sometimes God sends down the elites to earth to help humans, to protect them, guide them into their destiny, and for whatever reason it may be. Humans also call upon God for angelic help, but that help is delayed when angels have to fight their way down to earth. The shield will give the elites control of the second heavens, and the elites will no longer have to fight their way down as the demons will no longer be able to ascend to the second heavens. The elites will be able to descend with ease. The elites will face resistance on earth, but getting control of the second heavens will be less of a burden."

Something caught her attention, and she looked up at the sky. "Our meeting has been brief, Arden, but I will see you again, and we will fight together in battle."

I looked at her in confusion, but before I could speak, we were surrounded by pure light. I could no longer see her, and I was floating higher toward the highest heaven.

I was engulfed by pure light, and I felt God's presence enveloping me. I was still wearing my white robe, and I could feel God's presence in front of me. This reminded me of when I was first facing God when he created me. I could not see him, but his presence was powerful.

"You are ready, Arden, you are strong my warrior. I will give you the choice, valiant warrior, are you ready to return?" he asked.

I was filled with his grace, and I felt restored. I know I will meet Reinaya again, but I was ready to return back. "Yes, Lord, I am ready," I said.

I was no longer wearing my robes, but my armour. I felt myself descending, and I was now facing God.

"Well done, my faithful warrior."

# CHAPTER 12

I stood before God in the palace. Michael and Gabriel were standing on each side of God.

I was not alone. The palace was filled with cheers, and the angels burst into song and dance.

"Holy holy holy is the Lord God Almighty."

I bowed down before God and joined the other elites on the side. I could not see Nikolai and Valiana. Gelin walked from the back and stood beside me. He didn't say anything, but his presence brought comfort. I knew he was happy to see me, as were the other elites.

An angel was leading the worship; she had long silver hair, and she wore a long purple robe. She had a gold crown on her head.

"That is Asteri, one of the worship leaders here in heaven," said Gelin.

Angels followed her and danced with her. I could see many angels near God's throne playing the harp.

"Lord, we praise you, we give you all the glory and honour. We worship you Lord, the maker of all that was, that is, and that will be," said Asteri, bowing her head.

God looked at all of the angels in delight and smiled.

"Here we come, come before you
In honour and praise
Let all the angels sing your holy name," sang Asteri, and the angels sang along with her as well.

"Here we stand, strong and in awe
Of your majesty, whom we all adore,
Let there be love in all we do
For we give you praise forevermore
Sound of heaven and hope is born
For we are your creation
We love you more and more..."

She turned away from God and toward all of us.

"The time is near when we will all be under one house. Humanity is being reconciled, and they are returning home to us. There will be no more division, no rebellion, and no more fall. A glorious crown awaits for every single spirit returning to heaven," said Asteri, and the angels praised God and cheered.

"Light of heaven, pure and love
You sit enthroned, high and above
We sing your name, we praise your works
For we are your creation
We love you more and more."

Asteri and the angels behind her bowed down before God, and the angels at the front stopped playing the harp. God stood up and thundered his staff, and I felt a powerful energy surging across heaven. I was filled with joy, and I could feel God's unconditional love and his authority. His authority was overwhelming, and his power shook the heavens. There is no greater power than God's, and for the first time, I realized how brave I have been since God created me. It was God alone who empowered me to face and overcome every trial that came my way, and I passed. Now I get to be with God forever.

The palace was filled with silence, and God looked around at all of us. He was about to address the heavenly court.

"Today is a glorious day because my plan is coming into ful-fillment. The time is near where my people will be reunited with all of us. Heaven will be filled with joy, with love, just as it once was.

Never again will evil and pride dwell in heaven. This time, there will be everlasting peace. I celebrate you all my angels, my beautiful creation. I love you all, and I honour you all."

He sat back down on his throne, and we all bowed before him.

"Peace be with you," said God, and the angels began to walk out of the palace.

I didn't want to leave God.

"I will wait for you outside," said Gelin.

The palace was quiet, and I was now alone with God.

God stepped down from his throne and sat on the steps, inviting me to join him.

"How did you like the procession?" asked God.

"It was wonderful, I enjoyed the choir and Asteri's voice," I said. I looked around the palace and enjoyed looking at the gems gleaming from the walls. Those were my favourite decorations in the palace. "It is good to be back, Lord."

"It is good to have you back, Arden."

"What exactly happened?" I asked, remembering Zaphael piercing me, and I remembered the pain tearing through my spirit.

"It was an ambush. Satan assigned Zaphael to you, to stop you from using the shield. I watch his every move, nothing surprises me, I am always ahead of Satan. What he intends to bring to pass, I foil it, and instead, I bless every situation, and I let it happen according to my will. I brought you from Reynak, before Zaphael could hurt you more. You healed in me. The fallen are suspecting that you have been destroyed, and I let them believe that. I created angels as eternal spirits, and I put great thought into how I create an eternal spirit. Every spirit that I form is unique, distinct from others. I thought very carefully when I created you, Zaphael, Nikolai, and Valiana. I faced rebellion a long time ago right here in heaven. I needed to put you all through many trials and tribulations, and I wanted each of you to be worthy to receive the mark of legion, to spend eternity with me, and to be obedient to me. I tested your spirit, and you all submitted to me, except Zaphael. I allowed Satan to get close to you all, and all of you resisted except Zaphael. It was Zaphael's choice, and he chose Satan, and just like the rest of the angels I have condemned to hell, he will join them too."

I soaked God's words in, and I thought about it carefully. "Did you suspect that Zaphael would rebel against you, Lord?"

"I never impose my will onto others. I create a plan, I put it into motion, and it works depending on the spirit's obedience or disobedience. I want to be with those who want to be with me, sincerely, with no malice or deceit. Yes, I suspected, and I saw doubt and pride in Zaphael, and Satan used that to lead him astray. Once Zaphael made his choice, I made mine. I do not allow angels to repent. If they did, many of them would not be locked in chains in hell. I only allow humans to repent, angels serve both humans and me. Humans are made higher than the angels, but this doesn't make any of you less worthy. Let him go, Arden," said God gently.

I knew he was right, and I realised that the Zaphael I knew on Alvinor was truly gone. I only saw hatred in his eyes on Reynak. "I know," I whispered.

We spent time together in silence, and I enjoyed God's presence. As I did, the memory and the pain I felt on Reynak began to fade away. I felt at peace.

"I liked meeting Reinaya," I said, and God smiled.

"I knew you would. It was in my will for you to meet her, though not in those circumstances. Nevertheless, I am happy that you learnt how to use the mark of Cain from her," he said.

"Will she come back to us?" I asked.

"Yes," said God. "I am proud of you, Arden, you are exactly where you are meant to be. I have everything under my control. There is no need to be intimidated by Satan, both now and when your paths cross with his in the time to come."

"What happens now, Lord?"

"Keep walking forward, just as you were, and everything will unravel before you, just as it is meant to. Keep your gaze fixed on me. I am with you, trust in me, valiant warrior."

"I love you, Lord." He held me close, and I rested my head on his shoulder. I sat there for a little while longer, and I then went outside of the palace.

133

Gelin was standing outside. "Good to have you back," he said.

"Good to be back," I said. "Where are the others?" I asked.

"They are all on earth, watching over some humans who have recently come to Christ. They will be with them for some time."

"What have I missed?" I thought about Johann and Kitana.

"Nothing out of the ordinary. On earth, new wars have started between nations. I have been watching over Kitana. She is safe. I'll walk you to your quarters," he said.

We walked toward the grand citadel, and I could see the many quarters sitting below. "I spend more time on earth than actually in my quarters," I said, and he laughed.

"I know the feeling," he said. "I'm curious, Arden, what does it feel like?"

"The mark of Cain?" I asked, and he nodded. "It is heavy, I can feel the burden, but God has alleviated some of that heaviness. It is part of my spirit, yet still distinct. Reinaya showed me how to use it."

"How is she?" he asked.

"She is well. She still sees all that happens in heaven and on earth. She said when the time is right, she will come back."

"I understand, we do miss her. She is a fierce archangel, along with Michael and Gabriel. She has been through many battles, I know she needs more time before she comes back to us," said Gelin, and I saw that we were now standing before my quarters. "Rest, Arden."

I thanked him and he walked away to his own quarters.

I saw the mirror standing on the side and the fragrance of the flowers spreading across the air. God created my quarters exactly to my liking. It reminded me of my quarters on Alvinor. I changed from my armour and into a long white robe. I picked up the Bible and sat on the bed. I began to read one of my favourite verses, Psalm 23.

"The Lord is my shepherd, I lack nothing. He makes me lie down in green pastures, he leads me beside quiet waters, he refreshes my soul. He guides me along the right paths for his name's sake. Even though I walk through the darkest valley, I will fear no evil, for you are with me, your rod and your staff, they comfort me. You prepare a table before me in the presence of my enemies. You anoint my head with oil, my cup overflows. Surely your goodness and love will follow me all the days of my life, and I will dwell in the house of the Lord forever."

I closed my eyes, and I felt that the Lord was pulling me into a vision. I could not see him, but I could feel him.

I was walking through a forest, surrounded by beautiful tall trees with light green leaves. Wildflowers were blooming, and I realised I was on earth in this vision. I could hear water rushing from a distance. That must be a waterfall nearby. I followed the sound. I was alone; there was no one else, no human in sight. It was daytime on earth, and I could feel the warmth of the sun.

"Further ahead," said the Holy Spirit.

The trees were clearing, and I saw a beautiful waterfall and a small lake. The sound of the water was peaceful. I sat on a rock and admired the waterfall. I realised that this was the first time I have seen a waterfall on earth and in a vision.

"Where is this, Lord?"

"New Zealand," said the Holy Spirit. "It's a beautiful nation in the southern hemisphere of earth. You will like it there."

I wondered why God was showing me this vision, but I decided to let it be and enjoy the scenery. I must visit this place with the other elites. They will like it here as well. I know Valiana will. She likes nature and being around forests and waterfalls.

"Rest now, beloved," said the Holy Spirit, and I sat on the rock until dusk.

I felt a powerful surge of energy, and I came out of the vision. I felt uneasy, and I could feel evil, and it was coming from earth. I closed my eyes, and I focused on earth. I began to search for the energy signature. I saw Kita's penthouse. It was night in Sydney, and I saw Zaphael standing over her bed, and Kita was sleeping. There were no other elites to protect her.

I descended immediately and faced Zaphael. He stumbled back but then steadied himself.

"I thought I destroyed you," he whispered.

"You clearly underestimated God's power. What are you doing to her, Zaphael?"

"I can feel all that power in you. Give me the mark of Cain, and I will let her go," he commanded.

"No, now tell me what you are doing to her?" I said.

"I am teaching her astral travel, to harness her potential. You know of her heritage, and you have done nothing," he sneered.

"What is this?" I turned around and saw Kita staring at both of us in shock.

"She can see us?"

"She can see clearly in the spirit realm. You have come unprepared," said Zaphael.

He orbed out of the room, and I was alone with Kita.

"I know you, Arden," she said, struggling to sit up.

Before she could say anything else, I orbed, and I followed Zaphael. I could sense his presence. He was standing on the lower deck of the Eiffel Tower, Paris. It was night, and it was raining in the physical realm. I met him there at the top, facing him with my bow ready.

"Why can't you leave me alone, Arden!" he shouted this time.

"I want you to leave Kita alone, Zaphael. You are on the losing side of this war," I said. "Zaphael, stop interfering with Kita's destiny. She belongs to God. As for the mark of Cain, I do intend to use it in Reynak."

For a moment, the anger in his eyes faded, and I saw something else. I couldn't read it, and for a moment, it looked like he was about to let his guard down, but then his anger returned.

"Stop trying to save me, Arden! Give up, Arden, I will destroy every part of your precious Kita, and I will make sure she suffers in hell like the rest of us!" he shouted again.

I felt something that I had never felt before. Rage. I felt rage. I started to have flashbacks of Reynak, Zaphael hurting me, and I charged toward him, but he stood still.

I grabbed him by the neck and hurled him up toward the iron bars.

"You deserve pain, you deserve the fire!"

He smiled and closed his eyes.

We were suddenly surrounded by a strong silent energy, and a bright light flashed around us. I no longer had any control over him; he was standing a few feet away from me, and we were both facing God. I could not see anything else, and I didn't know where we were. Everything was bright around us, white pure light.

I bowed down, and I knew that God didn't approve of what I did. Zaphael knew what he was doing.

"I do not want to see you!" said Zaphael. "Get me out of here." Zaphael fell to his knees, and he began to scream. "What are you doing to me?" he screamed.

"The evil in you cannot stand being surrounded by my power. You are surrounded by the purest form of love and goodness," said God.

I felt a shift in the air, and Zaphael stood up, and he was no longer struggling. "Your grace means nothing to me!" he shouted. He spoke to God with so much hatred. "Why?" whispered Zaphael. "Why didn't you save me when I screamed, when I asked for help!"

"I gave you strength, but there was a part of you that wanted power. Pride ruled over you, just as it did with Satan. You had one chance, but you chose to follow power. You chose Satan over me," said God. "You chose fear over faith, Zaphael, and I do not give angels second chances. Yes, I put you through a trial, I tested your faith, and you chose to experience freedom with Satan rather than obedience and surrender under my authority."

Zaphael stood quietly, and this was the first time I saw fear in his eyes.

"You are free to leave, Zaphael," said God softly. Without looking at either of us, Zaphael orbed.

"This needed to happen sooner or later," said God. He waved his right hand, and the bright lights disappeared. I saw that we were standing in the palace, and God sat down on his throne holding his gold staff in his right hand.

"You are not pleased with me, Lord, forgive me," I said, bowing my head.

"For the first time, I have seen rage in you. Rage is not of me, and Zaphael was able to bring this out of you. Zaphael knew I would intervene, but he did not expect to see me," he said.

"Lord, I sensed dark energy, and Zaphael was teaching Arden astral travel. She was unprotected. I thought the elites were protecting her."

"Kitana has been growing stronger in her abilities. A lot of time has passed by on earth when you were healing in me. I have allowed Zaphael to get this close to her, but not tempt her. The elites have been guarding her when I order them to. Astral travel I allow, and I am allowing Zaphael to awaken Kitana's dream life. What the enemy intends for evil, I turn it around for good. Arden can clearly see into the spirit realm. She still has much to learn, and I am teaching her as well. I am holding her steady."

I kept still. I stayed silent.

"I am not angry, Arden, nor am I disappointed. It is hard for you to let go of your past with Zaphael. You say and believe that you can let go, but facing him tonight, seeing you filled with rage, that is not of me. Rage clouds your judgment, and it gives Satan the power to manipulate you."

"What happens now?" I whispered.

"You need to grieve. You have been going at full force since I created you, and now, I am calling you into a time of rest, spiritual rest. You need to forgive yourself and heal. Once you are healed, Zaphael as well as the other demons will not be able to plant deceptive thoughts into your spirit."

I didn't like this, not when I had the mark of Cain and knowing that I can use it right now and vaporise Reynak.

"I know you don't like it, but this is my will for you, do you yield?" asked God, but I stayed quiet for some time.

"What about Kita?" I asked.

"You need to trust in me that I have everything under my control."

I didn't want to yield; I was struggling. There is so much to prepare for; war is on our doorstep; Kita needed me.

God waited patiently.

I bowed down and stood back up. "I yield. What are your orders, Lord?"

I met his gaze, and there was only love. I thought he would be angry with me. He was right, I should not have allowed myself to feel rage.

"You will go down to earth. You will travel around the world and learn about the world. You are not to intervene in human affairs or in battle with the other elites against the principalities. You will be able to see demons, but they will not be able to see you. You will be shielded. You will keep away from both Johann and Kitana. Satan would be well aware of what happened between you and Zaphael. Do not worry, he will not come near you. Heaven will be watching over you."

"You are sending me on a holiday, as the humans call it?"

"Yes," he said. "Know this, Arden, should you choose to intervene and use your power, your shield will no longer be effective, and the demons will be able to locate you easily. Zaphael was able to attack you even though you carry the mark of Cain because you were not on your guard. The force field becomes weaker. No demon has ever harmed Cain because he remained guarded throughout these thousands of years. If you remain obedient and guard yourself, the mark of Cain, as a forcefield, becomes stronger."

"I understand, Lord."

"I release you, Arden. You may descend now."

I bowed down again and descended to earth. I was now standing on top of the Harbour Bridge in Sydney, and it was dawn. I could see Kita's home from here. I must not interfere.

I orbed, and I descended to Singapore. It was a few hours before the sun would rise here. I sat along the shores of Sentosa Beach; there were no humans in sight. The breeze was cool.

I succumbed to Zaphael's deception, and this was my price. In the midst of an impending war, God has ordered me to go on a holiday. For the first time since I was created, I feel lost. When I was in battle, there was purpose, direction, and I enjoyed wielding my bow.

"May I join you?" I could feel his presence before turning around.

Gelin sat next to me, and we both admired the ocean and the waves gently hitting against the shore.

"I saw what happened, between you and Zaphael, and then you both became invisible. When I was able to see you again, I saw you sitting here," he said.

I told Gelin everything that happened and what God had commanded of me, and he listened intently. "Is this a test, Gelin?"

"We can't fathom the mystery of God, Arden. There is always a lesson to learn, there is wisdom in every situation and all that God has purposed. You forget one important thing, you haven't been here since the beginning. God has created you, you are new to all this. You are incredible and powerful, but there is still so much that you have to learn and know. God is very well aware of the wars to come, in heaven and on earth. Trust in him, he is not angry with you. If he has commanded you to travel the world, with his protection, with no demonic interference in the physical and the spiritual, trust me, that is a blessing. Use this time wisely, rest."

"Thank you, Gelin."

"So why start with Singapore?" he asked, and the air around us became lighter.

"I like the atmosphere here, the heat, nature, and the people. I'll start from here and see where I go. There are still many places I have yet to visit."

"Sounds great!" he said and got up. "You might want to change from your armour to begin with." He laughed and made his farewell.

The sun was beginning to rise, and I realised that humans would be walking out and about. I changed into my usual blue jeans and black top and white sneakers. This was my usual attire on earth.

I looked wistfully up at heaven knowing that the Lord was watching me.

"Here I go, Lord."

# CHAPTER 13

I spent two weeks sightseeing around Singapore. The weather was nice and humid, and I spent most of the time walking around in the physical realm. I would usually rest sitting along the beach. I saw demons walking with humans and taunting them, but I didn't interfere, and they didn't see me. I enjoyed wandering around the Gardens by the Bay, especially at night. People would gather at night watching the light shows and fireworks. I love Singapore and its people. There are always celebrations, and the nation celebrates different cultures, talents, and also life.

Sitting here on top of the rooftop bar at the National Gallery, I admired the Marina Bay Sands lit up with different colours. I wanted to see the fireworks before I left.

The rooftop bar was busy; many people were celebrating and laughing. The music went well with the atmosphere too.

"Excuse me, ma'am, can I get you something to drink?"

"Oh no, thank you, I will be leaving soon," I said.

"No problem," he said, smiling and then curiously gazed at my right wrist. I followed his gaze and saw that he was looking at the mark of the legion. "That is a very odd and unique tattoo. Where did you get that?" he asked.

I have been wearing tops with no sleeves since God relieved me of my duties as an elite. I did not have to worry about any demons hunting me as I was invisible to them, so it felt nice to have the freedom to show my mark.

"It is just a tattoo I stuck on with a design template, it's not real," I said. This is what I told all the humans who asked me about my tattoo. It felt easier to explain it rather than telling them its origin. They would not believe me anyway.

"It looks very real though." He stared at my wrist intently and then gazed up at me and blushed. "I'm, Daniel," he said, holding out his hand, and I shook it.

"Arden."

It was nine o'clock, and the fireworks thundered above from the Marina Bay Sands. Beautiful, colourful displays lit up the sky, and the crowds cheered from the bar and from the park below.

The firework show continued for ten minutes, and then the sky became quiet.

"It was nice meeting you, Daniel," I said. He half smiled, and he also looked disappointed but then retreated inside.

I grabbed my jacket and went downstairs, walking down to an alleyway where there were no humans. I shifted into the spirit realm, and all was quiet.

I thought about the other elites, about Kitana and Johann. It has been hard focusing on this holiday that God sent me on.

Why was God doing this? Was this a test?

I knew it was up to God to end this holiday; he knows when I will be ready to come back. I was confused, but I found comfort in Gelin's words. There is always a purpose to everything that God ordains.

I orbed to Amsterdam. I have made many memories here. I remember Satan bringing me here, around the evil and the sins that humans take part in. I stayed in the spirit realm and saw demons prowling about, tempting humans. I walked past many, but they didn't sense my presence.

It was daytime, and I saw a cathedral sitting in the middle of the city. The cathedral was grand and tall. I walked inside and shifted into the physical realm, and I saw that the roof was covered in red shields, and everything around me was red. The sunlight reflected through the red shields, and the ambience was hauntingly beautiful. I could clearly see the interior architecture as red lights bounced off the walls.

A beautiful choir erupted from the middle of the cathedral, and I saw both men and women wearing white robes, singing. People sat around them as the soft melody echoed.

"Lord, I will not hide
In you, I shall abide
I will rest in you, I will walk with you
You answer my prayers, and you lift me up from the depths of the earth.

Lord, I surrender, I will obey to all your precepts
I will never bow down to the ways of the wicked
I will stand tall, I will stand with you whatever may befall.

You bring me up to the highest mountain, so grand at the highest of heights
There is no one like you, Father, you strengthen my frame and shower me with your delights."

The choir then began to gently make melodies without words, and the cathedral began to get more crowded. I went into a corner, and I shifted into the spirit realm. I orbed farther out from the city and descended on the side of a windmill.

The sun was at its peak, and the weather was pleasant.

I could see many tourists walking about down below. A large lake was next to me, and I could see people rowing on boats. I remember reading about this place, Zaanse Schans. The green wooden houses stood out.

I shifted into the physical realm and saw a small church down the road. I walked a few hundred metres and stepped inside. An elderly woman noticed me and encouraged me to sit down on one of the benches. The pastor was just about to give the sermon.

"Just in time, what is your name?" she asked with a sweet smile.

"Arden."

"Welcome, Arden, my name is Marnie." She began to usher in other people walking into the church.

I looked around the church and saw musical instruments at the front. I remembered the harps on each side of God's throne. I had never seen these before; I wonder how humans played these instruments. I have only heard them sing. There were many windows around the church, with plants and flowers decorated along the ceiling and the walls.

"Welcome, ladies and gentlemen, to this beautiful Sunday church. For those new here and those who have come to visit, I am Pastor Nathan, and it is a pleasure to have you here. Today, I want to share with you some words that the Lord has spoken to my heart. Prophetic words to edify you all in these times, words to sustain you and give you hope.

There are many Scriptures that speak of having confidence in the Lord. Let us look to the Lord, for our help and salvation comes from him. We can have confidence in God, for he has chosen us, set us apart, and loves us unconditionally. His love is pure.

So we say with confidence, "The Lord is my helper: I will not be afraid. What can mere mortals do to me?"—Hebrews 13:6.

Let us not be weary of doing good, dear ones. We must have confidence in God, that he will give us everything we need and he will answer our heart's desires. He is a faithful God, he keeps his word, and he keeps his promises. Mortals are powerless against a powerful God. People can do only do so much, wicked people who want to see you stumble, but the righteous will never be shaken. God upholds you firmly, have confidence in the most powerful being in the universe that he knows what he is doing and he will part the Red Sea and make a way for you—every single time.

This is the confidence we have in approaching God: that if we ask anything according to his will, he hears us—1 John 5:14.

It is good to fear the Lord, knowing that he is in absolute control and authority. Fear is not being frightened of God, hiding ourselves from God if we do something wrong and think that he will harm and punish us. That is not who God is. Fear is living in humility before the Lord, being faithful in doing all that he has called us to do with integrity. And if we sin or stumble, we don't hide away. We seek the

Lord in repentance, and we ask God to help us and to strengthen us. God does not like the wicked who wilfully serve the evil one and harm his people. God's wrath is toward them. Have confidence in God, have trust in him, and no matter how many times you slip, don't turn away from him, go back to him. He loves you, he wants to help you, and he is always ready to make things right and sort it all out for you.

Such confidence we have through Christ before God. Not that we are competent in ourselves to claim anything for ourselves, but our competence comes from God—2 Corinthians 3:4–5.

God has called you, and he will make you competent in everything that he has called you to do, in every season of your life. He will never lead you into a situation blindly and unprepared. Sometimes you wonder if you can actually do it, if you can make it, and if you actually have it in you to go all the way in your calling. Fear not, beloved, God has chosen you, he goes before and ahead of you, and he will prepare your heart to receive his blessings in fullness. If there are challenges, don't be disheartened, those challenges will only strengthen you to help you become all that you are meant to be in God. Not all challenges are from the evil one. And if it is, God will turn it around in your favour every single time so in the end, it benefits you. Have confidence in the Lord, that if he has called you to it, he will bring you through it.

And now, dear children, continue in him, so that when he appears we may be confident and unashamed before him at his coming—1 John 2:28.

Never give up on your dreams and in your calling. Choose salvation, keep your salvation, and don't lose it by following the evil one and indulging the flesh in sin. Be on fire for God, be zealous for everything he has called you to do. We all wait for that glorious day when Jesus descends mightily through the clouds with his angels. We don't want to see him and cover our face in shame, knowing that we have not pleased him and that we have not lived our life in obedience. We want to see Jesus standing confidently and unashamed and knowing that "yes, it has all been worth it, Jesus, you are worth it." Live your life in a way that will never hurt God's heart, live in such a way that everything you do glorifies Jesus. When you are opening a door for someone, a stranger, you are opening the door for Jesus. As you show hospitality to someone, you are showing hospitality to the Lord. Spread love everywhere you go, never allow deceit to creep into your heart. Keep Jesus in your heart always, never allow and make any room for wickedness.

Now this is what the Lord is saying directly to you. The more you dwell on the opinions of others, the deeper into negativity you will go. Dwelling, and obsessing on those thoughts, is the enemy's plan to keep you constantly distracted. Again, worry thoughts are an offensive attack from the kingdom of darkness. People don't always appreciate you, especially those closest to you. They make you feel unworthy, and you succumb to their critical spirit. You are not the problem. They are intimidated, they still have one foot in the kingdom of darkness, and this allows the enemy to taunt you through them.

Worry thoughts make you go deeper into a state of fear. You then begin to question my plans and all that I have promised. You begin to doubt. Listen to my voice, not those who are not of me. Look to me, learn from me. I celebrate you, though others not. I adore you, though others may not. I will never forsake you, though others will. Let them be, and let them go. I am bringing new people into your life who will love you, who will be loyal and kind and of me. You have often been disappointed by those who constantly use you when they want to and abandon you. You have faced rejection, and you have deep open wounds. I will heal you, and I will help you. The future is bright, and you will celebrate with people who will be with you throughout your entire life. They will never reject nor they will abandon you. They are good people, my people, wonderful people, and you will enjoy spending every moment with them. You will laugh, you will be full of joy, and you will never have to worry about being disappointed or rejected again. Good things are coming your way, my favour is in every area of your life, and you will indeed step into a season brimming with opportunities. You often find yourself reflecting on the pains of your past, those memories that put you down and make you feel as if you have accomplished nothing in your life. You feel like you have not done anything for my kingdom, as if you don't feel worthy of anything. There are days when you feel like wishing you didn't exist. Timidity, intimidation, and grief becomes you, and you become hopeless. Shadows whisper these thoughts from their dominion, unkind and dark words that are not true. It overpowers your mind, and you succumb to their lies. Let me just say that you are worthy, that you are actually doing powerful things for my kingdom. I allow the evil to get this close to you so you can become stronger. The more they persist, the more you resist and the more you become aware of what is of me and what is not of me. You'll realise that in time that you'll easily discern these failure thoughts, and you will instantly be steadfast in combating those lies with *my* truth. I am training you, and you are training right at the epicentre of the battlefield. This is good for you, and I am right there with you, through it all, just as I have always been.

Beloved, you are stronger than you think. You have accomplished much. If you get a paper and down your accomplishments, you'll see that you have actually achieved wonderful things in your life. That is just the beginning. There is so much more to come. Grand things are coming your way, fulfilment of the promises I have made to you and desires of your heart coming to pass.

This is what the Lord your God is saying to you all today, in this hour. Do not lose hope, there is much to hope for. There is much to look forward to. Praise be to the Lord our God who trains our hands for battle. Thank you, ladies and gentlemen. I hope you enjoyed this short teaching today. As you all know, we have a picnic down by the river, you are all welcome to join us and fellowship today."

The people in the church clapped and cheered, and then they began to walk down toward the river.

"Will you be joining us, dear?" asked Marnie.

"Okay," I said, not knowing what to expect. I had never fellowshipped with other people before.

The walk was only a few minutes from the church to the river. I was standing on the opposite side of the windmill, where I first descended to Zaanse Schans.

I saw children playing and running around and their parents sitting and eating together on blankets. Some were sitting on the tables. I saw Pastor Nathan standing near the water, admiring the view.

"Pastor Nathan, that was a wonderful sermon," I said.

He shook my hand and began to smile. "What is your name, dear?"

"Arden."

"Arden, like the garden of Eden, a place of peace and beauty. I have never seen you here before," he said. He kept his gaze locked on mine.

"I come from far away."

"I see," he said. "I had a vision when I touched your hand. I saw a road, a long road, and on each side of the road were bushes with long thorns sticking out. I saw you walking forward, but you were struggling. The more you walked forward, the closer the thorns surrounded you, growing further into the path." He began to look concerned and then returned his gaze out to the water.

I didn't say anything, but I realized something about myself ever since God sent me to earth. I have become more at ease when speaking with humans, sometimes feeling like I was one of them and not an angel.

"What is it like?" he asked. He faced me again, and I knew that he knew who I was. "Don't worry, I'll keep it to myself," he said reassuringly. "How did I know?" he asked, and I nodded. "I see many things, Arden, I could feel your power in the church. I knew at that instant that the Lord's angel was with us. I have faith and supernatural sight. I discern the supernatural with ease, it is a gift from the Lord."

I didn't retreat, and I trusted in his word. "It is beautiful, like nothing you have ever seen on earth. The peace and joy that is in heaven, is perfect," I said, and he sighed.

"I long to see his face. I yearn for him every day, to see his face," he said, looking down at the ground.

The Holy Spirit stirred within me, and I felt the Lord was wanting to say something to him through me. "Tell him it is not his time yet, tell him that his strength will never wane and that he will go to his grave in vigour. There is much ahead for him, more adventure and enduring peace."

I passed on the message to him, and he smiled.

"There is much ahead for you too," he said, resting his hand on my shoulder. "Goodbye, Arden, it has been a blessing meeting you. Peace be with you," he said, walking away to join the children playing in the middle of the field.

I admired the families and the water for a little while longer before orbing to my next destination.

I descended in France, right before Mont Saint-Michel. I needed more time to be here. I looked up at the top of the abbey and remembered that this was where I met Cain in human form for the last time. I decided to walk through the crowd in the physical realm.

There were many restaurants and shops inside the island, and the weather was warm in the afternoon. It was becoming less crowded as I walked up toward the abbey. I found a staircase and began to climb. There were many small windows through the spiralled staircase. It was low tide around the island, and I could see the beautiful greenery and flowers surrounding the abbey.

I finally made it to the top of the abbey, and inside, I saw a few people sitting on the benches. This was sacred ground, holy and peaceful. People sat quietly in solitude and contemplation.

I walked around to the front of the abbey; light beamed in through the windows. This reminded me of my time on Alvinor, when I sat in the observatory and the light of heaven comforted me.

"It is beautiful, isn't it?"

I turned around and saw a woman walking behind me alone. She smiled at me cheerfully, but in her eyes, I could see deep sorrow.

"It is, I like the peace," I said. "What is your name?"

"I'm Jade, and yours?"

"Arden. What brings you to Mont Saint-Michel, Jade?"

"I am here with my sister and her husband. They should be up here soon. I am visiting from Australia. I love cathedrals and architecture. I have always been drawn to cathedrals."

We sat down on one of the benches toward the front.

"How about you?" she asked.

"I am from far away. I came here a while ago, but I didn't have enough time to explore this place. Now that I have a lot of free time, I can travel with ease," I said, and I saw she was studying my eyes.

"The colour of your eyes, I have never seen anything like it."

"Thank you, I do get that a lot."

Before she got too curious, I began to ask her about her life and adventures. She was very easy to talk to, trustful and vulnerable. She knew she could trust me, and I could sense the gift of discernment in her. She talked about her childhood, her time growing up in Australia, and her desire to travel all around the world.

"Do you go to church?" I asked.

"Oh, I am not a Christian. I don't go to church," she said.

She held both of her hands tightly, and she appeared to be deep in thought.

"I don't know who I am and where I belong," she said sadly. "I am still searching, searching to be found."

"Do you believe in God?" I asked.

"I want to, I know there is something or someone out there, but it's like my eyes are covered. I'm walking in blindness, but I want to see the light."

She was lost in her thoughts again, and we sat together in silence.

The Holy Spirit began to stir in me, and he began to speak to my heart. "Jade is a child of God. She was chosen by God since the time she was in her mother's womb. I have hidden her from the evil one who prowls about seeking to steal and kill the young in that secret place. I have chosen her and set her apart. She has been through many trials, deep grief, and unfathomable heartache. But here she is, searching for me, looking for me. In a few years' time, she will come to Christ, and she will receive salvation. She will soar high. This is my decree for her, she will tear down nations and destroy the strongholds of the wicked, and she will build up nations, and in it, they will find peace, find me. I have ordained her to be the prime minister of Australia, and she will lead Australia in a way like no one has ever seen before. Australia will be a nation at the forefront of my blueprint in these last days, and she will set alight the hearts of many and destroy every demonic fortress that now surrounds that nation."

I couldn't help but smile.

"You are smiling," she said, and she also began to smile.

"It's funny, normally I would not talk to strangers in foreign places. I also don't have the confidence too as well, yet with you, I can say anything. I feel comfortable with you. Thank you, Jade."

"Jade! Let's go have lunch." We turned around and saw a couple standing near the entry door.

"That is my sister and her husband."

"May I pray for you before you go?" I asked.

"Of course," she said.

I placed my right hand on her shoulder, and we both closed our eyes.

"Lord Jesus, I thank you for this wonderful meeting and for precious Jade. She seeks you, Lord. She longs for you with all her being. I can see her heart, and it needs your touch, Lord. Touch her, Father, touch every part of her life, and bring it under your watchful eye, your grace, and your authority. As Jade walks out of here, I pray that you please release your warrior angels to lead her, help her, guide her, and protect her. May peace lead and follow her all the days of her life and those who love her and whom she loves. Direct her footsteps, let it come to your doorstep, and may every door open before her as she steps forward in faith. I ask for your will to be done, Father, in Jesus's name, amen."

She began to weep, but she was smiling and weeping with joy. "What is happening?"

"The Lord has touched your heart. There is a God, who loves you and know this, that he has wonderful plans for you. You are safe, you are loved, you are chosen, and you have a great destiny ahead of you. Be strong, be valiant, be full of courage, and know that he is with you wherever you go."

We said goodbye, and she walked away to join her family.

I sat there for a little while longer and felt God's presence enveloping me. "You did well, my valiant warrior. You are learning, keep going," he whispered to my heart, and I smiled to myself.

I travelled around France for another three weeks, visiting the city and the countryside too, exploring nature and ministering to the hearts of people as the Holy Spirit led me. I never interacted this way with humans on a personal level, getting to know them and their testimonies. Maybe this was part of God's plan after all? I liked being on earth.

# CHAPTER 14

I walked through the forests of Honduras, exploring nature and trekking through the terrains. This forest had many waterfalls spread throughout, and there were many humans trekking in groups as well. This time, the Holy Spirit chose my destination.

I have been in the city for some time, and I saw many demons walking in the spirit realm, following humans. Territorial demons were swarming all over this nation, and it was hard to be in the city. I needed to get away, away from evil, and the Holy Spirit led me to the north, deep in the jungle.

I was close to the ocean; I could hear waves crashing against the rocks from a distance. "No, go further in, further into the woods," said the Holy Spirit. I passed by a big waterfall, and I could see a small settlement in front of me. "Shift into the spirit realm," said the Holy Spirit.

As I did, I saw many demons walking beside humans. The settlement was primitive, and there were many huts spread throughout the forest. People were cooking outside, and I saw children running around.

There was a big hut sitting in the middle of the forest; it stood out from the rest. I walked up the stairs and went inside. It was eerie and dark inside, the only light came from the candles circling the hut. Black candles and bones surrounded the people sitting in the middle.

There were no demons inside the hut in the spirit realm.

An old man, wearing a white robe, sat at the front, and before him was a bowl. Sitting in front of him was a young girl and her mother.

He was wearing a necklace made of bones, and I saw dirty water in the bowl.

The young girl was sitting quietly, she looked confused, and her mother was crying.

"Please help us, we don't know where else to go," said the mother.

"You have come to the right place, but before I start, it would be wise to make the payment. The spirits will be pleased," said the man.

The woman got money out of her purse and placed it before his feet.

"What is this?" I asked the Holy Spirit.

"Voodoo," he said.

"What is the problem?" asked the man.

"My daughter, Nila, is having bad dreams. She is having trouble learning at school. She also needs medical treatment, and I have no money to pay for her treatment. We need help, please help us," cried the mother.

The man closed his eyes and began to chant. He was speaking in demonic tongues, and he began to shake violently. The young girl looked scared, but her mother comforted her.

The man became still, and I saw a demon kneeling beside him in the spirit realm.

This demon was in his armour; he had black hair falling down to his shoulders.

"Tell the woman that her daughter will have dreams no more, but she is to bring her daughter to you once a month, to give an offering. Her daughter must continue to pray to the idols in her home, and she is now healed," the demon whispered in the man's ear.

The man spoke the demon's message, and the woman looked relieved.

"Thank you, we will do as you say," she said and gave him more money.

The demon went away, and the man began to chant in demonic tongues again.

"I will see you both in a month," he said.

He suddenly shifted his gaze toward where I was standing and then began to speak in demonic tongues again. I needed to go from here.

I walked quickly away from the settlement and toward the ocean. I stood on the cliff and shifted into the physical realm.

"What was that?" I asked the Holy Spirit.

"Voodoo, a great evil, practiced by many humans throughout earth. Servants of Satan, who willfully sacrifice their soul to serve him and gain his favour, wealth, and supernatural longevity. The little girl's destiny has been stolen. Though healed of her sickness, Satan has trapped her destiny, and her years are cut short because the man has stolen it."

"That is wicked, cruel," I said. I have seen wickedness in other nations but not so much as this, especially to children.

"That is one of Satan's many schemes, to steal destinies of the young and to create strongholds so those people will not be able to receive Christ because their heart has become hardened," said the Holy Spirit. I needed to get away from here. I orbed back into the main city and descended in a quiet alley. I shifted into the physical realm and walked to the main street. It was noisy, and people were screaming and shouting. Lots of women were marching, holding banners and holding their right hands up to the sky.

"We will stand, we will fight, we will not give up, and we will strive," they chanted.

I saw many police officers trying to stop their protest, but the women kept on marching.

"We will stand, we will fight, we will not give up, and we will strive."

I saw a woman standing on the side of the path, and she watched them silently. "What is happening here?" I asked.

"Woman in Honduras are getting murdered and abused almost every single day, and our government is doing nothing to help them. We have endured enough, this is us fighting back. We want our voices to get heard," she said. She looked solemnly at the crowd. "Not all men here are bad, there are good men who treat their women and children with kindness. But there are also evil men who beat us, keep us living in fear, we feel unsafe living here. We have no money and no means to escape this country. I am afraid to sleep at night. You are not from here?" she asked.

"No," I said.

"You mustn't stay here for very long, go back as quickly as you can to your home. The longer you stay here, the greater the danger you are in."

She retreated inside the shop. I stood there not knowing what to do. I couldn't intervene in human affairs. I could not stay in this nation any longer; I needed to leave.

I remember Nikolai talking about New York. I orbed immediately, and I descended into the spirit realm in New York. It was night, and the street was crowded with people and cars.

I closed my eyes and focused. I listened.

"Hallelujah, hallelujah!" I could hear people shouting and praising from a church at the end of the long street. I walked quickly toward the church and sat at the back of the church, still in the spirit realm. There was only a small group of people gathered in the church. I saw a pastor standing at the front, giving a sermon.

"Well, folks, it is just us today. I have a wonderful word for you from the Lord. We will do some worship and some prayer after this."

"Amen," the people shouted.

This is where I needed to be, away from evil, I felt weak being around evil. Being here in the church, I felt stronger.

"Today, I want to talk to you about faith. Humans are curious. We find the future fascinating, wanting to know what lies ahead so we know what we have to look forward to. At the same time, wanting to know what calamities lie ahead so we can be prepared for it or avoid it all together. Curiosity can turn into obsession, and obsession into bondage, and bondage into stronghold. Before I was a Christian, I had an obsession of wanting to know my future. I was living in confusion, hurt, and I lived everyday with not much to hope for. I thought that it would be exciting to know that would happen in the future so I can hold on to that. This was through my teenage years. I would go to psychic readers, tarots, opening door after door to demons. I would also buy my own set of tarot cards, trying to figure out if I could read them. All of the cards said something intriguing. But then I threw those away because something didn't feel right. The occult becomes an obsession. We want to walk by sight, not by faith. We want to rely on ourselves, not on God. Through occultism, we go deeper and deeper into strongholds and despair. Even if we know that we shouldn't trust psychics, we still go so we can find some kind of closure and relief from our reality. We want to connect with something spiritual so we don't feel alone. That is what it is like for the Gentiles out there. They are yearning to find and to be found. They are seeking God, but they are looking at all the wrong places. The more they participate in the occult, the more Satan puts curtains over their eyes so it's hard for them to see the truth.

"After being saved, I still had an obsession with the future. I still relied on my own strength and having control rather than relying on God. I was still living in fear. It took me years to get out of this mindset and to rely on God. In Satan's kingdom, there are false prophecies, fortune-telling, sorcery, divination, all for the purposes of leading people astray. In God's kingdom, there are gifts of prophecy and His Word for the purpose of leading people into salvation and building others up.

"This is what God wants you to know, he wants you to walk by faith and not by sight. If he tells you everything now, you will be excited, but over time, that sense of excitement and hope will diminish. He has blessings, recompense, and adventures for you. He wants you to be able to enjoy it as it comes. He wants you to have faith in him. He doesn't harm his children. You worry, a lot, unnecessarily. You put too much burden on yourself. You worry about everything. Your mind is full of fear and anxiety.

"He needs you to trust in him that he has everything in your life under control, that is obedience. Yes, he does put challenges across your path, that is not to punish you, but to strengthen you. He has lessons that he needs to teach his children before eternity. He is preparing you. Challenges sent by him are a blessing. Challenges sent by Satan are a nuisance, but he turns it around into a blessing anyway because he loves you. Satan loses every time. Walking by faith is obedience, therefore, beloved, trust that he knows what he is doing.

Even when things don't make sense, keep walking by faith forward with your eyes fixed on him. It will make sense as you keep moving forward, and you will be delighted."

The people began to clap, and they praised the Lord.

"Before we go into praise and worship, I want to talk about spiritual endurance, which is a perfect addition to what I have just talked about. Faith, coupled with spiritual endurance, is a powerful combination," he said. "Let us chase God's heart. Let us do what is in God's heart. Let us never break God's heart. God's heart is the most precious thing in the whole universe. Like David, let us do everything that God wants us to do. David served God's purpose, David completed his race, let us do that too, with great perseverance, endurance, faith, integrity, and obedience.

John 16 chapter 33 states that this world is ruled by the devil. In this world, we will have tribulations, but fear not for Jesus has overcome this world. In him, as heirs of God's kingdom, we are over-comers too. We are more than conquerors, Romans 8:37. God has called you. He has called you to fulfil his purpose for you on this earth, while experiencing a full human life and also being able to enjoy the earth he has created. Our feet grounded on earth, our eyes fixed on heavenly things.

As Kingdom Warriors, we run our race, not in competition against each other, but with comradeship. We cheer each other on. God has given each of us our own specific track to race on. If we look at other people's race and we become envious, looking to the right and left, we will slip, perhaps stumble if we lose sight of the traps and temptations that the enemy might be putting on our track ahead. That's why it is important to keep your eyes straight ahead, your heart fixated on God and with obedience, focused on what he has called you to do. If you see your brother or sister fall or stumble, go over to their lane, and lift them up. Steady them so that they gain the momentum to continue running their race. You won't fall behind, you'll still have the same momentum.

It's not about running at full speed. What God has called you to do, go at a slow and steady pace, build your strength and your faith. If you keep ministering without taking a break, if you keep working overtime in your business and career, you will burnout and crash. Spiritual endurance is about enjoying your calling, your life at a steady pace, while balancing it with your health, family time, and alone time while you take time off to recharge. It's about knowing when to take a spiritual rest and when to continue your race with joy and vigour.

As you continue growing in Christ through your race, you will grow spiritually stronger, your endurance level will rise. Your spiritual muscles will be in good shape. When the enemy comes and tries to push you off your race track, you won't crumble. You will resist, you will keep your feet steady on the ground. You will ignore his lies, and you will keep your eyes fixed on the Lord. You must keep your eyes on the Lord, through all the seasons of your life, every day. You will stand firm, you won't budge. Endurance is the ability to be steadfast in the Lord, running at a steady pace, knowing when to pursue your calling with full focus and knowing when to take a rest, recharge, and have the momentum to continue running your race with the same energy, passion and joy.

Let us stand and praise the Lord for being so faithful, he is so good to us."

I stood up with everyone else. A young man led the worship and people walked to the front of the church, swinging from side to side and lifting up their hands in worship.

"Lord, we come to you,
Lord, we take shelter in you
For you have cleansed us, washed us, love us, and guide us
Watch us, help us, and make us glorious
In your name, we pray
Every night and day
No matter what others say
We will stand by you no matter what comes our way
Lord, we take refuge in you
Lord, we sing your holy name

For you make us strong and keep us firm
Honour belongs to you, glory follows you
Your blood has washed us clean, and because of you, we are free
In your name, we pray
Every night and day
No matter what others say
We will stand by you no matter what comes our way."

The music played softly in the background while the worship leader spoke.

"What a mighty God we serve. He is always for us, never against us. He is with each one of us, in the middle of miracles and in the middle of storms. If you need prayer, please come to the altar, and we will pray for you."

I saw one family lead a young man to the front. I followed them to the front; something was about to happen.

"This is my nephew Ethan. He wants to give his heart to the Lord, he is ready," said the woman, and everyone clapped.

"Welcome to eternity, son," said the pastor and he laid his lands on each side of Ethan's shoulders. Everyone began to pray, surrounding Ethan and the pastor.

"Do you wish to receive Jesus as your personal saviour and the lord over your life son?" asked the pastor.

"Yes," whispered Ethan.

"I will lead you to say the sinner's prayer, the salvation prayer."

"Heavenly Father, I come to you in prayer asking for the forgiveness of my sins. I confess with my mouth and believe with my heart that Jesus is your Son, and that he died on the cross at Calvary that I might be forgiven and have eternal life in the kingdom of heaven. Father, I believe that Jesus rose from the dead, and I ask you right now to come into my life and be my personal lord and saviour. I repent of my sins and will worship you all the days of my life. Because your word is truth, I confess with my mouth that I am born again and cleansed by the blood of Jesus, in Jesus's name, amen."

As soon as Ethan finished saying the last words, a strong supernatural energy surrounded him. I looked up to heaven, and the heavens opened, and there I saw clouds of witnesses, rejoicing. I saw angels in the palace celebrating. I felt dark power leaving Ethan, and I saw light pouring in from heaven and into Ethan's soul. The light entered from the top of his hand, and I could see pure light surrounding his frame.

Ethan began to weep, and the others embraced him. "Welcome to the Body of Christ, my son. Peace be with you," said the pastor. "Well, folks, same time, same place, have a blessed weekend," said the pastor.

"Fifteen Azalia Avenue, Miami," said the Holy Spirit. The Holy Spirit wanted to show me something; I could sense the urgency.

I closed my eyes and focused on the address and orbed in the spirit realm. I descended into a house, in someone's living quarters. A girl was crying, writhing, and she was surrounded by three women. The women were praying for her.

"This is deliverance. The women are casting evil spirits out of the girl," said the Holy Spirit.

"I command every spirit of hatred, lust, pride, and envy to come out of Raelle right now in the name of Jesus," said one of the women sitting closer to the girl.

"No, she is mine," said the girl. I could sense that it was the spirit talking through her.

The women began to pray in the spirit, and each of them placed their right hand on the girl's shoulder.

"We soak Raelle's entire being with the precious blood of Jesus Christ, and in the name of the Lord, we command you to get out of her now and go back to hell, in the name of Jesus, amen."

They began to pray in the spirit again, and the girl began to shake violently. The women held her down gently and continued to pray fervently. The girl began to scream, and as she did, I saw a dark figure come out of her mouth. The dark figure howled, and it approached toward me in the spirit realm.

It was not a demon. It was a shadow, malice and evil. It was deformed, but then it began to shapeshift into a human form. It had no human features; it appeared to look like a shadow of a human.

It stretched out its hand, as if wanting to touch me but then floated back.

I thought God said that I would be invisible to the demons in the spirit realm.

"Evil, yes, but not a demon. This is a dominant, former Nephilim from of old," said the Holy Spirit.

I studied the shadow, and it floated in front of me. It lingered there for a little while longer and then floated away, disappearing into the night. It could see me.

"Don't worry, they will not harm you. They are powerless, and they cannot come near anyone that is good and pure," said the Holy Spirit, and I felt comforted by his words. "You are learning quickly and well. You are gaining strength," said the Holy Spirit.

I stood there silently, looking at the women who were comforting the girl.

"You are free now, sin no more, child. Keep your eyes fixed on the Lord, and he will lead you in the way you should go," said the woman who embraced the girl. She was weeping, but I could sense that her burden was gone; she was free indeed.

"You are stronger than you know, Raelle," said the woman embracing her. "We often lose sight of our strong points and moments throughout our life where we needed to be courageous and take bold steps. Constant thoughts of failure can rummage about, and we then begin to dwell on our failures rather than our strengths. That's only a lie coming from the evil one. Notice it, observe it without getting attached to these failure thoughts. Don't obsess on it, and start filling your mind with wonderful thoughts.

I left their home and walked down the road. I saw demons following some of the humans. I also saw angels walking with some of the humans too. They acknowledged me as I passed by them. I recognised some of the elites from heaven. They didn't stop to talk, but I knew they were on a mission.

"Where to now, sweet Holy Spirit?"

I felt power, strong energy surging through my spirit.

"Israel."

# CHAPTER 15

I descended to Israel in the spirit realm, and I was in the middle of a conflict. Bombs were being bombarded and I could hear people running and screaming. I remember observing the war in Israel from heaven. I have seen many humans die. The spirit realm was swarming with demons and elites. They were fighting, and I saw some elites leading the humans to safety.

"I think this is the way, it feels right," said a man. He was holding his child in one hand and his wife's hand on the other.

Why did the Holy Spirit send me here? I have been ordered not to intervene in human affairs or in spiritual warfare.

"Holy Spirit, what do I do?"

He didn't say anything, but I knew I was supposed to be here.

"We are running out of weaponry, we need more ammunition, more soldiers, more men to fight with us. No other nations are coming to help us," said one of the soldiers. He had authority, and I realised he was a commander.

I ascended to the north, away from the epicentre of the battle. I saw many villages from above and saw many ruins. Houses were destroyed, and I saw people were living in tents.

I orbed further ahead and saw that there were no humans nearby.

I noticed a church; it appeared that the roof was destroyed.

I descended and sat on a bench at the front of the church and shifted into the physical realm. I studied the architecture. Some of the windows were still intact, and the glass-stained windows were shattered in pieces on the ground. There were broken tables and chairs at the front, and I looked behind and saw that only some of the benches were still stable.

I looked up and saw the night sky. There were many stars tonight.

I was away from the war, from the sound of bombs, and in here, I found peace.

I wish I could do something, I wish I could fight, but I must try to resist the urge to break God's rule.

I heard footsteps behind me and saw an old man walking up toward me. He had grey hair, he was short, and he had a walking stick. He must be from the village nearby.

He sat beside me and put his walking stick down.

"Hello," he said with gentleness.

"Hello."

"What brings you here at this time of the night, are you well?"

"I am well, I am new here," I said.

"I like to come here at this time and look at the stars from here. This is where you get the best view, under an open heaven."

"I was in the city, but there was war, and I came here. It is quiet here," I said, and the man smiled sadly.

"You never know how long it will be quiet here for. War came here once. It left, but it will be back again." He signalled to the destroyed roof. "My wife and I escaped the war, and we managed to find a small place just around the corner from here. We have known peace only for a little time. We never know when it will be our last day here, so I come here, watching the stars and spending time with the Lord. Do you have a place to stay?"

"Not at the moment," I said.

"Please, you must stay with us. It is dangerous for a young woman to wander alone, especially in this mountainous region. My wife and I will look after you."

"You can trust him," said the Holy Spirit.

"Yes, I can go with you," I said, and he looked delighted.

He picked up his walking stick and beckoned me to follow him. He led me through a path just below a mountain. He began to tell me about the city of Caesarea and his life in the city during the war.

"Oh my goodness, how foolish I have been. I have been talking for so long that I didn't even ask you your name."

"Oh, that is no problem at all. My name is Arden," I said.

"And I am Elias."

His home was not too far away from the church. I saw many large tents scattered under the mountain. He led me inside toward the tent that was blue, and it looked sturdy.

A woman came out from behind the curtains, and she was holding a pot. She was surprised when she saw me and then welcomed me with an embrace.

"Arden, this is my wife, Maya. Maya, this is my friend, Arden. She is new to town. She was sitting alone in the church, and she didn't have anywhere to go. It got too dark, and so I invited her to stay here with us."

"Certainly, we are happy to have you here, Arden. You must be tired. Come, have a seat." She motioned me to sit on a small cushion on the ground. Maya had long grey hair, olive skin, and she was taller than Elias. She walked very slowly and gently.

Their home was comfortable and peaceful. I saw a small bed standing on the back corner and a large curtain covering that part, separating the living area from their room. A small lamp hung from the top of the tent, and it was gently swinging from side to side.

"You have a very nice home, Maya and Elias. Thank you for having me," I said, and they both smiled.

"We do our best with what we have. As long as we have Jesus, that is enough for us," said Maya. "You must be hungry, come, I have prepared some food," she said.

"Oh, I am not hungry. I am very sorry."

Elias studied me for a moment and then encouraged Maya to let me be.

"Okay, dear, I will prepare your bed."

She went into her room and came out with a small mattress and a blanket and spread it on the side of the table.

"I hope this will be comfortable for you," she said. I thanked her and then lay down. Elias didn't ask me about my belongings, and I am happy he didn't. I did not want to reveal myself as an angel.

I closed my eyes, and I was drifting into a vision. I was standing between a valley, and in front of me was a path that I was to follow.

As I was walking ahead, thorns began to appear from the forest trees, and they began to prick me. I tried to evade them, and I tried to move forward, but the more I walked forward, the more they surrounded me. I woke up suddenly and realised it was close to dawn. I must have been in the vision for the entire night. I didn't want to disturb Elias and Maya, so I left their tent and made my way toward the mountains.

A few humans walked about, but they were busy setting up their tents and working. They didn't notice me, and I am happy they didn't.

I walked deeper into the forest and found a meadow filled with many wildflowers. This reminded me of heaven. I remember sitting in heaven with God in the meadow. I sat down and looked around. The sun was rising slowly, and all was quiet.

Light illuminated through the trees, and I felt at peace. Suddenly, I heard a noise coming from behind the trees, and I saw Elias walking toward me. He looked relieved as soon as he saw me.

"There you are, Arden. I have been worried about you," he said, sitting beside me and putting his walking stick on the ground. "May I sit here with you?" he asked, and I nodded. "I often come here with my wife to spend time with the Lord. We pray here, we praise. It is dangerous to praise the Lord where we live. If soldiers heard us, they would kill us. I'm tired, Arden, I am old, and I am weary, though I don't look it. Weary that is," he said and he laughed, and I smiled.

"I have travelled to many places on earth. I have seen freedom, but I have also seen evil. I have seen life, but I have also seen death," I said.

"You have deep pain inside of you, something you are hiding deep in your heart, you struggle to heal from it, you struggle to let go," he said. I was surprised and he chuckled. "Gift of discernment," he said, and he looked pleased.

I began to talk about my visions and the vision that pastor Nathan spoke to me about, and he listened intently. "You need to move on from someone, someone who is holding you back from your potential. You need to move forward, you try, but the thorns, the past that you can't let go of, it keeps haunting you."

"It is not that easy, Elias. I try, but it is hard."

"Forgiving others is hard, but forgiving yourself is much harder. You will know when you truly forgive someone else and yourself. Your heart will feel light, you will gain momentum, and you will experience freedom, a release."

I could see pain in his eyes, and I realised that he has experienced loss. "You lost someone, someone you loved very much," I said.

"I lost my daughter and her family, we all lived together in the city. Then came the war, and we lost everything. She had a daughter of her own. Her husband went to battle, and a few days later, we found his body lying on the street. We were trying to escape. Our daughter gave my wife and I some time to escape so we could catch the train here, but the enemy soldiers grabbed her daughter. She went back to get her daughter, but they never came back, and we ran for our lives."

He began to weep, and I comforted him.

"The enemy says this is a holy war, but it has become all about greed and power. We want peace, but the soldiers from both sides are fighting for nothing. Satan is devouring both our nations, he is stealing peace and has killed many. Some believe that by taking over a land, they are living according to the Old Testament, but that is not true. Those are the old ways, they will wither away. God has done something new, a way out, and his name is Jesus, people fail to understand this. Lives have been lost from both sides, and people live in fear."

"I'm sorry to hear that, Elias, I wish I could do more," I said, and he smiled, wiping away his tears.

"But you will do more, you are far away from home, but you are going to do mighty things, angel of the Lord," he said and laughed. I couldn't help but join him.

"You know?"

"I know," he said. "I suspected at first, for I have met many angels, but there is something different about you. I asked the Lord last night after you went to sleep, and he confirmed to me that you were indeed his angel."

I didn't know what to say, but the Holy Spirit told me to trust him, and I felt peace when I was around Elias and Maya.

"Though my body is weak, my spirit is still strong. I have been walking with the Lord for a long time. Come, let us go to church where we met yesterday. Some of us gather there at this time to pray and encourage each other. We only stay there for a little while so we don't get caught."

I helped Elias get up and gave him his walking stick. I held his arm, and we both walked away from the meadow.

"Arden, I'm glad I met you, and I'm glad that you are my friend."

"So am I, Elias, so am I."

The path to the church was quiet, and no one was in sight. As we walked inside the church, I noticed Maya sitting on the bench at the front. She was with two other women and a child. Standing at the back were two other men.

"Hello, everyone, it is good to see you all. Thank you for being here. Samuel, I hope you were not followed," said Elias.

"No, Elias, we have been careful, but I think next time, we should gather somewhere else. I have a feeling that people are watching us closely."

"We can talk about this later," said Elias. "Everyone, meet my friend Arden. She will be joining us in prayer today. Arden, these are my friends. This is Samuel, his wife Allira, and their daughter Samina." Samina was shy, and she hid behind her mother.

"And this is Daniel and his wife, Alisha." She greeted me politely, and we all sat together in a circle on the benches that were still sturdy.

"My wife, Maya, will be leading us in prayer today."

Maya lifted her hands in praise and bowed her head.

"Heavenly Father, we come here today to honour you, to praise you, and we thank you for keeping us strong. We ask that you surround us with your love and grace, strengthen us, Lord, and bless us with your healing touch so that we may continue to do all that you have for us with vigour and joy. In the name of Jesus, we pray, amen.

Brothers and sisters, I understand our time together today is short, but I do have a wonderful word to share with you. A soldier, on a battlefield, is well armoured and well equipped. The soldier is aware of his or her weakness, so they can best defend themselves should the situation arise. No matter if the soldier is on his or her territory or in the enemy's territory, an effective soldier is always prepared to face any kind of situation.

On earth, there are wars. Wars can begin anytime, and it can end anytime. Now you are a soldier of Christ on a spiritual battlefield. On a spiritual field, the battle never ceases. There is no ceasefire between the devil and God's people and angels. It is constant. There are demons operating from the second heavens and on earth, who work with great care and precision to lead people astray. Demons are the cause behind every wicked thing on earth. They manipulate, lie, tempt, and they will do anything to make sure that you are separated from God forever.

As a warrior of God's kingdom, it is an honour to participate in spiritual warfare. But just as a soldier trains first, on earth, as a spiritual soldier of Christ, you must train too. The good news is that the tools for spiritual warfare are already made available to you, and you can access it anytime.

It is vital to stand firm during spiritual warfare. You may be living a holy life, you are walking in obedience, you are doing everything right—but you must know that the enemy of your soul can come out of nowhere and attack you. All is well one day, then all of a sudden, the devil will heap discouragement and fear on you. You will need to be prepared.

He will try to overwhelm you with fear, doubt and frustration. He will attempt to make you lose hope and make you believe that God will not come through for you.

Satan will remind you of all the people and events in your past that have traumatised you. From there, you will become consumed with resentment and unforgiveness. This opens the door for the devil to infiltrate your mind. The enemy will play wickedly. There is no rule when it comes to attacking the people of God.

The enemy will tempt you to sin. He will pour an overwhelming amount of desire that you will want to sin.

When these things happen, you will need to be ready in the moment and start acting on it straightaway. Don't wait for an hour or tomorrow. Start acting on the offensive and defensive immediately.

Notice it. Do not make a rash decision or react when you suddenly feel these rush of emotions that the enemy hits you with. Be still and notice it. There's an art to being still and answering the enemy's taunts with poise and precision. It takes practice, and you will get better as you continue to stand firm on the spiritual battlefield.

The enemy will want you to lose control and will want you to feel weary—emotionally, physically, and spiritually. This is the deciding factor of whether you will succumb to his lies or maintain your victory in Christ Jesus. As soon as you become aware of the attack, you can do one, a few, or all of these things: Start speaking in tongues immediately. Call upon the Lord, and pray to Him that He will release His warrior angels and fight on your behalf. Put worship music on, and begin to praise, sing, and dance wherever you are. If you feel downcast, frustrated, weary, confused, fearful, stressed—you praise God. Praise and worship God no matter what season you are in. Start declaring Scriptures into the atmosphere. God's Word holds power. You don't say, 'Leave me alone, Satan.' You declare God's Word, Holy Scriptures, and when you do so, demons flee and the atmosphere will change.

The enemy will come back to remind you of your sins. You'll feel that pressure in your mind. You'll think that you have disappointed God, that God might be angry with you. That is a lie so you remain stuck and unable to move forward. You must keep marching forward and know that God knows that it's not your fault. God knows that Satan is a crafty liar. God knows your heart. You must believe that God has forgiven you. Remind yourself that you got this and God's got you. Let go of guilt and shame, and keep living your life serving the Lord, keep enjoying your life, and keep praying.

You can pray for deliverance, wisdom, and guidance during your alone time with God. You can receive healing and prayers from other people whom you trust. You can also look up videos on YouTube. Be careful and pray for discernment when watching videos on YouTube.

There are many false teachers and followers of the beast on YouTube. A wise soldier uses their resources well. You must too.

The evil operates from second heavens and from earth. You are seated with Christ in the highest heavens, the third heavens, where God is. Therefore, your authority is higher than those who are in the second heavens and under. Those principalities are under your feet. You have been given power and authority to operate from the third heaven and to trample on snakes and scorpions. First, you must know your identity in Christ Jesus. You must know that Satan is a defeated foe. You are already victorious. You are royal and a child of God. Wear that crown of splendour with humility, not with pride. When you pray, see yourself in God's throne room. Imagine what it would look like. You have God there right by your side. You are praying with fervour and are praying with command and authority straight from the throne room. Your prayers are releasing fires of heaven, and those fires are burning every plan of the enemy. Get creative in your prayer."

We all joined in another prayer and rested together in silence. I could feel deep sorrow and grief. Everyone in the room had experienced loss, but they appeared to be strong. God was keeping them steady.

Suddenly, I could feel darkness emanating from the spirit realm and into the physical.

"I can feel it too," said Elias, watching me shift around on the bench.

"What's wrong, Elias?" asked Maya.

I could hear screams coming from the village, and I saw many people running toward the church. Some fled into the forest, and some ran past the church. I could see large trucks coming from behind them, and they were shooting at everyone.

"Run, my friends, run and don't look back. Run to the forest and hide," ordered Elias, and they moved instantly, except Maya.

"I am not leaving you, Elias," she said.

"I know," he said, embracing her.

The trucks got closer, and I saw soldiers running on foot with guns in their hands.

"You can't run, my love, I must help," said Maya. Before we could say anything, Maya ran outside from the church and began to wave to the soldiers and began to run away from the church. She was distracting them so they could ignore us.

We heard guns, and we heard Maya screaming, and then it stopped.

Elias appeared to be shaken, he stood still as if in a trance.

I didn't know what to do, God has ordered me to not interfere in human affairs.

"Arden, you need to go," whispered Elias.

"No, Elias."

"Arden, we will meet again, now go," he said. "I'm glad we met, I'm glad I got to be your friend."

I wanted to scream and shield him from the soldiers, but I didn't want to be disobedient. The trucks got closer, and the soldiers were walking toward the church. I shifted into the spirit realm and saw hundreds of demons in the spirit realm. They were surrounding the trucks and the soldiers too. If I intervened, they would see me.

A soldier signalled others to follow him to the church. "Ah, boys, look what we have here," he said, pointing his gun toward Elias.

Elias gripped his walking stick tightly and stood firmly. "I serve a mighty God!" he shouted.

"We will show no mercy," said the soldier at the front.

"Neither will my God," said Elias. The soldier shot Elias between his forehead, and he died instantly.

"No!" I screamed.

The demons stood still and looked around the spirit realm. A powerful surge of energy burst across the spirit realm.

The soldiers left, and I heard the trucks move further into the east. Suddenly, everything became quiet. I shifted into the physical realm.

His eyes were still open. I bent down and closed his eyes.

"Until we meet again, my friend."

I went over to Maya, and I did the same.

I went over to the villages and did the same for the others too. So much heartbreak, so much injustice. I saw children lying on the ground. No, I could have had the power to stop the attack. Rage began to churn, a familiar and unwelcome feeling. I must stop them. I must foil their plans.

The heavens opened, and Gelin descended. He was wearing his armour this time instead of his usual black human clothes.

"Steady, warrior," he said.

"What are you doing here, Gelin, why have you come now?"

"I have been watching over you since you left heaven to come here. I know what you are about to do, don't do it. That rage twisting your spirit, let it go."

Grief consumed me, and the rage grew stronger. Gelin slowly came closer. "Arden, I got close too. I intervened, and look where I ended up. This is not your fight. Stand down."

I changed into my armour in the spirit realm, and he sighed.

# CHAPTER 16

"They were my friends, Gelin."

I didn't give him a chance to speak and ascended into the middle of the city in the spirit realm. I stood in the middle of the battlefield. Bombs were bombarding, and buildings were being destroyed. People were running for their lives.

Hundreds of demons were working with the army and fighting the elites.

Gelin descended next to me. "I know how you feel, Arden, believe me I do, but God has not commanded you to intervene. You must resist."

"Then why did the Holy Spirit lead me here?" I asked, wielding my bow.

"I don't know, Arden, but if you engage now, you will be exposed, and the demons will attack you. They know you have the mark of Cain, and now is not the time to use it. Control it," he said.

I could see the demons were overpowering the elites in the middle of the city. I orbed to the middle, and I decided to attack with the help of the mark. Gelin was right, now was not the time to use it, but I could use it in the short-term. I remember how demons were caught off guard when Cain first gave me the mark in the battle. I channelled my rage, my power into the bow, and I descended toward the ground with speed. My bow hit the ground, and it released a strong energy, and the spirit realm shook. The demons flew back and fell to the ground. The elites gained momentum, and they didn't waste any time in casting the demons. Some demons fled, and some stayed.

I was no longer shielded, and the demons steadied themselves, their gaze fixed on me. More demons thundered down from above.

"Don't let your guard down," said Gelin, and he began to fight the demons.

I shifted into the physical realm and destroyed the army tanks and the trucks. The humans saw me and stood still.

A bomb was fired into the building on the other side of the city, and I saw that many humans were in that building. They didn't have time to flee. I orbed in front of the building and hovered at the top. I crossed my arms and channelled the mark of Cain and released it toward the bomb. The bomb was destroyed, and I saw that some of the soldiers were chasing some of the people who were running from their homes. I descended and blocked their path.

"You don't want to do that," I said, snatching their guns.

"Who are you?" said the soldier. He stood in a trance, and I realised what was happening.

I shifted into the spirit realm and saw a demon whispering in his ear.

"Hurt them all, kill them all," he said.

The human broke his gaze, and I could see he was struggling. "I can't stop," he cried out. This wasn't a war between humans; it was a war between demons and humans. They were not in control; the demons were. The demon looked at me and snarled.

"This is our territory, filth!" he said. I didn't waste any time; I attacked him with my arrow, and I cast him away.

The soldiers didn't stop, they continued to chase the humans.

Ten demons swarmed around me, each holding their sword. They stood there, waiting for me to attack.

"You can't win here, elite," said the demon leading the other nine. He looked familiar; I remember his face. He was in hell when I was there the first time; he was pushing souls into the lake of fire. "Yes," he said, as if reading my mind. "You remember my face."

I held my bow in my right hand steadily and blocked his sword. The others were attacking me relentlessly, and I spun my bow around shielding myself from their attack. I channelled the mark of Cain through my bow, and I hit them against their armour. They flew back, and this gave me the momentum to cast them out. One by one, I pierced the arrows through them, and they vanished into black smoke, back to hell, where they belonged.

I orbed back to the middle of the battlefield and saw Gelin was being pinned. It was Zaphael, his cape and armour stood out. He was the only commander in the battlefield. I wondered why the other commanders didn't join this battle. Zaphael hurled Gelin to the other side of the field and charged toward him. I could see that Gelin was starting to grow weary.

I orbed toward Gelin and stood in front of him, shielding him from Zaphael.

"There you are, unprotected, unguarded," said Zaphael, summoning his weapon away. "All that rage in you, I can smell it on you," he said, taunting me.

I kneeled down to Gelin, and I could see he was injured. His wound on his neck was deep. Light beamed from it. Zaphael stood silently.

I remembered what Freydah taught me; I could heal him. I hovered my right hand over his wound, and I could see it closing.

"I'm sorry, Gelin, this is my fault," I said, steadying him. An angel descended, and I saw Freydah standing on the other side of Gelin, helping him stand steadily, but he was still weak.

"I'll take it from here, Arden," she said, and she ascended back to heaven with Gelin.

"Stop this, Zaphael."

He wanted me to attack him. I didn't want to fall into his trap, and I summoned by bow away.

"What are you waiting for, Arden, I am right here in front of you. All the rage and all that fear, your desire to do justice, punish me," he yelled.

I sighed and retreated, and I resisted. "I'm sorry it had to be this way, Zaphael, I really am, and I wish that you were still with us, pure and good."

He growled and leaned in closer.

"I forgive you, Zaphael, and I forgive myself. The past cannot be changed, and what has happened, has happened. I'm sorry it can't be changed. I release you from my spirit. I set you free."

For a moment, he looked confused but then shifted his gaze away from mine and turned back. He ascended and disappeared.

There was a sudden shift in the spirit realm, and I saw the heavens opened. Light beamed from heaven and down to the spirit realm on earth. The demons and the elites stopped fighting and looked up.

I could see Michael blowing the trumpet loudly, and the spirit realm shook. We were being summoned back to heaven. I saw the elites summoning away their weapons and ascending to heaven.

This has never happened before. I stood on earth, and I didn't know what to do. The demons were still standing there; they noticed me, but they didn't engage.

Michael stopped blowing the trumpet, but heaven was still open. "You too," said the Holy Spirit gently.

I struggled; I didn't know what would happen. I stood on earth for a little while longer, and I saw that heaven was still opened for me.

I ascended and stood before God's throne. He was sitting on this throne; he was wearing a gold crown on his head, and a purple sash adorned his white robe.

I kneeled before God, bowing my head, afraid to look up.

"Why are you afraid?" he said softly. He wasn't angry; he spoke to me lovingly. "I love you," he said, but I didn't look up to him. "Look up, beloved," he said.

I met his gaze, and I grabbed his hand as he steadied me up. He was not angry; he was gentle. I looked around and thought there would be others in the palace, but I was alone with God.

"I have already addressed the others while you were standing alone on earth. Remember, you were still inside time, but here, time doesn't exist. I said what I needed to, but I wanted to see you alone."

"You are not angry with me, that I disobeyed your orders, that I intervened?" I asked.

"You forget that I have just created you. The other angels have been here long before you. They have learnt their lessons, and they have become wiser, through experiences. You needed to rest, you needed to have a human experience, to know the good and the bad," he said.

"This was a lesson?" I asked.

"A lesson and an experience before your next journey. I am ordaining your footsteps. You need to learn obedience, Arden. You must try to take control of your emotions, no matter what injustice you see. It is hard, I know, but you must learn to follow my commands, be obedient, and if I have not authorised it, don't do it. You need to trust that I have everything under control. Nothing comes as a surprise to me."

"Yes, Lord."

"I am proud of you. You did something that I didn't expect you to do so soon. You didn't give in to Zaphael's taunts, you resisted, you forgave him, and you forgave yourself. He no longer has any hold over you, and you can move forward now." God was smiling, and his glory radiated through the palace. "Now you have experienced first-hand the darkness that befalls over humankind. You have seen good, you have seen sorcery and divination, you have seen how demons lead humans astray, and you have also seen my people fighting the good fight. This will help you in all that is to come," he said and put his gold staff against the wall.

"Yes, Lord."

"What happens now, Lord?"

"You will go back to earth, and you will train Kitana. You will be with her. You don't need to focus on any other missions for the moment. Guard yourself. Vintore and the others are focusing on Johann and Reynak. You are specifically to keep watch over Kitana. You can travel between heaven and earth as you need to."

"What do I need to do, Lord?"

"The Holy Spirit will guide you. I have been training Kitana myself, she can see into the spirit realm at will, but do not worry, she is stronger than you think. The more you spend time with her, the more you will know what to do and how to lead her."

"Yes, Lord," I said, and I changed into my human clothes, wearing my usual blue jeans and black top.

I kneeled before God again, and his grace filled my spirit.

I decided to see Gelin in the grand citadel before leaving for earth. He was sitting on a bench on the side of the arena. He was alone.

"I'm glad you are better, Gelin. I'm sorry you got injured."

"It wasn't your fault, but I'm happy to see you are here, safe. It is easy to get attached to humans, you want to help, but you can't interfere with their free will, despite what is happening to them," he said. "You do put too much pressure on yourself, you forget that we have been here no longer than you. It doesn't make you less powerful, but there are always lessons to learn, before the final judgment, and then God will destroy time." I listened quietly, and he placed his hand on my shoulder. "You are strong, never forget it, there is much ahead," he said, and I smiled. "So what now?" he asked.

"God has assigned me to Kitana on earth," I said. "Do you know what the others are doing?"

"Nikolai and Valiana are assigned to some humans on earth. I am keeping watch over Johann Vandel, Vintore, and the others are in Reynak. Remember, Arden, be on your guard," he said.

We sat there silently for a little while longer, and I descended to Sydney.

I stood in Kitana's apartment in the spirit realm, and it was night, and it was heavily raining in Sydney.

She was in her living room, looking outside through the window. She shivered and then turned around. Her gaze met mine, and she was calm. "I used to think that I was going mad, but then God opened my eyes, and here you are. I have always wanted to see angels. I noticed that you were different when I first met you, I just couldn't quite put my finger on it," she said.

I smiled and shifted into the physical realm.

"Better," she said. "I was wondering when I would be seeing you again. It's happening, isn't it? The time is close," she asked, and I nodded. "I'm glad, God has assigned you to me?" she asked.

"Yes," I said. "I am here to help you, to prepare you. I will spend my time between heaven and earth. You are protected."

"You have seen his face, what is he like?"

"He is beautiful, perfect," I said, and she started to become teary.

"I wish I could go to him now," she said, sitting down on her couch.

"You will, but not yet," I said, and she sighed. "Kita, how much do you know?"

"I can see the spirit realm clearly. I can see demons and I can see angels. The demons don't come near me anymore. They used to, but for some time now, there has been peace. I don't have nightmares anymore."

"Have you seen Zaphael lately?" I asked, and I remembered the time when he was teaching her astral travel.

"No, I have not. The last time I saw him was when he was in my room with you, you were both arguing, and then you disappeared. God was allowing him to teach me astral travel. I used to have dreams where I would heal people in other countries. I would do deliverance and help people from trouble. I wondered what that was, but now I know it. Astral travel can be good and used in the right way, but the enemy distorts it and helps the wicked to astral travel for his own agenda."

We talked a little more about her dreams, and then she went to sleep. I looked out the window and admired the Sydney skyline. I shifted into the spirit realm to make sure Kita was safe from demons.

"It is good to see you again, Arden." Yalina came out of her realm and stood next to me.

"I have been on a lot of adventures," I said, and she smiled.

"I have no doubt about that," she said. "She is now awakened. God has revealed to her of her Nephilim heritage, her abilities, and a little of what is to come for her."

"How did she feel at first?" I asked.

"She was quite fearful at first, but God gave her the grace and wisdom to understand. She still has much to learn."

We both admired the rain, and Yalina then retreated to her realm.

I spent many weeks in Sydney. Kita took some weeks away from work and spent most of her time at home; she called it a time of Sabbath. I got to know her more, about her past, her life before Jesus, and her life with Jesus. She was completely sold out for Jesus. She trusted me, and we became good friends. There were still no demons in the spirit realm around us, and I wondered when Satan would intervene.

I wanted to go back to heaven, so I told her that I would return and will keep an eye on her from heaven.

I ascended and walked inside the top tower of the library. I was alone. I could see elites walking down below and people sitting together in fellowship near the trees on the edge of the forest. I went through the scrolls; I needed to learn more about Nephilims. I saw the Book of Elohim sitting on the table and flipped through the pages. This was written by God to help the elites. I stopped when I saw a sketch. It looked like the dominant I saw on earth.

"They hide, cower, and wait to devour,
They go as they please, soul to soul
Those who are lost, those who serve the evil one
The righteous will cast them out, with power and thunder
Earth will tremble and the darkness will be no more."

God loves to write poetically.

"Hello, Arden."

I looked up and saw Nyla walking toward me. She was wearing a long orange robe, and she was holding a book in her hand.

"Perhaps this will help," she said, handing the book to me.

"I have been watching you and Kitana from here. I am very pleased with how everything is going. It is good seeing you getting along well. She will need you in the time to come. This book has my own notes about dominants if you want to understand them more, I wrote it for you."

"Thank you," I said. "Nyla, who is Kita up against, Johann or the dominants?"

"Both. Kitana will lead many people in a time of great calamity and sorrow. Johann, the Antichrist, will lead many people astray. He will torture many. Kitana will strengthen the hearts of many, and she won't be alone. She will have you, and she will also ally with another powerful woman of God. I believe you met her in France."

I thought about who she meant, and then it clicked.

"It was no chance meeting," she said, smiling.

"Jade!"

She nodded. "Jade will lead Australia into battle with other nations. For the moment, you are to focus on Kitana." She talked about her own life on earth before saying goodbye.

I read through the pages and stopped when I saw "Gateways."

"When humans sin, intentionally or even unintentionally, they expose their soul to the demonic, to dominants who take delight in living a human experience. Dominants do not like being shadows. They want to be in human form, but they cannot enter a vessel until they have been invited to. When humans indulge in desires of the flesh, their spirit becomes weaker, and this makes them vulnerable to dominants and to demonic oppression."

I went through the pages and saw that Nyla drew sketches of the dominants, just like God did in the Book of Elohim.

"The dominants feed on fear. You must teach Kitana to walk in faith, not in fear. If she walks in fear, the armour of God on her will become weaker, and she will become vulnerable. Doubt, worry, and fear gives more power to Satan and the dominants."

She also scribbled notes at the bottom of the sketches.

"Where your doubt is, there is God's wisdom.

Where your hurt is, there is God's healing.

Where your burden is, there is God's freedom.

Where your self-condemnation is, there is God's grace.

Where there is spiritual battle, there is God's supreme power.

Where there is pain, there is God's love. God's love is pure, unconditional. God's love will never be taken away from you, for His love is everlasting."

"After the descendants sacrificed their collective power, the dominants could not complete their ritual, and they became formless. They served Satan on their time on earth as Nephilims, and they still serve him now. They will linger on earth until the final judgment. Though it is easy to cast out a demon and send it back to hell, you can't do that for a dominant. They roam about the earth, seeking to devour souls. They answer only to Satan, and in the end, they will dwell in the lake of fire with Satan for eternity."

I saw a small note stuck on the last page of the book, and it was a prophetic word for Kita. Nyla wrote the instructions to give the paper to Kita on my next visit to her.

"From the time you were in your mother's womb, I have declared you as my own. You are one of mine. Yes, I have known you in that secret place and have given you wisdom and taught you, communed with you, and have loved you. I declare my love for you, and it is everlasting. Do not let the enemy bring disharmony, and do not give in into his torment. I have declared you to be mine, and you are mine alone. I have had plans for you, and it shall come to pass in my perfect timing, and it shall come to pass in its rightful season. You belong to an eternal kingdom, my kingdom, and my kingdom is everlasting. Do not fear death for death has no hold on you. I have written your name on the palm of my hand and have declared you as my child. Keep me close to your heart as I keep you close to my heart. Have I not declared that I have set my people apart? Indeed, I have set my people apart to celebrate the kingdom that is to come soon. Yes, very soon, and it shall be glorious for all to see. All will see, all will know, and all will hear that I am the Lord of all. Do not give up so easily, I am with you. It can be daunting, wearisome, and hard to keep enduring, but let me assure you, what's waiting for you on the other side is worth it. I am with you in this season of your life, and I will be with you in every season of your life. I will never forsake you. I have lived in the world, and I know it's ways. But you are not of this world, therefore, you must not succumb to its ways. You are the sheep of my kingdom, and I am your shepherd. I know where I'm going, and I know where I'm taking you. Follow my voice, and never stray from the path I have set before you. I bring you good things, and I take care of my sheep. I love every single one of my sheep, and I keep an eye on every single one of my sheep. My understanding and ways are higher than yours, my child. I am with every single one of you, at every hour of the day. Your prayers reach me no matter where you are. Abide in me just as I abide in you. Fear, worry, and anxiety are things from the enemy. I have overcome all these things, and I have overcome it for you. I say, beloved, you are mine. Don't doubt my plans for your life.

"Don't doubt my love for you. Have I ever disappointed you? Have I ever led you toward a path that makes you unhappy or one that steals your joy? I only give you good things. I want you to enjoy your journey with me on earth. The more you doubt, the more you worry and obsess on those fears, the more power you give to the enemy, who takes delight in watching you suffer. I want to teach you, to train your mind to become aware of his tricks and then protect yourself from his lies. Allow me to do that by renewing your mind when you read the Word, My Word. Pick up the Bible, and get into the habit of reading and putting my Words into practice. I do not like idleness, I want my people to be steadfast. There is no magic formula from getting one place to the next on a spiritual level. People want things to happen in a blink of an eye. I don't operate like that. If you want growth, if you want change, if you want what I want for you, then you must get into the Word, every day. I have said that spiritual growth is slow, therefore, do not expect to be at the top of the ladder in one go. Climb gently, build your strength, and remain prayerful in all you do. I am with you."

# CHAPTER 17

I spent some time in heaven with Nyla, getting to learn more about the dominants and about her life as a human on earth. While keeping watch over Kita, I also spent time training with Gelin and Quiff. I needed to grow stronger with the battle looming ahead of us.

"I see you are gaining momentum. I can feel the difference, you are much stronger in your offensive than you were before," said Quiff.

"I agree," said Gelin.

"Thank you, I think it is time for me to go to earth now. I have been up here for some time," I said, changing from my armour and into my human clothes.

We said our goodbyes, but before I descended on earth, there was something that I needed to do. Something that I have been leaving for far too long.

I went into the palace and saw God sitting down on the stairs before his throne.

"It is good to see you, Arden. I suspected you would come and see me before you went back to earth. Your confidence is shining," he said.

"You want to talk about earth," he said, knowing me all too well.

"I do, Lord. I have become bolder in approaching before you since you created me, and to this moment, I can feel the change, a good change, and it is as if my spirit is glowing."

"I know, I see it, and others can too," he said.

"I feel ready to talk about it now, though I was not before. I have seen many things, Lord, the good and the evil. Demons relentlessly attack the humans, humans taking part in sorcery and divination. Do they not know what that is ahead of them? I have been to hell, Lord, that is not where they belong."

"One of my child's testimony can help you understand this," he said. He waved his hand, and I entered into a vision, and I was on earth. God was standing next to me. We were in a house; a girl was standing in front of a small group of people, both young and old, and she was sharing her testimony.

"Hello, everyone. Today I would like to share with you the difference between Christian spirituality and New Age spirituality. Christian spirituality is about having an abundant spiritual life, where you are walking in sync with the Lord and being in a loving, intimate relationship with him, for God loves you dearly. There are many different Christian spiritual practices that will help you develop an effective prayer life. This will be discussed one at a time in the coming weeks. I will share with you of the practices I learnt from my studies as well as my own experiences and as the Holy Spirit leads. Christian spiritual practices are Christ-centred, it helps you mature in Christ, to grow stronger in discernment, and to be able to hear God with clarity. God is a creator, he is creative, and there are many different creative ways we can connect with him and to transcend to higher levels with and in God.

New Age Spirituality, on the other hand, is completely demonic. For example, meditation in the New Age movement is about focusing on oneself, whereas Christian meditation is about focusing on the Lord with your heart in adoration. There is a two-way communication between the Lord and yourself. There is joy in being in God's presence.

Some of the many New Age spiritual practices involves kundalini and chakra meditation, palm and psychic reading, tarot reading, reading horoscopes, exposure to voodoo priests, and exposure to witchcraft either through practice or being subjected to it. People are curious, and they have a deep yearning for the supernatural, to something higher. They want to fill a void, and they believe that these things can fill it. This is the enemy's plan to lure them in the occult, to have an addiction to these things, to give them just a little experience of the supernatural but leave them wanting for more.

This creates strongholds, and people are tricked by the devil to give demons legal grounds to meddle with their life.

Now I've done all the above practices before I was a Christian, and it's true. Horoscopes are addictive, and I used to read it every single day for about two years. I would constantly look for something good so it could make me feel better about myself. Once you get into that habit, it's very hard to let go of, and after you begin to read horoscopes, the urge to dive into the New Age spirituality only grows stronger. My encouragement and warning to you, dear ones, never give a thought about trying to study New Age, horoscopes, Ouija boards, palm reading. The enemy will try to tempt you and make you wonder about these things, but when the enemy does, just ignore him and start praying. Resist the devil when he brings these thoughts, and he will flee from you."

God went over to the girl in the spirit realm and placed his hand on top of her hand, and she began to prophesy.

"The Lord wants to say something," she said and everyone gazed at her intently.

"A spirit of rebellion is at work in the world. It goes about, skilfully, corrupting the hearts of many, including those from my house. It is the latest weapon from the enemy's vault, and when it's intended work is done, many more attacks will follow, wave after wave, succession after succession. Why? Because the time is near. My people keep questioning me, losing heart and doubt my Word when I say, 'The time is near.' They come to doubt and lose faith in me, and this gives Satan the perfect loophole to lead them into his dominion. Hearts are weakening, their body gives way. They turn to hollow promises of the servants of the evil one and follow their ways into sin, lust, and drunkenness. I go to them, I want them to come back to me, but they desire to be in the company of the wicked. They forget the price they will pay. They think of eternal death as nothing and indulge in sin and pleasures of the flesh. I chose them for a purpose, to be leaders so many could come to Christ, but instead, they have disappointed me. Multitudes will come to Christ in the time to come, a time of great sorrow and calamity. But multitudes will fall away. I say this not to scare you but to warn you, warn you with my rod so that you don't fall away, even what you perceive to be just a little temptation. I desire perfect purity and perfect holiness. If you do this, then you will enter my kingdom. I am looking for leaders, leaders to unveil false prophets, leaders to stand on the trenches, leaders to go to the ends of the earth, even if it means losing their life on earth. I have many leaders in my *kingdom*, they are faithful to me, they will do anything I tell them to do. Yes, I have faithful people in my kingdom. And now I am looking for people to come before me and yield. I am looking for people who want to be leaders. Leaders who will stand guard and protect their flock no matter what. Too many people are still in darkness and captivity. Some seek me, but the enemy brings them back into the dungeon. I am looking for leaders to go wherever I tell them to go and lead the lost from danger. When you make the choice, you will need to understand that if you intend to sin and fall away, you will not come back. Think wisely. I am looking for those who are stout in heart. Eternal treasures await for you in heaven. A fleeting moment of suffering on earth for the sake of many but a glorious crown of valiancy in heaven. You will not be alone. I will be with you wherever you go."

Some of the people sitting in front of her began to weep, those words ministered to them.

God waved his hand again, and we came back to heaven.

"That makes sense, Lord. Thank you for showing me that. I understood everything else I saw, Lord, but why did the Holy Spirit lead me to Israel?"

"It was in my will for you to be there, Arden. I am not angry that you did what you did, but I know that you have learnt your lesson when it comes to being obedient and yielding to my authority. They are stubborn and obstinate people who after all these thousands of years still live in disobedience and sin. You have read the Old Testament, when I led my people out of Egypt with signs and wonders, but they still choose to worship idols and commit sins."

"Many people have lost their lives, Lord, from both sides of the war. Will it end?" I asked.

He waved his hand again, and we both stood in the spirit realm on earth. We were in Israel, in the middle of the warfare. I remembered those buildings, and I saw soldiers releasing bombs. The sky was filled with ashes, and I saw men, women, and children running away from the battle. I saw demons and elites fighting as well, but they didn't take notice of us.

"We are shielded from them," said God, discerning my thoughts. "Satan and his demons have limited power on how much they can tempt and steal a person's salvation. I give my people strength to overcome it, but their fleshly desires overpower their spirit, and out of their own free will, they choose sin over holiness."

"What about the innocent?" I asked.

"They will come back home to me. They will dwell with me forever," he said.

"Will the demons and elites continue to fight?"

He nodded and studied the elites and demons fighting. "They will fight until the end of time. There are some people here that will not die on this battlefield. I have declared that they will live and not die, and they will find a haven in other nations and continue to walk forward in their walk with me. The demons do not want this, and the elites fight them and give the humans time to flee and allow the elites on the ground to help the humans escape."

We walked further into the battle and saw an elite leading a group of humans to safety. He was wearing his human clothes, and I could see the mark of legion on his right wrist.

"Come now, hurry. I will lead you to the border, and there you will find safety," said the elite, and he led a family out from the city and toward the forest. I noticed a demon running toward them, but an elite attacked the demon with her arrow, and the demon vanished into black smoke.

"I still watch over the innocent in this nation. I am still in control, therefore, fear not, warrior, my will, will be done on this nation. After all these thousands of years, people are still fighting over land. They choose land over relationships and power over peace."

"Yes, Lord, I understand now."

He returned us to the palace again.

"Thank you for showing me and teaching me, Lord. I understand now," I said, and he smiled gently.

"Kitana is waiting for you. Go along now," he said, and I descended on earth.

I saw her standing on the rocks before a large lake surrounded by mountains. "I needed a holiday. Welcome to New Zealand," she said, sensing my presence.

I was standing next to her in the physical realm. It was early morning, the breeze was cool, and the sun was still rising.

"Queenstown is my favourite place to come to. It is like an extension of heaven," she said, admiring the view. "That is the Remarkables," she said, pointing to the mountains in front of us.

"It is peaceful here, I like it," I said.

"Have you travelled here?" she asked. I thought about my vision. I remember the waterfall when I was in heaven. I described to Kita what I saw from my vision, and she started chuckling.

"I know which waterfall you speak of. That is on my itinerary for this morning, Purakaunui Falls. It is about a three-hour drive from here."

We got in the car she hired; it was a small red car with a sunroof. I sat next to her, and she turned on the radio.

I realised that this was the first time I have been in a car. I told this to Kita, and she laughed.

"There is always a first time for everything. Enjoy the ride and the scenery."

The air was crisp and cool, and there was not much traffic.

"My life in Sydney is fast. I am always on the go, and though there is time to rest and slow down, coming here is like stepping away from time and into eternity. I come here every year, and the flight is short too." She focused on the radio and turned the volume higher.

"God is not going to show you or give you something if you are not prepared for it. Only God knows if you are truly ready for something, mentally and spiritually.

I used to ask God to show me what hell looks like. I wanted to know because I was curious, and I wanted to know what I've been saved from. I don't do it anymore.

If God did, then I think I would crumble, mentally. I don't think I would have been able to handle it in that season of my life. I didn't just want a glimpse, I wanted the full experience. I believe God did give me a glimpse, only what I could take.

In the dream, I was sitting on a small boat as if I was in an amusement park but in hell. Under the boat was lava. I felt a demon sitting behind me, and in front of me there were other people. It felt like I was on a roller coaster, and the lava was splashing on us, and we were in pain.

The splash of the lava, the feeling was not like something I've ever known or felt on earth. The pain and the feeling was not of this earth. It was indescribable. I believe I only experienced limited pain, as if God was allowing me to experience only a certain measure of pain.

From this, I have learnt to pray and ask God for things and revelations with a mature mindset. That is, 'God, I am open to receiving, to grow, experience, and learn anything you want me to. I pursue and thirst for you, for the things of heaven. My will is yours, I surrender.'

I've heard of testimonies where God would show people hell through dreams and visions, and he would call them to testify of their visions to warn other people. Not to put fear in other people but to warn people. The topic of hell is no joke, it does need to be talked about, but in a way that helps people to run to God and to make things right with Him. The past is over, it is never coming back, and tomorrow is not guaranteed. All that matters is now, right this very moment, and you have *this moment* to repent, to be saved, and to make it right with God. It doesn't matter what you have done yesterday, last week, last year, or ten years ago—God does not want you to live in condemnation. He wants you to be free and to live a wonderful life filled with purpose and power in and with him.

Once you accept Jesus into your heart, it will make sense. Where nothing has made sense before and you have wandered about, lost, confused, hopeless, but when you make Jesus the Lord and Saviour, your fate is sealed in heaven, and you have been gifted with salvation and promised an eternity in heaven with the very One who created you.

You never really know when the process really starts, truly for a person. I was formally saved in late 2016, as I have said in many of my testimonies. But I remember when I was about fifteen years old, I had this DVD laying around about the life of Jesus, and one day I just decided to watch it. I enjoyed it so much. I felt light and a kind of joy that I had never felt before. At the end of the DVD, the narrator was leading and inviting the viewer to commit their heart to Jesus and to say the salvation prayer. I prayed that prayer out loud. Something happened that day, I still can't put my finger on it, but something good happened.

Dear ones, if you want to give your heart to Jesus, or if you want to recommit your life to the Lord, say this salvation prayer out loud, with a sincere heart, confessing and repenting of your sins. Jesus is offering you a free gift. It is free because he has already paid the price. The gift is eternal life, a place of pure joy and peace with an awesome God and dwelling in His house with your awesome brothers and sisters."

"That is quite a testimony. I know this woman, she shares very powerful testimonies, Ohana Veronica," said Kita. She turned the volume low and focused on driving again. She was lost deep in her thoughts. "Sometimes I think of him," she whispered. I knew she was talking about Aaric. This was the first time we have talked about Aaric. I knew she would talk about him when she was ready to. "I believe you met him," she said. I knew she was referring to the time when she was in a coma. "He talked about you. He was curious about you, but I told him not to investigate you."

"He was very polite, sharp, and kind," I said, and she chuckled.

"I assumed that you have seen everything that happened between us," she said, and I nodded.

"The first time I laid my eyes on him, I felt something. It started as a crush, I was young, and I was desperate for love and the need to be loved. I didn't even know how to talk to boys. He never talked to me, and I was quite shy. He never really looked at me, but as years went by, I really started to fall for him. I tried to stop what I felt because I knew he didn't like me back and he never approached me anyway. I liked that he was honest, straightforward, kind, and he was the kind of person who would make sure that you were heard and safe. I felt safe around him. I had to leave that workplace, God got me out of that workplace because my season there was over. I wanted to leave, but I struggled. I had this hope that perhaps one day, he would like me back and that there would be a chance that he would feel something for me too."

"But he didn't right away," I said, and she nodded.

"It was painful, especially when I didn't get to see him almost every day. It was hard to let go. I believed in him, and I saw his potential. I wished that he was of Christ too. A few years later, our paths crossed, and we became friends at first, but then it turned into something more. He wasn't ready to be in a relationship back then, and he admitted his feelings for me. We spent the next few years getting to know each other, we travelled, we were head over heels in love with each other. But there was one thing that didn't feel right in my spirit, that he was not a Christian, and I know that you can't force someone to be a Christian. I always had this hope, he knew it too, and it always came between us. When I saw what happened in the city that night, I ended it, that is not how a man of God behaves. I have forgiven him, and deep down, I somehow know that it would not work out no matter how much I wanted it to, and we both tried our best to make it work."

"I'm sorry, Kita."

She sighed. "Me too," she said. "I will intercede for him. I will stand in the gap for him and pray without ceasing so that he receives salvation."

We drove silently through the countryside for a little while and saw many sheep sitting on the farmlands. "We are close," she said.

"You should know that the Lord has revealed to me my future spouse. After I came to a place of acceptance, God showed me my husband in a vision. I remember some months ago, I had a dream that I was in a market, and a man was hugging me, embracing me, and I felt so safe and happy being with him. His name is Mikhail Azera. He is from Colombia."

"Have you met him in person?"

"No, not yet," she said. "We have a mutual friend. He was studying at the same place as my friend, and she was working on a documentary that I was part of. He was part of the camera crew, but then he could not make it to any of the locations. I was keen on meeting him, and I was confused. The project ended, and some months later, I was doing housework, and God dropped this revelation into my spirit and revealed to me that he was going to be my spouse, that I will marry him."

"How did you feel?" I asked. I was happy for her.

"Happy, though I did not know much about him. God revealed to me more about him throughout the weeks and months, and he is a Christian, he is completely sold out for Christ, and we are very similar to each other. We both love creativity, and we appear to be in sync. I am excited to meet him, and the more God reveals to me about him, the more I like him. I am waiting on the Lord to bring us together."

"I am excited for you, Kita, I really am, and you deserve the very best," I said, and she smiled.

"Thank you, Arden, good people are coming into my life, and I'm glad you are a part of it. Oh, we are here," she said, parking the car on the side of the road, and we were surrounded by large trees, and I could hear water thundering down from the right side of the forest. "It is not that far from here, only a short walk from here."

There were many other people walking through the forest toward the waterfall.

I shared about my time in heaven to Kita; she was very curious and keen to learn more about heaven. I gave her the note that Nyla wrote. She began to weep as she started to read it.

I didn't tell her who Nyla was; we had only talked a little bit about her Nephilim heritage. I told her a friend from heaven gave the prophetic word, and she didn't question me about it.

I gasped as we stood in front of the waterfall. This was the same as the one I experienced in the vision from heaven.

"You are exactly where you are meant to be," whispered the Holy Spirit.

# CHAPTER 18

S tanding on top of the Harbour Bridge, I admired the Sydney skyline. Kita and I had a wonderful time in New Zealand. She was right; it did feel like an extension of heaven. She returned to working at the library, and I continued to protect her and learn more about her. God was protecting her from demonic interference, so was I.

The stars were shining brightly; I had never seen so many stars over Sydney.

"Great minds think alike, no other place like Sydney."

It had been a long time since I heard his voice. A familiar voice, almost friendly.

"Emrail, I didn't expect to see you here."

"But I did," he said.

He was in his armour, but he didn't appear to be aggressive. It almost felt comforting to him here with me. We stood there, in silence. It was midnight in Sydney. Kita was sleeping; she was safe.

"All that energy in you, I can feel it," he said. I realised he was talking about the mark of Cain. "You are not afraid that I will attack you?" he said calmly, raising his eyebrow.

"Surprisingly no. If you wanted to attack me, you would have. You have already witnessed its power," I said, referring to the last time I saw Emrail in battle when Cain gave me the mark, and he chuckled. "I don't think Satan will like it if he sees you here with me," I said, and he sighed.

"Satan is currently busy in hell, and he can't be everywhere at once. I made sure I was alone before coming here. War is coming, and I know my fate, Arden. I want to tell you something, something

I want you to know," he said. "I am not here to hurt you, Arden, this is not a trap."

I shifted uncomfortably, but then I studied his eyes, it was sincere, almost as if he was one of us. There was evil in him, I could feel it, but there was something else too.

"I will listen to you," I said, and he looked relieved.

"I loved God once, when I had grace. Satan was very crafty, he put malice in the spirit of angels. He only went to those who he had assurance that they would side with him. He targeted those, and he put pride in them. One by one, the angels conspired in secret. We were foolish, believing we were hidden from God's supreme power.

"Satan promised me that I would be one of the commanders in his army, that I could do anything I want, that I didn't have to serve other spirits, and that I could have any luxury I wanted. I gave in, and I succumbed to this deception. Commander I became, but I became a slave and a puppet. After God banished us to earth, after the fall, many of us realised our mistake. We repented and asked God to bring us back. But he didn't.

"When he didn't, some of us hardened our spirit, and we lost hope, so we willingly served Satan and did his bidding. We mated with women before the flood and after the flood, bringing forth Nephilims, a scourge in God's eyes. Some of the fallen who realised their mistake, they started to help the humans, intervening with their free will, and this did not please God. They were already condemned to hell. God has kept them in chains in the dungeons in hell."

I started thinking about Idora; she helped me when I was in hell. She was taunting Satan when I was trying to find Zaphael. "If you repented, why didn't God put you in chains?" I asked, and he winced.

"I needed to be careful. We were on earth first before the humans. Some of the fallen became renegades and isolated themselves from Satan and then began to help the humans. Satan retaliated by capturing some and putting them in chains in hell himself. God then intervened and shielded the renegades from Satan. Those renegades continued to help the humans, and then God put them all in chains. They were getting out of control, they wanted to punish

Satan, they blamed him for losing their grace. Arden, in the battle ahead, I need you to do something. I need you to cast me to hell."

I was not expecting Emrail to say this. He looked at me expectantly. Now it made sense when he was looking at me in the battle when Cain gave me his mark. Emrail could have easily attacked us, yet he chose not to.

"Emrail, what will you gain by being cast into hell?" I asked.

"I am tired of working for Satan, torturing humans and fighting with the elites. I accept my fate. If you cast me to hell now, Satan will not cast me into the lake of fire. He might put me in a cage, or I might linger in hell doing nothing until the final judgment. I need this to stop."

"I don't know what to say, Emrail."

"Say yes, Arden."

His gaze broke off mine, and he diverted his attention to the east. "I can sense it, Satan's agents are coming. I must go now, Arden, remember what I told you."

He shifted into the spirit realm, and I could no longer feel his presence. I saw two crows flying toward me. They flew around me, circling me, and then flew away.

I didn't expect this from Emrail, I had never met a demon who willingly wanted to be banished to hell. I knew God was watching, for he always is. Will Satan punish him in hell, or will Emrail get what he wants? The breeze was getting colder, and I shifted into the spirit realm. It was quiet; there were no demons, no elites, and no wind.

Suddenly, I was surrounded by a strong silent energy. It was eerie, evil, and it radiated across the spirit realm.

"Arden."

It was a soft whisper, and I knew he was in trouble.

I concentrated on his location, delving in deeper into my vision, and I saw him on the ground, surrounded by demons. He was in a parking lot near the airport in Melbourne, Australia.

I descended and saw a man standing by his car with his bags. He looked confused and upset.

A demon was next to him, speaking into his ear, and I could see that the man was getting very anxious.

I saw two demons holding their sword against Nikolai, pinning him to the ground. I summoned my bow and attacked the demon near the man. He vanished into black smoke before he noticed I was even there.

The other two demons were charging toward me, but I channelled the energy from the mark of Cain, and they both flew to the other side of the parking lot. One of the demons threw his sword from across the lot, and I diverted it away with my bow. I aimed by bow at them, but they both ascended.

I helped Nikolai up and saw he was wounded. A faint light was coming from his arm; it was a small cut.

"Thank you, Arden, and I'll be okay," he said, gazing at his arm.

"Here let me," I said. I remembered how Freydah showed me how to heal, and my right hand hovered over his wound. I concentrated, and the cut was starting to close.

"Brilliant," said Nikolai, admiring his arm.

"Courtesy of Freydah," I said, looking pleased with my work.

The man knelt to the ground, looking exhausted. He began to pray.

"Lord Jesus, thank you for protecting me. Soak me with your precious holy blood, and bring healing and restoration. I pray for clarity and guidance, strength, and wisdom. Lord, watch over me as I go home in peace, and surround me with your warrior angels to protect me and keep me company. In Jesus name, I pray, amen."

"A man of God," I said, curiously studying him. He had olive skin and thick black hair. He didn't have an Australian accent like the others I met here. I think he was of Spanish descent. He looked relieved and then drove away in his car.

I saw three elites descending from heaven and hovering over his car, travelling with him as he drove away from the airport.

"Who is that man?"

"God has assigned me to protect him. He is of Christ, but lately demons have been attacking him. Breakthrough is near from him, that is why, and they want to stop him from meeting his destiny," said Nikolai.

"What is his name?"

"Mikhail Azera," he said, and I couldn't help but grin.

"Why are you smiling like that?" he asked.

"I know that name, though this was the first time I had seen him face-to-face. The human that God has assigned to me, Kitana Denali, Mikhail Azera is her God-mate, her husband, her destiny."

"I see," said Nikolai, looking amused.

We both ascended and orbed to Mikhail's home. I saw his car parked on the street, and I could see him entering his apartment. He lived just on the outskirts of the city.

The three elites stood guard around his apartment. I recognised the elite standing near the front door.

"Vana, good to see you here," said Nikolai.

"Nikolai, Arden," she said, acknowledging both of us. She had long red hair, and she was holding her bow in an offensive position. "God has assigned Tariel, Kifiz, and myself to protect Mikhail. We will take care of him. He needs you in heaven when you are ready," she said.

He thanked her, and we went inside. His apartment was filled with many camera gears.

"I have only observed him from the spirit realm and protected him from the demons. Usually, it is one or two demons trying to lead him astray, but today they overpowered me, and I was caught off guard."

"He is safe now," I said, and he nodded.

I studied Mikhail for a moment as he sat down and began to have his meal. He was a little taller than Kita, he appeared to have a reserved nature. He does look like a good fit for Kita, they would both complement each other very well.

"Why are the demons constantly attacking him?" I asked.

"Mikhail has a breakthrough ahead of him, God is bringing him into his next season, a season of marriage and a season of moving forward in doing things that God has called him to do. Satan is attacking him because this man is going to lead many people to

Christ. Satan knows that this man is powerful and with Kitana, now that I know that she is his spouse, they will be very powerful together as a kingdom couple. Satan does not want this to happen so he is attacking Mikhail's mind, filling his mind with fear and worries."

We watched over Mikhail for a little while longer before Nikolai ascended to heaven.

I remained there in the spirit realm. The spirit of God began stirring in me and I knew he was about to give me a prophetic word about Mikhail.

"This man of God, Mikhail Azera is Kitana's Denali's husband. God has ordained them to be together since the beginning of time. Together they will bring the kingdom forward and God will do many miracles, signs and wonders through them. He will use his creative gifts and his calling as a shepherd to influence and inspire both the young and the old."

Mikhail broke his gaze from his meal and then looked toward me. He frowned and also looked a little confused, but he then went back to eating his food.

His phone began to ring, and he put it on speaker.

"Hello, aunty, how are you?" he said.

"I hope I haven't called you at a bad time, Mikhail," she said.

"Not at all, aunty, how is everyone back home?"

"We are all well," she said.

They talked about his work and her family, and then she asked something that turned my attention to him again.

"So have you met her yet?" she asked, and he chuckled.

"Soon, aunty, I have been waiting on God's timing, but I can feel it, it is almost here, as if on my doorstep. God will bring us together, he will lead me to her, and I will find her," he said, smiling to himself.

"Oh, my baby, I'm so happy for you. You deserve the best."

"Thank you, aunty."

"Okay, I won't keep you long, but let me pray for you before I go. Lord, I give you honour, praise, and glory for all the wonderful things you have done for Mikhail's life and the blessings that are coming his way. As you close this season of his life and open

WAR OF THE REALMS

another, let him transition forward with ease, peace, and joy. Father, as the time comes close for him to meet his wife, I pray for their first meeting to be memorable, patient, and exciting. Let everything go according to your will and purpose, and let your will be done in every area of Mikhail's life. In Jesus's name, I pray, amen."

"Amen, thank you, aunty," said Mikhail.

"Anytime, baby, I love you, and I will call you next week sometime."

Mikhail appeared to be lost in his thoughts, as if daydreaming. He was smiling to himself, and I couldn't help but smile to myself as well. God sure has created a perfect match, Kita and Mikhail do complement each other well, I can feel it in my spirit, though I will not tell Kita about my visit to Melbourne. I did not want to worry her, and it would be best if I allowed their first meeting to be a surprise.

I went back to the top of the Harbour Bridge, it was still early hours, and Kita was still sleeping. The spirit realm was silent, and I could feel malice near me. I could not see any demons around, but I could not put my finger on this energy that was flowing toward me. I summoned my bow and held it steadily.

"That will not be necessary," he said, standing beside me. He wore his black suit, and he looked at me calmly.

"Why are you here, Satan?"

"I am here to show you my grand plan," he snickered.

"Not interested, Satan."

"I wasn't asking."

He held my hand, and we orbed instantly to the top of the Eiffel Tower in Paris.

I thought about ascending to heaven, but at the same time, I was also curious. I knew God was watching me, and I could ask for help any time.

"I see the Nephilim is under your protection, it's a shame really, she had so much potential, and now it is going to go to waste," he said.

I stood silently in the spirit realm. The streets were filled with many people and festival rides at night.

"Why bring me here?" I asked.

"I will display my splendour in this city through my chosen one. He will perform many wonders, signs, and miracles in my name. France is strategic, the territorial demons are at work and are leading many astray. The force field powered by the Christians here is getting weaker. You might want to switch from your armour?" he said.

I changed into my normal human clothes, blue jeans and black top. Satan frowned when he saw me and didn't look pleased.

"We are going to Club Nirvana, one of the most prestigious and luxurious club in the world. You are going to go in there looking like that."

I rolled my eyes and looked ahead and saw Club Nirvana written in neon sign. It was a rooftop bar on a high-rise building in front of where we were standing. I could see men wearing tuxedos and women in fancy dresses. I visualised wearing a gold sequinned dress just above my knee and gold high-heeled shoes.

"Better, said Satan. "Though something is missing."

He conjured a necklace, sapphire and diamond, and placed it around my neck.

"Perfect," he said, smiling menacingly, and I shifted away from him.

"No tricks, Satan."

We descended on the corner of the building, away from the crowd where no one could see us. We shifted into the physical realm and went inside, to the top of the building. I could hear jazz music playing in the background and people dancing on the dancefloor. Some people began to bow before him.

"My human servants," said Satan.

I saw a sign that said private residence, and we were led by two men upstairs to a terrace.

It made sense when I saw who was standing by the terrace, looking toward the city—Johann Vandel.

"Arden, it is good to see you again," he said.

He was wearing a tuxedo like the others, and his hair was tied back into a small ponytail.

A woman sat on a couch, looking between us.

"My apologies, Tia, this is Arden, an angel. Arden, this is my girlfriend, Tia."

She admired him lovingly and glared toward me.

"My Lord," said Johann, bowing before Satan, "what brings you both here, to my favourite city?"

"I'm here showing Arden a small part of our plan," said Satan.

"Why?" I asked.

"Johann?" said Satan.

"I am going to do many wonderful and evil things, but you see, Arden, I also know that your God is going to challenge me with the human you are protecting. So if she, and you, are going to be my opponents, then I want you to be worthy opponents. I want you to train her well. I like a good challenge."

His gaze burned into mine, and Tia shifted uncomfortably on the couch and went to stand next to Johann. He held her chin and kissed her.

"You brought me here for a pep talk?" I said, feeling exasperated.

"More or less," said Satan, and Johann went to pour more wine in his glass, trying to hide his smile.

"Get me out of here, Satan."

"Remember what I said, Arden, until we meet again," said Johann.

We shifted into the spirit realm, and Satan waved his hand. There was a burst of energy radiating across the spirit realm. The city around changed, and we were now standing in the middle of a desert.

"Where are we?"

"Back in time. I want to show you something," he said, snapping his fingers, and we were now standing inside a room. It was primitive and simple. It was afternoon, and I could see from the spirit realm that the sun was about to set.

A man came into the room; he was wearing a long white robe. He had black curly hair falling down to his shoulders, and his eyes were green. I could feel his gentle spirit. He faced the window and held out his hands.

"Lord, I come before you with a humble spirit. Thank you for your wisdom, thank you for keeping your people safe and for watching over our ways. Create in me a pure heart, O God, have mercy on me, O God, according to your steadfast love, according to your abundant mercy, blot out my transgressions. Wash me thoroughly from my iniquity, and cleanse me from my sin! For I know my transgressions, and my sin is ever before me. Against you, you only, have I sinned and done what is evil in your sight, so that you may be justified in your words and blameless in your judgment. Behold, I was brought forth in iniquity, and in sin did my mother conceive me. Behold, you delight in truth in the inward being, and you teach me wisdom in the secret heart. Purge me with hyssop, and I shall be clean. Wash me, and I shall be whiter than snow. Let me hear joy and gladness, let the bones that you have broken rejoice. Hide your face from my sins, and blot out all my iniquities. Create in me a clean heart, O God, and renew a right spirit within me. Cast me not away from your presence, and take not your Holy Spirit from me. Restore to me the joy of your salvation, and uphold me with a willing spirit. Then I will teach transgressors your ways, and sinners will return to you. Deliver me from bloodguiltiness, O God, O God of my salvation, and my tongue will sing aloud of your righteousness. O Lord, open my lips, and my mouth will declare your praise. For you will not delight in sacrifice, or I would give it. You will not be pleased with a burnt offering. The sacrifices of God are a broken spirit, a broken and contrite heart, O God, you will not despise."

"This is Daniel," I said, for the Holy Spirit spoke his name to my spirit.

"This is Daniel," said Satan.

Satan waved his hand again, and we were now standing on a terrace with Daniel and another man he was talking to. It was early morning, and there were many people leaving the city.

"Our people are free now, set free from captivity, though I will stay here as God has willed it so," said Daniel. "I saw something, a vision," said Daniel, and the man waited patiently.

"What did you see, Daniel?" said the man, looking concerned.

"A man, not of this world, evil in his heart, and under the power of the evil one. He will cause many to suffer. Many will lose hope, and many will come to the Lord. An angel of the Lord came down from heaven and showed me all that is to come, my friend. Great sorrow and suffering, injustice and calamity."

"What does this mean, Daniel? When will this happen?"

"In the future, how far, I do not know. I fear what is ahead, but I give the people of the Lord hope. They must endure no matter what."

Satan waved his hand, and we came back to the top of the Sydney Harbour Bridge. I changed back into my armour.

"Why did you show me that?"

"To let you know that you cannot do anything to stop what is coming. My plan will go forward, and there will be suffering. You already try to stop my army, but to no avail. No one can stop me. I have the ultimate power. Nations will fall, people that are now in faith will lose it and serve me. They will fall into sin, and they will like it."

"That was a gigantic waste of time, Satan. Your plans don't interest me. I am interested in my God's agenda, not your propaganda. You bore me with your unwelcomed visits. Please go away and bother me no more."

Satan glared at me and disappeared into the spirit realm without saying anything back. I had many questions, but not for Satan.

"There is no power greater than mine," God whispered to my spirit. "I have the ultimate authority and supreme power. Satan is a nuisance, he is trying to distract you, to make you sway, but even he is blind to your awesome power and resilience in me. Do not fear, all that I showed Daniel long ago will indeed happen as it is meant to. This is what I have chartered and as I have declared, so shall it be. All will see, all will know, and all will hear that I am Lord of the universe, the Holy One of Israel."

"Amen, Lord."

# CHAPTER 19

The tower at the top of the grand citadel was filled with many elites. Some were sitting in groups, studying books and looking through scrolls. Other elites appeared to be socialising. I sat on the armchair near the window, overlooking the forest. Since Satan showed me Daniel in his time, I have been curious about all that is to come. My memory is limited, and God had only given me memories of heaven before the fall and the creation of earth.

I flipped through the pages of the Bible and stopped at the Book of Revelation. I began with the prologue. Revelation chapter 1, verse 1 to 3: The revelation from Jesus Christ, which God gave him to show his servants what must soon take place. He made it known by sending his angel to his servant John, who testifies to everything he saw—that is, the Word of God and the testimony of Jesus Christ. Blessed is the one who reads aloud the words of this prophecy, and blessed are those who hear it and take to heart what is written in it, because the time is near.

The time is indeed near, the angels know it; we are preparing for one of the biggest battles the universe has ever known.

I flipped through the pages and read through the events that will happen on earth. As I read through it, I began to feel down-hearted, and I felt my spirit becoming burdened by everything that the Antichrist will do. I needed to talk about this. I held the Bible and walked out of the citadel and toward the palace.

"Hello."

I saw a man approaching me. He was wearing a white robe; he had short black hair, olive skin, and green eyes.

"Hello," I said.

"There's no need to go there. Perhaps I can help you with your questions," he said.

"Who are you?"

"I am John, and you are Arden. You are going to God to ask him about the Book of Revelation." He noticed my surprise and chuckled.

"He doesn't miss anything, does he?"

"God told me to meet you on your way. He said I can answer your questions, and may I say, you are an extraordinary warrior. I have seen you in battle on earth and in the second heavens, very extraordinary."

"Thank you, John."

"Come, let us sit here," he said, pointing to a bench sitting under a canopy made of branches and flowers. "I remember everything that the angel showed me vividly," he said. He appeared to be lost in thoughts, remembering his time on earth.

I waited patiently for him to speak.

"The Word of God," he said.

I gave him the Bible, and he flipped through the pages.

"Humans need to know how important it is to read the Word of God. It sustains the weary, lifts the lowly, and strengthens the weak. It is the sword of the spirit, the greatest spiritual weapon on earth, and when I look down to earth, I can only see a small number of God's people using it effectively. Time is short."

He put the Bible on the bench, and I knew he was ready to tell me about the final chapter of the Bible.

"Many will come to Christ in a time of great sorrow and calamity, and many will harden their hearts and turn away from God. There will be wars, disasters, and evil on earth that humans have never witnessed since the creation of earth. All these things are to happen before the end. This is a holy war that Satan started, but Christ will end it. It is a test, God wants to be with those who want to be with him and desire to be with him over all the pleasures of earth. They need to fight and be steadfast. God desires purity, holiness, and obedience, and it is hard to be these things when you are surrounded by evil, malice, and darkness. Humans will need to have courage and keep overcoming the evil one, to resist and maintain their salvation."

"The Antichrist is already walking on earth, Johann Vandel. Satan is preparing him," I said, but John did not look surprised.

"Yes, I have been watching them both. Johann Vandel, on the outside, he may appear to be civil, but in his heart, there is hatred and malice, a kind of hatred for God that I have never seen in a human before. There is no going back for him. He has sealed his fate, and his allegiance is to Satan. The Nephilim you are protecting, you will need to keep strengthening her and stand by her side for all the days of her life. Though the Antichrist will do great, powerful evil things, Kitana Denali will foil many of his plans. She will strengthen the hearts of many, and she will lead many people out of the darkness and into the light. There is always hope, and God will use her mightily to keep foiling Satan's plans. You must understand, Arden, God does not want any soul to perish. Every single soul is precious to God. Before Christ descends, God will give many people a chance to repent. People will experience evil, they will see truth, and they will hear the Gospel. Some will come to Christ and be saved, and some will continue in their sin, and even after knowing the truth, they will still follow the evil one. Cities will fall, cities will rise, nations will fight other nations, blood against blood, and good against evil. Christ is coming soon, his reward is with him, and he will give to each person according to what they have done. The righteous ones will go through the gates into the city."

I was encouraged by John's words, and he told me about his adventures with Jesus on earth and the miracles that God did through him. He said I could visit him anytime in heaven; he knew Daisy, and he lived opposite her.

I studied the Book of Revelation, and I felt the Holy Spirit stirring in my spirit. "The time is now," he said. I had an open vision, and I saw myself hovering over the black lake in Reynak with my bow. I was ready to release the mark of Cain over the second realm.

"Yes, the time is now," said the Holy Spirit.

I saw Kita, and she was safe in her home. I could see four elites surrounding her, watching over her from the spirit realm. I orbed down to the middle of the arena, and I summoned the elites.

One by one, they descended, wearing their armour. Quiff, Gelin, Nikolai, Valiana, Izralina, Elandriel, Vintore and Azarey.

"It is time," said Vintore, studying me carefully. I nodded, and I saw everyone's demeanour. They were all calm, ready, and excited.

"I can feel it," said Quiff.

"Where do we start?" asked Valiana.

"Izralina, Elandriel, and I will be in charge of equipping and directing the battalion," said Vintore. We will need to prepare carefully.

"Arden, will you be leading this war?" asked Vintore, and I shook my head.

"No, I don't think that will be strategic, as much as I would like to lead this war," I said, and I looked to Gelin. Others did the same.

Gelin chuckled, but we all looked at him intently. Nikolai was trying to hide a smile. "Oh, you are serious?" said Gelin, still amused.

"Yes, Gelin, who better to lead us in one of the greatest wars in the heavens since the fall. You are meant for this, we believe in you," I said and stood silently for a while.

After much thought, he finally spoke. "Alright. But first, Arden, how did you intend to use the mark of Cain?" asked Gelin.

I told them everything that Reinaya showed me. "That is why I need to be on my guard and be focused on using this shield strategically rather than leading the war. I will need protection against the demons when I do use it. I will be vulnerable when I begin to summon and release all that mystical energy. I must not get attacked this time."

"Understood. Quiff, Azarey, Nikolai, and Valiana, I will assign all four of you to protect Arden. Do as she says, and make sure the demons don't get anywhere near her," said Gelin.

"Understood," they all said together.

"Will Michael and Gabriel be joining us?" asked Gelin.

"God has not said anything yet, they are on important missions on earth. Even if they don't come, we will need to go ahead and be prepared," said Vintore.

"Alright, I believe a surprise attack will do. We will descend on Reynak and cast out demons at will. Commanders or demons, doesn't matter, we will show no mercy. If some descend on earth, don't follow them, we can deal with them later. The main aim is to take over Reynak and get control of it. Arden and the four of you will need to come through another path, quietly, and do what you need to from there and onward, Arden."

"Sounds like a plan," said Vintore.

"The battalion will descend first, then the five of you," said Gelin, and we all came into agreement.

"Let us all go and alert the battalion," said Vintore to Gelin, Izralina, and Elandriel. Quiff and Azarey followed them.

Nikolai and Valiana stayed with me in the arena; we sat down on the ground.

"The three of us have come a long way, we have seen many victories," said Valiana.

"Indeed," said Nikolai.

"What has been your highlight so far, Arden?" asked Valiana.

"I like to be at the top of the Sydney Harbour Bridge and watch the skyline in the physical realm. Even in the midst of battles on earth and in Reynak, when I am there, there is peace and stillness."

"Nikolai?" asked Valiana.

"Travelling across the world and talking to humans in the physical realm, experiencing what it means to be human, and using my angelic abilities at the same time to protect them."

"What about you, Valiana?" I asked.

"I like fighting the demons on Reynak, right at the source," she said, and we all chuckled.

"Valiant Valiana," said Nikolai, and I agreed.

"It is the eve of battle, I can feel it, and it will be glorious," she said.

"I think it is best that we all spend some time in solitude before we gather again," I suggested, and they agreed. We parted ways; Nikolai decided to retreat to his quarters, and Valiana joined the other elites in the grand citadel.

I knew where I would go. I walked to the palace rather than orbing there.

I thought the palace would be empty, but it was filled with many angels and elders. Asteri was leading the angels in worship.

"You are, the Lord Almighty and of all creation
The one, who was, who is and who will always be
Here we are, bowing before your power and your loving grace
We stand together, in awe, in praise and we sing of your holy name
Holy, your name is full of glory
Majesty, your name is known forevermore
Elohim, we adore you with our spirit Lord
For it is you who brought us to life
Your promises, stands firm, over all the angels and your creation
That is, who you are and who you have always been
Here we are, bowing before your power and your loving grace
We stand together, in awe, in praise and we sing of your holy name
Holy, your name is full of glory
Majesty, your name is known forevermore
El Shaddai, this is our praise to you
For it is you who brought us to life."

Asteri and the angels danced around the palace, and God stood up from his seat and joined them. This was the first time I saw God dance, and he was a wonderful dancer. He stood in the middle of the palace, and the angels were dancing around him. They began to sing the chorus again, and the elders sitting on the upper part of the palace began to sing too.

"Holy, your name is full of glory
Majesty, your name is known forevermore
El Shaddai, this is our praise to you
For it is you who brought us to life."

I stood on the side, and I raised my hands up worshipping God too. I had never done this. I usually liked to stand quietly on the side with the elites and watch the worship, but I felt joy in my spirit and I began to sing.

"Holy, your name is full of glory
Majesty, your name is known forevermore
El Shaddai, this is our praise to you
For it is you who brought us to life."

I could see the angels were slowing down, and they all bowed down before God.

"We give you all the honour, all the praise and glory Lord. We love you," said Asteri.

"I love you all, forevermore," said God and sat on his throne. He wore a gold robe today, and I studied his sandals. His sandals were beautiful, carved in gold and coloured in red and blue. His robe also had red and blue designs on it, it looked similar to the carvings on our armour.

He thundered his rod on the ground, and the angels began to leave the palace.

"My valiant warrior, I'm glad you came just in time for worship. I was happy to see you singing and worshipping along too," he said. He sat down on the stairs, putting his rod on the side of the throne and beckoned me to join him.

"I like spending my time alone with you, Lord."

"As do I. You are excited, though you are also nervous," he said, discerning my thoughts.

"It is time to use the mark of Cain. We are prepared for battle," I said, telling God about our strategy, and he was pleased with it.

"You doubt if you will be able to succeed in doing it. You doubt yourself and your abilities as an elite," he said, and I nodded, sitting quietly there for a long time. "You were made for this, I created you for such a time as this. I have set a path before you, and so far, you have never let me down. Yes, you have intervened in things that you should not have, but you never turned away from me, and you have grown stronger. Your faith in me has always been strong, and you never questioned your allegiance to me. I created you thoughtfully, perfectly, and you have the ability to do everything that I have called you to do, and you will do it well."

I felt peace in my spirit, and the heaviness that I felt was lifting. "Your peace is perfect, Lord."

"Indeed, it is," he said. "You are ready, Arden. Trust me, valiant warrior, you will succeed. Have faith," he said, and I felt my spirit becoming stronger.

God's words healed me and strengthened me. I heard Gelin calling me to the middle of the arena.

I prayed before God before leaving to go to the arena. I remember Psalm 23 from the Bible; it was Kita's favourite.

"Lord, you are my shepherd, I lack nothing. You make me lie down in green pastures, you lead me beside quiet waters, you refresh my being. You guide me along the right paths for your name's sake. Even though I walk through the darkest valley, I will fear no evil for you are with me. Your rod and your staff, they comfort me. You prepare a table before me in the presence of my enemies, you anoint me head with oil, my cup overflows. Surely your goodness and love will follow me all the days of my life, and I will dwell in the house of the Lord forever."

"Lord, let your will be done in this war of the realms," I said, and God smiled warmly.

"My will, will always be done," he said with authority.

I orbed to the arena, and when I descended in the middle of the arena, I saw that we were surrounded by the battalion. The numbers were beyond what I have ever seen in any battle I have been a part of. It was a glorious sight. Every elite was in their armour, and they had already summoned their weapons.

They were all cheering, and I joined them too.

Gelin held up his lance, and we became silent.

"Elites, we have waited, and we have fought valiantly from the beginning. We are about to descend to the second heavens. Some of you have been there, and some of you have not. Cast all that you see, do not stop, and fight the good fight. This is the battle, the victory is already ours," said Gelin, and I knew that he was the right choice to lead the battalion. I studied the elites, and I did not see any fear or discouragement in any of them. I noticed Freydah standing near the door of the citadel; she was also wearing her armour.

Gelin held up his right hand on a fist, and the battalion became silent again. "Elites, on my lead," commanded Gelin.

There was a moment of stillness, and then Gelin descended to Reynak. The rest of the battalion followed him until it was the five of us standing in the arena.

"The demons must have known that sooner or later, the mark of Cain will be used. I wonder if they are prepared in Reynak too?" asked Valiana.

"I guess we will find out," said Quiff, grinning.

"Wait, Arden, what is the plan from here? Gelin mentioned that we will need to be in stealth mode," said Azarey.

"We will need to be away from the camp, that will be the epicentre of the battle. We will need cover," I said. It had been a long time since my last visit to Reynak.

"The trees," said Nikolai.

"We will need to descend on the trees and glide through it and not on the ground, just on the edge of the camp," said Quiff. "Arden, where do you intend to release the mark of Cain?" asked Quiff.

I remembered the vision that the Holy Spirit showed me and shared it with the others.

"We must go now," said Quiff.

"Alright, I want each of you to put your right hand on the left side of the elite standing on your right. We will be in sync and will descend where I want us to," commanded Nikolai, and we all did as he said.

I felt the mark of Cain, the mystical energy stirring and becoming heavy. We began to glow, and we descended on Reynak together and then quietly stood on the branches of the trees. All of us were here, and we were alone. There were no demons in sight, but we could hear the warfare.

I could hear horns being blown and screams.

"It has begun," whispered Valiana. She was standing on the branch on top of me. The others were standing on the tree next to us.

We glided through the trees with Nikolai leading the way. He held his hand up, and we all halted. I saw a swarm of demons running below with their weapons. I recognised Ilthezar. He signalled others to stop running, and they all became still. We hid behind the trunk of the tree.

I glanced at Nikolai, and he shook his head. Ilthezar walked toward the tree that I was on.

"Ilthezar, they need us!" shouted one of the demons. He snarled and glanced toward the trees again.

He led the others toward the battle and didn't look back. He sensed something, maybe it was the mystical energy I had in me. Could that alert the other demons? If it did, then I needed to be quick.

I remember what Reinaya showed me, that I needed to channel all that power toward the bow and release it on the ground with all my might. She said it was a matter of using it at the right time.

We continued to glide through the trees, and we came upon some ruins.

We came down from the trees and slowly walked behind the ruins. Nikolai led us, I was in the middle, and Azarey was behind us, making sure we were not being followed.

Nikolai held up his hand again, and we all hid behind the ruins, kneeling down. I could feel evil coming. I heard voices, and it grew louder as they came closer.

"What do we do, Carinz? There are too many of them, the entire battalion is here."

"Preemptive strike, they intend to use the mark of Cain, Balnor," she said.

"Should we not fight with the others? What will Satan say?" he asked, and Carinz sighed.

"It is better to go to earth and be free than be here and be cast into hell for eternity. Balnor, we must leave for earth. It is the best thing to do," she said. I could feel their evil energy; it grew stronger as they were beginning to descend, but then they stopped.

Azarey summoned her bow, and Valiana summoned her tridents.

"Stop, do you feel that?" asked Carinz. I could hear Balnor walking toward me, and he broke apart the ruins I was standing behind.

They didn't waste any time talking and began to attack us. Nikolai tore apart Carinz's cape, and she stood still, as did Balnor.

"You will pay for that," she snarled. She attacked him relentlessly, but Quiff went to help Nikolai.

Balnor stood in the middle of the ruins. Valiana, Azarey, and I surrounded him. He held his sword ready for a defensive attack.

"There will be great bloodshed on earth, and the angels will be powerless," he said.

The three of us attacked him; he was strong, and he was quick. He pushed Valiana, and she flew back toward the forest. She recovered quickly and gained momentum.

Azarey hit his knees, and he kneeled to the ground. She held his neck, and he struggled to get up. I aimed my arrow to his arm, and he screamed. I let Valiana do the honours.

"Have fun in hell," she said, and with each of her blades, she pinned it to each side of nis neck, and he vanished into black smoke.

Carinz was overpowering both Quiff and Nikolai, and when she saw that Balnor was cast away, she orbed away.

We were alone again.

"I wonder why they didn't call in for reinforcements?" asked Valiana.

"Perhaps we caught them off guard. Come, let's take cover," said Nikolai.

We climbed the trees again and moved toward the lake. I climbed to the top of the tree and saw the camp. There was warfare and I saw both demons and the angels flying through the battlefield. The field near the lake was quiet, but I knew that it would be swarming with demons once I started to summon the mark of Cain.

We reached the lake, and all of us stood on one of the trees.

"We were not followed. We are alone," said Azarey, meeting us on the tree.

I studied the field; it was not very far away from the camp. I looked further ahead, and I remember Emrail, and I used to battle there. Emrail asked me to cast him away the next time we would meet in battle. Was I ready to?

"Leave Emrail to me," I told the others.

"Arden, you will need to lead from here," said Nikolai.

I studied the field again and saw where I wanted to release the mark of Cain. It was just before the lake that stretched toward the edge of Reynak, to the valley. The lake was deep, if demons did come and we threw them down the lake, they would struggle to orb.

"I will hover just before the lake, and I will summon the mark of Cain. It will take some time to build up the mystical energy and release it. I will be defenceless, I will need each of you to surround me and shield me."

They all nodded as we stood ready to orb to the field.

I met Nikolai and Valiana's gaze, and they stood steadfast.

"Here we go," said Nikolai.

I looked to the empty field and knew what we were about to be bombarded with. "Here we go."

# CHAPTER 20

hovered over the field, and the others surrounded me with their weapons ready.

"Lord, let your will be done," I prayed.

I closed my eyes and focused on the mark of Cain. The energy was strong, and I began to feel heavy. I felt the energy overpowering me, and I struggled to hover over the field. I saw Nikolai looking concerned, and he was about to come to me.

"Steady," I said. "I've got this."

I summoned my bow, and I began to glow. Powerful energy radiated from me, and it began to flow out of me. I began to feel pain, a distinct pain, the same pain I felt when Cain was transferring his mark to me.

I saw movement in the trees; the others saw it too. I needed more time.

Demons thundered down to the field, and they began to charge toward us.

I concentrated harder to summon the mark of Cain, and it began to stir, and the pain grew stronger too.

"We've got you, Arden," said Azarey.

As the demons were about to attack, dozens of elites descended between us and the demons, and they began to fight.

I started to gain momentum and knew the time was close.

I heard Nikolai screaming, and I saw Eliel's blade tore through him.

"Nikolai!" I screamed.

"Focus, Arden!" shouted Quiff.

Eliel pulled back his blade, and Nikolai was falling down. I could see his wound, and the light was beaming from his shoulder and back.

"Focus, Arden!" shouted Valiana.

I saw Freydah descending in the field, and she caught Nikolai. Just as she caught him, they ascended instantly. He will be okay. Eliel's gaze met mine, and he smiled menacingly.

There was a loud thunder, and Gelin stood between us.

Gelin pointed his lance to Eliel, and he stood firm.

"If you want her, you will have to go through me," he said.

"Gladly," said Eliel.

"Keep going, Arden," said Gelin.

I focused on the mark of Cain, and I began to channel it to my bow. It was happening.

I felt a sharp pain, and a demon hurled me down in the lake. I was deep in the lake, and I felt the demon's hand on my neck, pushing me deeper.

I struggled to open my eyes, and I could see a familiar face. It was Ilthezar, leader of Reynak's army.

His grip on my neck was strong, and I could feel the mark of Cain fading back into my spirit.

My spirit began to feel weaker, and I was losing my strength and my will. I was being drawn into a vision, and I felt the heaviness of the water overpowering me. The heaviness disappeared, and I was standing on top of the Sydney Harbour Bridge. I was surrounded by pure light; it was not day, and it was not night. There was no evil, no darkness.

I felt a familiar presence standing beside me. His brown eyes were gentle, and his love was tangible.

"Lord Jesus," I whispered. His presence overwhelmed me and strengthened me.

"I can see why you like it here so much. I, too, sometimes come here," he said, admiring the view.

I admired him, and he smiled.

"Keep fighting, warrior," he said with authority.

"What you do right this moment will be the deciding factor in the war of the realms. You are starting to doubt again," he said.

"The demons are putting in a good fight, Lord, the more I try, the more they overpower me."

"You are stronger than you think, powerful than you believe," he said.

"I can't do this alone, Lord," I said.

"You won't have to, my valiant warrior. You can do all things through me for it is I who will give you strength."

The vision began to fade, and I felt the heaviness of the water again. Ilthezar's hand was still on my neck. I felt my strength returning, and I met Ilthezar's gaze. I grabbed his hand and pushed him off me. I gained momentum and orbed upward. I used the mark of Cain to radiate a strong energy, and it blasted across the field. The demons and the angels flew across the field; the angels quickly regained their offensive position and saw me.

One by one, they lifted their right hand up to the sky and began to chant, "I will fear no evil for you are with me Lord."

The chant grew louder, and the angels began to reassemble. I met Gelin's gaze, and he looked at me and nodded in triumph.

More demons began to descend near the lake. I saw Zaphael, Eliel, and Demiriz descending far ahead of me and were charging toward me.

The heavens opened, and a powerful energy radiated through the battlefield. The angels and demons stood still, and we all looked at the sky.

The sound of a trumpet thundered across the second heavens, and a big beam of light thundered down to the battlefield, and it hovered in front of me.

The light began to fade, and the presence felt familiar. She held her bow, and her silver armour began to shine as the light faded away, and she revealed herself. Reinaya.

The demons began to flee as they saw her, but the commanders stood firm. The angels looked at her in awe, and they began to cheer. She rallied them, and they gained momentum. Our eyes met, and she didn't need to say anything. With one gaze, I regained hope, and she began to fight for me and shielded me from the commanders.

Her arrows soared across the battlefield; I had never seen any angel release her arrows so quickly and cast many demons with that speed.

I saw Emrail standing in the distance, and our eyes met. There was no emotion, but I knew he was waiting for me to attack him, but I needed to release the mark of Cain. Reinaya orbed and stood between us, and he didn't fight.

She didn't say anything, and with one move, her arrow pierced Emrail, and he vanished into black smoke.

"Arden, now," she commanded.

I orbed higher; I needed altitude. As I ascended higher, so did Valiana, Quiff, and Azarey. They shielded me.

I pointed my bow toward the ground and channelled the mark of Cain to it.

I began to glow, and I was surrounded by a ball of light.

I felt a hand touch my arm gently, and I could feel my spirit getting stronger.

"I am with you, valiant warrior," he whispered gently. Jesus was standing next to me on Reynak, in the air, and he gave me strength. "You are ready," he said.

I darted toward the ground with my bow pointing toward the ground. I hit my bow against the ground, and I released the mark of Cain from me and over the second heavens.

I felt the energy leaving my spirit, and as I hit the ground, the force radiated powerfully across Reynak. The energy vaporised every demon on the field, and they all vanished into black smoke. I could feel it, the evil was fading.

Cheers erupted around the field, and the angels were cheering.

Valiana, Quiff, and Azarey met me on the ground and celebrated with me, though I was feeling weak.

I could feel the power of the shield covering the second heavens, an invisible mystical energy between heaven and earth. No demon will ever enter this realm again, and the angels can go to earth without any hindrance.

Reinaya stood next to me and summoned her bow away. "Well done, warrior," she said.

"We didn't expect you," I said.

"It was time."

She acknowledged me and then went to talk to other elites who had not seen her for a long time. They were all happy to see her.

"Victory!" shouted Gelin, and the angels cheered again.

The heavens opened above, and there was a loud thunder. An angel was blowing a trumpet, and there was no longer any darkness covering this realm. The trees, the lake, and the ruins vanished, and light beamed in from heaven.

Instead of the dark sky, the colours changed to shades of purple and white. The ground beneath us disappeared, and we were hovering in the air.

God was changing the realm from his throne. Small cities, command centres, appeared across the realm, each one not too distant from each other. The city reminded me of Alvinor, only these ones were a little smaller.

"New command centres for the elites," said Gelin. "We have been waiting for a long time for this to happen, thank you, Arden," he said.

"I wasn't alone," I said, smiling and relieved that the burden of the mark was no longer melded with my spirit. I remembered Jesus's presence next to me and in my vision.

"You never were," he said.

Some of the angels ascended to heaven, and some us orbed to the command centres. Each of the command centres had an open roof cathedral in the middle, and the walls were covered in jewels. On each side of the cathedral, there were two quarters for the elites who would be stationed there.

Peace radiated across the second heavens.

"I assumed we would descend with Jesus once we took over this realm," said Valiana.

"Not yet," said Reinaya. "We will need to guard this realm, maintain our control until it is God's time. We have achieved a great victory, let us all rejoice in it."

"What does this mean for the demons?" I asked.

"Retaliation," said Gelin. "How will that look, I do not know, but I do know one thing. We have reminded them where they stand in this war and that the time is near. The war has not ended, but by taking control of this realm, we can do much damage," he said.

Reinaya and the others ascended to heaven, but I stayed behind. I felt the Holy Spirit stirring in me, and I knew there was one more task that I needed to do. A knowing.

I descended on the streets of Amsterdam and found my way to Fifty-Four Lancaster Avenue.

It was day time, and the club was quiet.

"The club is closed today, and how did you get in?" said Adrian, walking out from behind the bar. He halted when he met my gaze as if he recognised me.

I was in the spirit realm, and he could see me.

"When Cain left Adrian, supernatural residue stayed in Adrian," said the Holy Spirit. "I have called him to be ours. He will be a leader in my kingdom."

"I have been seeing things, you are an angel, Arden, I remember you, I remember everything. My mind has been flooded with memories, memories of another life."

"It is going to be okay, Adrian. The Lord has heard your cry, and he welcomes you," I said. "Do you wish to receive salvation?" I asked.

He began to weep and kneeled to the ground, "Yes," he whispered.

He reached his hands out to me, and I held it firmly.

The heavens opened, and the Holy Spirit poured into him. "I see it," he said. "I see the angels, they are rejoicing." He looked to heaven in awe and in bewilderment. "He is real," he said, weeping again.

"This is only the beginning," I said. "Welcome to eternity." I ministered to him and gave him Kita's contact.

"She will help you. She is in Australia. Leave behind this club. It is time to start again, a new life, a new purpose," I said, and he looked relieved. I bid him farewell and ascended to heaven in God's palace.

The angels were celebrating, and Asteri was leading the choir.

Michael and Reinaya stood on the right hand of God, and Gabriel stood on his left. The upper part of the palace was filled with elders, clapping their hands. I stood next to Nikolai, and I put my hand on his shoulder, happy to see him. We didn't need to say anything when full understanding was perfect. He was healed, and he was rejoicing with the angels.

"Amazing Lord, how sweet your sound
Awesome Lord, your grace abounds
Holy, holy, holy is your name
Glory, glory, gloriously you reign," the angels chanted.

God held up his hand, and the angels bowed down.

"Today is a glorious day for many reasons. We have Reinaya back with us," said God, and the palace was filled with cheers again. Reinaya looked around triumphantly.

"We have control over the second heavens. Reynak is destroyed, and the angels are now in control. This is a victorious day for us all. The time is near, but not yet. There are more people on earth that are yet to return to me. There is much work to be done, but know this, today, we have reminded the fallen that the end is coming for them, sooner than they believed. The second heavens will no longer be known as Reynak. Today, it has a new name, Arcadia."

We cheered again, and God thundered his rod, and the energy went down to earth.

"New anointings, new revelations, new destinies," he declared, and I felt a shift happening on earth.

"God has stirred the hearts of many people who are unsaved, that is his favour and grace now that we have taken control of the second heavens," said Gelin.

Asteri led the choir again, and the angels continued to celebrate. The elites bowed before God and took their leave. I stayed for a little while. I knew where I wanted to go after this.

It was dawn in Sydney. I stood on top of the Harbour Bridge in the spirit realm and saw that Kita was having breakfast in her apartment.

"Mind if I join you?" Vintore stood next to me; he was in his human clothing. "I wanted to see you before I go on a short vacation on earth," he said.

"Where will you go?"

"I'll start with Canada," he said.

We shifted to the physical realm, making sure we were hidden from the humans.

"One of the best views to watch the sunrise from," he said, admiring the sunrise. "You were made for this. In this point, everything you have done for heaven, for us, for the battalion, no one else could have done what you did. You are full of courage, you dare to go to places no one has ever ventured, and you do it with vigour and with a steadfast spirit. I admire you, we all do."

"That means a lot to hear that from you, Vintore. We would not have been able to do this without Cain. He surrendered his mark, despite knowing his fate," I said, remembering his sacrifice.

"He will be remembered," said Vintore. "Rejoice, the best is yet to come." He shifted to the spirit realm and disappeared.

"What now?" I thought to myself. Many demons were cast into hell during the battle, and some fled to earth. That means the demons will retaliate. What will Satan do now? Will there be more wars? How much will the demons interfere?

The Holy Spirit began to stir in me, and I knew that he was about to answer my question.

"Enjoy the now, enjoy this peace, valiant one. Vintore is right, the best is yet to come. There will be more battles, greater battles, but fear not for I am with you. The stage is being set for the final judgment. The stage is being set for the final descent of the heavenly armies," he said.

"What of the humans, Satan will answer our victory with retribution," I said, watching the humans walking below. I could see angels walking with them in the spirit realm, and I could also see demons following them.

"The remnants are rising," said the Holy Spirit, and I saw a vision of people, a great multitude of people dropping their spears and javelins, no longer bowing before Satan, but walking away from him. They are stepping away. Like soldiers marching in the rain, only this time, serving the Lord Almighty. A specific group of warriors, set apart, to do the good work that God has called them to do. No longer in bondage and chains, they are now holding steady the sword of the spirit, shield of faith, breastplate of righteousness, helmet of salvation, and belt of truth, and their feet are fitted with readiness that comes from the gospel of peace. Now, soldiers of heaven, reigning with Christ.

There is always hope.

I shifted into the spirit realm and orbed inside Kita's apartment.

She finished her breakfast, and she was watching the TV. She noticed my presence, and she was happy to see me.

"I was wondering when I would be seeing you," she said. "The angels were keeping me in good company while you were away."

I told her about the battle in the second heavens, and she listened to me intently.

"That is a powerful testimony, Arden. Thank you for sharing that," she said and then looked startled. I noticed the change in her demeanour. "The time is close, isn't it. It really is the last days," she said. She didn't appear to be anxious but was excited. I nodded, and she was lost in her thoughts again.

Her attention went back to the TV, and she turned the volume up. She was fixated on the man standing in front of the White House. I recognised him too. Johann Vandel was speaking to many reporters and crowds standing before him. I noticed his adviser, Henrik, standing behind him.

"Today is a great day. With my leadership, the world will know peace like never before. I will lead you into an age of glory, a world where this generation and the next will never know war, but only peace, utopia. And utopia can be achieved, and I will take you there. I hereby declare my decision to step down from my role as Director of the Security Council and assume my role as a candidate for the President of the United States of America."

Kita paused the TV and looked intently at Johann. "That's him, the Antichrist. He is here," she whispered.

"Yes," I said. Kita would not know this on her own; the Holy Spirit had revealed this to her. I needed to prepare her for all that is to come.

"Here we go," she said, looking at Johann again then at me.

I picked up the Bible from the table and gave it to her, and she smiled. "Here we go."

# ABOUT THE AUTHOR

Neekita Chand is based in Sydney, Australia, and she loves Jesus. She likes to encourage and empower others through her Christian ministry called Valiance Ministries. She loves learning about Christian spirituality, spiritual warfare, and the gifts of the Holy Spirit.

She loves the world of art and creativity, such as photography, painting, poetry, and cooking. Her current favourite holiday destination is Singapore. She adores the culture, food, festivities, and the adventure that portrays the beauty of Singapore. When she's not writing, she can be found watching movies and relaxing at home, sitting by the beach and journaling, daydreaming about her next travel adventure, and spending time with God in nature.

Neekita's love for writing began in high school, where she wrote many creative essays focusing on the world of fantasy and adventure. She wrote her first book, *Battle of the Legions*, inspired by God and her love for God's Word. Her passion about the heavenly realms and to continue the adventures of Arden and the angels inspired her to write the sequel, *War of the Realms*. Her hope is for those who read the books to be built up in their faith, to walk alongside Jesus with valiance, and to dream big, that anything is possible with God.

Printed in the USA
CPSIA information can be obtained
at www.ICGtesting.com
CBHW032134120724
11511CB00009B/58